"If only you knew what it felt like to be a clone,"

Sven raged.

"I've known you for five years," I answered. "You've given me a pretty good idea."

"That's what you think," he said, grabbing me by the shoulders and twisting me around until he forced me over on my stomach. He held me securely in this position, not letting me move as he entered me. All the while he gave me a running commentary. He spoke of a bomb, detailing all its intricate parts; he described the corridors and circuits of the Mivrakki Komsol in intimate terms that only he could know; he pictured the minute details as he placed the bomb; in slow motion he told how the whole building complex, the circuits, the relays, the consoles, burst into the air in shattered fragments. At the moment of his climax he yelled, "KILL THEM. KILL THEM ALL!!"

Evelyn Lief

The Clone Rebellion

The First Book of the Clone Chronicles

PUBLISHED BY POCKET BOOKS NEW YORK

Another *Original* publication of POCKET BOOKS

POCKET BOOKS, a Simon & Schuster division of
GULF & WESTERN CORPORATION
1230 Avenue of the Americas, New York, N.Y. 10020

ISBN: 0-671-83156-9

First Pocket Books printing June, 1980

10 9 8 7 6 5 4 3 2 1

POCKET and colophon are trademarks of Simon & Schuster.

Printed in the U.S.A.

To my grandmother, May Efron,
who gave me Time.

CHRONOLOGY

1936 A.D.T.T. (Terra Time)—First surgical experiments within the lobes of the human brain.

1993 A.D.T.T.—First documented experiment that produced a living cloned human being.

1997 A.D.T.T.—Cloning of human beings declared illegal.

2051 A.D.T.T.—Bypassing of Einstein's slower than light-speed axiom with discovery of space/time continuum; beginning of human colonization of the galaxy.

2150 A.D.T.T.—Growth of numerous colonies.

2191 A.D.T.T.—Plague B sweeps through Orion sector.

2221 A.D.T.T.—Plague B cured; Earth attempts to regain her domains; small wars throughout the galaxy.

2240 A.D.T.T. = Year One of the Galactic Era—Anselm Gabrol, the Peacemaker, negotiates trade agreement, organizes ConFederation.

Year One G.E. to 500 G.E.—Exploration and colonizing of more new worlds; growth of technologically over-dependent cultures.

545 G.E.—First successful Komsol-clone connection made by Dr. Paul Menard.

CHAPTER 1

Excerpts from Selena Menard's *Out of My Father's Seed: A Personal History of the Clone Wars, Vol. I.*

Whether my father, Paul Menard, will be cast in the role of the villanous creator of the Komsol clones, or as their eventual liberator, only future generations will know. But it is my hope that these personal chronicles will help, in the aftermath of these years of upheaval, to reveal the threads of truth entangled in the web of rumor and misinformation that has been fostered by MedComm. Indeed, I believe my heritage has uniquely placed me in a position to observe, and now to record, most of the significant people and events that have led to the overthrow of MedComm and the revitalization of our stagnating system.

But now, to help me to get my thoughts into some semblance of order, it is easier for me to begin at the beginning. My beginning.

I am not a clone. But I have always known that if science had not taken a hand in my birth, I would never have been born. My father was more than three hundred and thirty years old when I was conceived. All the many parts of his body had been replaced several times over. The sperm that issued forth to impregnate my mother's ovum came from an organ transplanted from a cloned replica of my father. I have often wondered how much difference there was between myself and an actual clone. As an only child, I used to imagine what it would be like to have sisters who were identical to myself. I would imagine playing tricks on my parents, who could not tell one clone-child from another.

Although my parents loved me well enough, and my friends and teachers at school honored me as Paul Menard's daughter, I have always felt myself somehow apart, somehow different. It was not only my personal identification with the clones. There was an added factor. Some small part of me, a feeling of the father's, perhaps, reflected in the daughter, regretted the scientific revolution he had engineered. My father's goal had been one of scientific progress, not of political power and economic exploitation. But, still, he did want the money and freedom to advance his own research—along with the trappings of power and fame —that came from the scientific community. So he shrugged his shoulders and turned the other way.

Surely, if he had not ignored the cruelty and exploitation being perpetrated by MedComm, I would never have been born. As a child derived from cloned organs, indirectly subsidized by MedComm, I have carried this guilt with me through much of my life. I can personally attest to the truth of that old adage about the father's sins being visited upon the child. But now that some of the harm has been undone, I can begin to breathe more easily. I have always been glad to be alive. Now, to be able to share this happiness with others, without that ever-present guilt, is a great relief.

Nevertheless, it has taken many years, of both inner and outer change, for me to outlive this guilt. I can only be thankful to have been given the opportunity to do so. But I must also take credit, for the choice to act, to become involved, was mine.

The first step was taken back on the planet of Kant, where I was born. My father had long ago moved there from Trattori, the hospital planet where he had carried out most of his early cloning experiments. In his later years he no longer wanted to be always the center of attention, to be pointed out as the great Dr. Paul Menard, the expert in cybernetics and genetic engineering, the creator of the Komsol clones and the perfecter of the hook-up between clone-brain and machine. (However, not to go overboard in praise of my father, I want to repeat here the well-known fact that as far back as the last quarter of the twentieth century A.D.T.T., the technique of cloning human bodies was already known. But it was not until the sixth century of the Galactic Era that humanity, tired of its obsession with its outward expansion to the stars, began looking inward once again, and returned to its exploration of the human gene.)

It is obvious that my father owes his fame (or his infamy, if you prefer) to being alive in the right time and place. This is not to say that he was not a genius. It was indeed he, and no other, who was responsible for creating the first all-powerful human-brain-directed Komsol in the year 545 of the Galactic Era.

Unfortunately, a by-product of these experiments was the production of cloned bodies as a source of transplant organs; and Med Comm, having financed my father's research, ended up as a group of semi-immortals whose long lives and accumulated wealth made them a controlling factor throughout the inhabited human worlds of our galaxy.

I still remember that last conversation I had on Kant with my father. I knocked. When I pushed the thick, oaken door I was still surprised, as I was every time, at the ease with which it swung open. My father was sitting at his desk, his back to me. He swiveled his chair toward me as I entered his study. The dark-complexioned but clear skin of his face, and his full growth of black hair, belonged to a man of thirty. But he was almost three hundred and fifty years old while I was the one who had not yet reached her eighteenth birthday.

I crossed the room, slowly covering the wide space between the door and his desk. I looked around me, partially aware that I was hoping to avoid this final confrontation, and partially knowing that this might be my last entrance into my father's sanctuary. I feasted my eyes on the walls paneled with rare wood; I breathed in the smell of the leather chair my father sat in; I drank the thick atmosphere of luxury that hung heavily in the room; I let my body shiver with the almost physical touch of my father's power.

And I exploded.

"How can you live like this?" I screamed for what must have been the thousandth time. "How can you just sit there and do nothing? How can you let this slavery and torture and murder go on? You, of all people, should know that clones are people, too. Don't you believe they have any rights?" But my tirade ended weakly as my voice trailed off into the overwhelming quiet of the study.

My father's tired eyes answered me before the words which followed. "Not according to the law."

"Then the law has to be changed," I argued, but my voice was still subdued.

"It's not up to me," he answered, in his impenetrably calm manner.

"Then who is it up to?" I demanded righteously, consciously forcing loudness back into the sound of my voice.

"Child, can't you let me rest? I've lived a long life and I think I've earned the right to let someone else deal with these problems."

"But it's your fault. You started all this. And you still let MedComm use your name."

"If you feel so strongly about it, go ahead and do

something. I give you my blessing. Just leave me out of it."

I had no new words, no great insights with which to answer my father. In frustration I wanted to hit him, to beat him until he said yes, he would help me, yes, he would do it my way. Instead, I clenched my fists, turned away from him and stomped across the room. But I did look back at him one more time as I yelled, "I will. I'll leave tonight." I didn't wait for the great Paul Menard to answer, but slammed that massive oak door shut behind me.

I rushed upstairs to pack and that night left my father's house forever. I have never gone back to Kant.

It was more than ironic that I should return to my father's old home base, the hospital planet Trattori. It was necessary. As the center of medical research as well as practical application, it was the best place for me to train as a psychomotor therapist. There I learned to use my physical knowledge of the body that I had gained from my background in dance. But no longer did I toil long hours to please bored aristocrats; now I lived to help people in trouble.

And it was me helping these people, not my father's daughter. Me, Selena Petard, as I now called myself. After four years of study I had graduated and become known as one of the most promising young therapists in my profession.

Yet, something was still missing. In my younger days (looking back, I laugh here at myself, because I was only twenty-two at that time), as a dancer, I would show off my tendus, pliés, my grand jetés across the floor. The movements were physically demanding and gave a certain aesthetic satisfaction when they were done well. But after each dance concert was over, when the applause had died down, I knew it was not enough. In the end, my dancing was only technique.

Now I had achieved content. I cared about my patients, helping one to learn to walk, another to use a damaged hand, another to readjust to society even though he still limped. I had a particularly soft spot in my heart for the ward of malformed children who had been part of a shipment of fetuses damaged in deep space.

But where were the clones? Where were those people I longed to identify myself with? Somehow, by coming to Trattori, the seat of my father's first experiments, I guess I had hoped to find a mass of poor, starving, mistreated clone bodies. But they were nowhere in sight.

Trattori was exactly what it seemed, a haven for the accident victims, the ill, the congenitally deformed of the galaxy; a center of research offering the newest technology, the most skilled practitioners. But there was no sign whatsoever of clones, organ farms, or horrifying experiments performed on helpless victims. Wherever the seat of MedComm's power might be, it wasn't here.

In the meanwhile, yes, I was helping my patients on Trattori. But what about all those proud and angry words I had spouted at my father?

When news of the incident on Mivrakki reached me, I felt as if I had missed out on everything. Someone or some group had dared to blow up Mivrakki's Komsol, and to help its clones escape!

How absolutely marvelous. Except that I had not been part of it. I stuck my nose in the newstapes, trying to dig up signs of unrest elsewhere. I was itching to be off and running, the Joan of Arc of some clone rebellion on some distant world. But all I could find was the disheartening news that MedComm had been forced to send a peace-keeping patrol to Mivrakki. Supposedly, the loss of the Komsol technology had left the planet in shambles. But I knew better. They were out to squelch the rebellion. There seemed to be no hope for the clones, or for anyone who wished to help them. I walked around moping for weeks, glaring at my coworkers, and generally of little use to my patients or to myself.

Finally, I began to wake up to what was happening around me.

A new patient had arrived on the west wing, attended by a prominent MedComm surgeon and seemingly well-guarded by a bevy of concerned followers. I began skirting the area surreptitiously, trying to peek past the rarely opened door. At least it was a diversion to take my mind off my own unfulfilled altruistic dreams.

Then one day I was invited in by the prestigious MedComm physician, Marcus Kasur.

At first he had stood there, in the hallway, a short, pudgy, balding man with the appearance of a person in his mid-forties. I was on my way to the exercise room, following the path of my now usual detour past the mysterious door, and trying to look noncommittal as this person eyed me up and down.

Just as I was about to turn the far corner, I heard my name being called.

"Petard. Hold on a minute, will you?"

I stopped dead in my tracks, expecting to receive that reprimand for nosiness I felt I so richly deserved.

Instead, he said, "I've been waiting for you. I know you usually pass this way about this time every day."

"What can I do for you, doctor?" I asked, letting politeness and propriety cover my schoolgirlish nervousness.

"I have a patient for you, a very special one. His problems are right up your alley. I've heard what good work you've been doing."

"Thank you," I said, meanwhile feeling the glee rise in me at the prospect of breaching that mysterious door.

"There's only one thing." His pudgy fingers gripped my elbow, but gently. "What you will see is strictly confidential. Not to be mentioned to your colleagues, or to anyone else. You understand?"

I shook my head up and down, thinking to myself, let's get on with it already.

"Okay, come with me," the doctor said. "If you have a few minutes?" he added as an afterthought.

I assured him I was available and followed him into that closely guarded hospital room.

I stopped at the foot of the hospital bed.

The bottom half of a body, sex indistinguishable, lay under the sheets. The top of the head was wrapped in a mound of bandages. In between was the face, neck, chest, and arms of an almost totally emaciated human—a male human I suddenly realized as I noticed the ragged patches of hair on his chest. I stared in horror, wondering how such an advanced state of deterioration could have been allowed. Not only was there no meat or fat on the skeletal form, but the muscles had begun to atrophy, leaving the fingers and arms twisting away from the body at odd angles. The hands, which lay on the bedsheets and twitched at random intervals, were grotesque caricatures of a witch's talons.

Perhaps it was the total horror of the physical condition of the body, perhaps the skeletal face, perhaps the disquieting lack of expression of the facial features, or the uncommunicative eyes, but it took me many long moments to realize who I was looking at. Then I gasped and forgot to breathe until I woke to find Marcus Kasur half carrying me toward a chair.

"No," I whispered. "Let me go." I pushed away his helping arms and stumbled back to the bed to stare at the misbegotten creature. It was a washed-out, distorted, but definite carbon copy of my father. I had finally come face-to-face with a clone.

After another long moment of silence, I managed to ask, "Where did he come from?"

"I brought him here. He's one of my patients," Kasur answered.

"That's not what I mean." I felt energy returning to my limbs as I swiveled to face the doctor, who stood behind me. "He's a clone."

Now it was Kasur's turn to gasp.

I continued. "Don't bother to deny it."

"How can you be so sure?" Kasur flung back at me.

"Because—" and I paused, "he's an exact replica of my father, Paul Menard." And then I shut my mouth because I hadn't ever planned to mention that name. I turned back toward the bed, and immediately my eyes were once again riveted to the emaciated face that lay enfolded by the soft white bandages. I was equally drawn and revolted by this caricature of my parent. And yet it was not really so surprising to have met one of my father's clones. After these many years there must be thousands of copies of Paul Menard floating around the galaxy.

At my side I heard Kasur's voice. "What do you plan to do about it?" he asked, his voice cold as the edge of a sharp knife.

Finally, I pulled my gaze away from the clone and forced myself to face the doctor. "I guess we each have a secret now," I said, smiling slightly to set him more at ease. "I don't want my identity made public, and you don't want it spread around that you're harboring a clone. Maybe even the Mivrakki clone?" Suddenly the pieces fell together. I knew I was right. I continued, "So let's strike a bargain. I won't tell if you won't tell. Deal?" I held out my hand.

He grasped my hand with both of his, pulled me away from the bed and over to the window. "I can't tell you how relieved I am," he confessed. "I took it on myself to invite you in, even though some of the others had objections. But, although I pride myself on my excellence as a surgeon, I'm not a rehabilitation expert. We needed someone like you, and after I asked around, it sounded like you not only could give us the medical help, but also might be sympathetic to our cause."

"Sympathetic," I murmured. "This is just what I've been waiting for my entire life. A chance to help. A chance to undo my father's damage."

"I understand." The doctor's eyes squeezed shut for a minute, and he said, "The need to atone, to purge oneself of past sins. Yes." He opened his eyes and reaffirmed, "I do understand."

"Then you don't mind about my father," I said, sounding inane to myself. "And you won't tell anyone else?"

"No, I won't tell," he reassured me. "We're two of a kind. We can help each other." He squeezed my hand. "Now, let me think what to say to the others."

I was quiet while he retreated into his own thoughts. But inside, my heart seemed as if it would leap beyond the ridiculous confines of my body. At last. At last I was part of the action. I had finally hooked up with the right people.

It never even entered my mind to wonder how an underground group, in rebellion against a government and with a "kidnapped" Komsol clone, would dare to walk right into a hospital complex as if they belonged. At the time it was so obvious it didn't need to be questioned. Trattori offered the best medical facilities in the galaxy; and where better to hide than right here, out in the open. Besides, Marcus Kasur was a renowned MedComm surgeon. Anything a MedComm doctor did was to be accepted without further discussion. It's only today, so many years later, that I realize what a coup they managed to pull off. At that time all I cared about was the excitement of the moment —that I was finally actively involved in the rescue of a clone.

I was sitting in a hospital conference room with two other women and three men. Other than a bubbling coffeepot set on a table in the corner, the place had an aura of disuse. We each sat in a hollow-backed uncomfortable chair not built to induce clear thinking. Each person carried booklets, newstapes, written notes, empty pads. But nobody referred to the piles of material placed on top of the rectangular table around which we sat. Instead, they spoke loudly and forcefully, waving their arms to make a point or quietly insisting that they knew the answer. Part of me was beginning to get bored with these endless, repetitive get-togethers; another part of me was unwilling to accept any hint of dissatisfaction. I was being included in these important meetings. That was all that mattered.

I looked around me at the group of "conspirators." To my left sat Marcus. I felt most comfortable near to his physical presence in these meetings, where, after only a few short months, I was still looked upon as the outsider. Next to Marcus was Toby Bentor, a thin, bony young man with a preoccupied look to his eyes that never focused directly on your face. His head was tilted off-center, and I always had the impression he was battling with undecipherable equations locked deep in the recesses of his mind. To state facts more plainly, he was an ex-comsol clone, one of those that had been partially hooked up to a small, solar-run computer unit. Toby had been lucky enough to retain a large amount of physical mobility, and it had not been that difficult for him to escape once he found someplace to go.

It had been even easier for the next person, Sindra Tellac. She, too, was a clone. But, being part of a corps of clones upon which various experimental tests and procedures were practiced, she had never acquired the dubious honor of being attached to any comsol. Sindra sat directly across from me, tall, lean, stiff-bodied with held-in anger. I couldn't help analyzing her state of mind from the physical symptoms. It's more than my job training now; it's become an automatic reflex.

Next in today's seating arrangement was a person almost diametrically opposed to Sindra. Lista Colman was a plump, middle-aged woman with unremarkable brown hair, who emanated a sense of motherly warmth that provided a firm base for her fierce determination. Just the way she sat, leaning forward, the palms of her hands planted firmly, face down, on the tabletop, told you she meant business.

Both Lista Colman and the next person, Daven

Migdal, formed the coalition from Mivrakki. It was interesting to note how we always paired off—these two from Mivrakki, the two clones, and myself and Marcus. We rarely crossed over these arbitrary lines. Today, Daven sat between Lista and me. He was a short, skinny man, a physically unimpressive sort of fellow who had a habit of absentmindedly playing with the rim of the old-fashioned thick eyeglasses he sported. I watched as he prepared to speak. First he fondled the frame of his glasses and slowly raised it above his forehead, then rubbed his eyes and squinted as if he could barely distinguish the forms seated around the table. As I watched this casual performance, I once again became aware of an unexpected magnetism, almost animal, definitely primal, in its force. His mild persona was only an unconscious attempt to keep in check his strong inner core. I could only wait expectantly as Daven finally pushed his glasses firmly back onto the ridge of his nose, and leaned forward to speak.

"I'm sorry, Lista," Daven said, "but I've had my fill of Mivrakki. If I can help it, I don't intend setting foot on that planet ever again."

"But it's your home world," Lista objected.

"All the more reason not to go back there. It's the place where my parents were killed. I'm tired of holding on to all those bad memories."

"But there are good memories there, too, aren't there? People who care?" Lista leaned across her corner of the table and touched Daven's hand lightly. He closed his larger hand around her small fingers.

"Yes," Daven said softly. "Without you and the others I don't know what I would have done."

"Then come back with me." Lista's voice was almost plaintive, but not quite.

"I'm sorry. I can't. I could never really be comfortable there."

"Will you be comfortable anywhere?" Lista's voice was a combination of matronly concern and a cold resolve to lay out the truth.

"I don't know. I can only try to find out. And meanwhile, hopefully, I can share the experience I've gained, fighting MedComm, with other worlds which need help. I truly see that as my part in all this."

"So be it, then," Lista said, giving Daven's hand a last squeeze before she sat back in her chair. "You know you'll always be welcome in my house."

"Thank you."

Sindra's shrill voice erupted into the quiet room. "If we're done with all this human emotionalism, perhaps we can get back to business. Which, as I understand it, has more to do with the liberation of the clones than with who is going home or not." If her eyes could flash real flames she would have burned to ashes the two people from Mivrakki. They, wisely, refrained from commenting.

"The question, as I understand it," Toby said, with his slow, deliberately placed words, "is what will be our next move."

"We have to rise up and fight." Sindra looked almost ludicrous as she banged her fist on the table.

"You know, we're not ready for that yet," Toby said in his calming tones. "The only real resistance that exists can be found in the bureaucratic services where I used to work. And those are still too small to manage any effective action. What we really need is to tap into the power behind the Komsol system, to find a way to contact the Komsol clones."

"We've got Sven." Sindra leaned forward with such energy that it seemed she would jump out of her chair. "He broke free of his circuits."

"But he's the only one so far," Toby answered. "Most of them have been kept so out of touch with human society that they're not much different from the electrical components they're attached to."

At this point I felt I had to speak. "Sven's development is going well," I announced, "but it will be some time before I can accurately gauge his abilities and tap into them. He's only just recovered his power of speech." Nervously, I found myself brushing my long black hair off my forehead, a useless gesture like Daven's fiddling with his eyeglasses.

"How can you ever expect to understand us. You're not a clone." The loudness of Sindra's voice reverberated in my ears. I had no answer to this bald statement of fact. I looked at the people sitting around the table and my eyes stopped with Daven.

His quiet, strong voice broke through the icy silence. "We're not strong enough yet to fall apart into factions. For the time being, clone and human have got to work together."

"Thank you, Daven," I said softly.

"You know I agree," Sindra said, directing her attention to Daven and not me. Her tone was still furious. "I wouldn't be here talking to you True Borns if there were any other way. But Selena should know, from the outset, that we intend to acquire enough power so that political and economic forces will no longer be able to persecute and exploit us. And she may not like the kind of power we're going to get."

"I don't like the kind of power that's being used against you," I said, holding my ground.

"That's why you're being tolerated. For now." Sindra leaned back in her chair, a smug expression on her face.

"Well, I, for one, welcome your help." Toby was speaking again. "I would like to tell Selena and Marcus and Lista and Daven that I'm grateful for every thinking brain that's willing to join our fight. And I'm afraid"—he turned to look at Sindra—"that even in this room there are four humans and only two clones. We just don't have the numbers to do it by ourselves."

Sindra glared back at her fellow clone. "Not yet," she said in an audible whisper. "Not yet."

"In the meanwhile," Toby continued, "I think we're just going to have to wait and work slowly. We need time to accumulate more resources, more power to back us up. Then, maybe, we'll be able to act."

How ironic, I thought, that even now, in the fore-front of the "revolution," I was still relegated to waiting. But no, I reminded myself. I had an important role to play. It was my job to help Sven build up his strength, to guide his entrance into the normal world of humanity—a place he had never before encountered during his cloistered nineteen years of life.

CHAPTER 2

Jeni

Jeni's mind walked the empty corridors of Komsol. Her thoughts passed along the giant computer's circuits. The neurons and synapses in her brain merged with the computer's copper wires. Human and machine, joined in electrical impulse, walked through soundless corridors. Human and machine, joined, shaped metallic walls, circuits, control switches. Flesh and copper transformed data into abstract equations to be interpreted by Jeni and stored in Komsol's memory banks. Together, they formed the nerve endings of sensors which picked up the sights and sounds of Callistra.

The entire planet was little more than a grandiose mining town. Located on a hot, sandy world, Callistra's people made their living by mining silicon. This chemical element was used to make the delicate wafers that formed the wings of the giant solar satellites that collected the solar energy used by most of the ConFed planets.

The people of Callistra lived in one centrally located

city, Callis, made of walls and domes that protected them from the uncomfortable weather. Small mining outposts were located at various strategic areas. Most workers would spend five days away at a mining site, then two days home, if their site was close enough. If located at a great distance from Callis, they spent three weeks on the job, and one week off. Wives and families, merchants and officials, lived in Callis where all the usual small shops, necessary government buildings, and cultural centers were grouped together under the domes. A short distance away from the domed city was the Komputer-Solar-Jeni complex.

The Komsol complex was inhabited by one small, deformed twenty-two-year old woman's body and one giant calculating machine whose movable arms traveled not only throughout Callistra but to the two solar satellites circling in distant orbits. Jeni and Komsol, joined, were the central control system and source of critical energy for the entire planet.

With such rapid speed that her actions were virtually simultaneous, Jeni inspected all the working parts of Komsol. This regular checkup was almost a function of her autonomic nervous system—the same system that kept her body breathing. Integrated circuits functioning. Proper relays open. Current passing along prepared paths. Spreading outward from her central point, she made sure the power lines were carrying their full load, that her energy was heating homes, cooking food, running farm machinery, providing electrical power to the silicon plants.

Wait. Back up. Something feels wrong.

It took only a millisecond for this realization to penetrate Jeni's conscious mind.

Click. Jeni and Komsol together.

Check incoming microwave intensity?

Too low.

Check ground temperature?

Too low.

But the silicon photocells on the space collectors?

Were still gathering.

And the transmitter to the ground?

Was still functioning.

The rectenna on the ground?

Was not receiving full capacity!

The power stations out in space were still collecting electromagnetic radiation, still transforming this radiant energy into microwaves which were being sent down to Callistra. But the rectenna was only receiving half its normal quanta of microwaves!

Where was the radiant energy being sent?

Click.

Not to the rectenna.

Click.

Somewhere else.

Click.

Open more relays. Alert emergency circuits.

Electromagnetic radiation, transformed and concentrated into microwaves, could act as a deadly beam, burning every human, animal, plant, and building in its path!

Click.

Jeni's mind sent out feelers. Small computer comsols began wheeling themselves away from Komsol, circling out and away from Jeni's center. The comsols circuited back information. Clear on the East. West. North. South showed a streak of black soot. Jeni sent two comsols to track the burned-out path.

Where was the beam headed? What latitude and longitude?

Click.

The vanguard of the beam at this moment in time: 32°S by 36°E, abstract binary digits registering. Translated to: a picture of gray ash heaped over whitened bones. Only the stubble of buildings remaining. It was as if some malicious enemy had wreaked a terrible vengeance, as if Jeni was viewing the aftermath of a doomsday war. The path of destruction stretched in a diagonal, through the city of Callis, as far as her comsols could project their inanimate vision; but the blackened strip was only a half kilometer in width.

On either side of the burned-out area domes still covered the gray and silver squat structures that hugged the ground; twisting roadways still circled above the flat network of homes and shops and offices. People ran in haphazard directions or stood gaping stupidly at the place where their houses had been or their children had played. Only a moment in time. So quick had the hammer fallen. The city was in shock.

But Jeni didn't have time for such a luxury. The chemicals pumping into her blood kept her mind alert; her fusion with Komsol, leaving her more machine than woman, gave her the coldly analytical view of her world that left her computing acreage of destruction versus lives and property still left intact. How much longer could the beam be left to run wild? How much time did she have to compute the area of malfunction as well as repair possibilities? What was the point of diminishing return when she must commit the ultimate action?

She sent out her own radar beam, up from Komsol, to connect with and probe the power stations circling Callistra. Station A was still sending its energy stream down the right path. It was Station B that was off the track. She had to correct the transmitter before it sent its solar radiation rampaging across all of Callistra.

What had caused the malfunctions? No time to find out. Quick. The source. The transmitter was rotating its beam, making a giant circle on the planet below. Reach for the control unit to send it back to its proper position. Not functioning. Go further back to the source of the energy, to the silicon wafers gathering radiant energy from Callistra's sun. Damp down the solar mirrors. Use the shield to stop the photocells from absorbing. Again, controls not functioning. And now, a second beam of destruction. Another wide circle of black appearing on Callistra's surface. Station A was malfunctioning too.

There wasn't any more time. She had to do it.

Self-destruct.

No!

Feedback from all circuits. STAY ALIVE. Jeni found that she wanted to exist. But if she destroyed the power stations the overload would feed back into Komsol's circuits, and maybe even back into her own brain. On the other hand, if she didn't do it, there would be no populace left on Callistra. Nobody would need her energy.

Still, there was a 50 percent chance she would survive the overload. Komsol would certainly die. But, she reminded herself, I am Jeni. Could Jeni once again become a separate living entity? Anything was possible.

There was no choice. She had to protect the people she served.

STOP.

Jeni shouted. She sent waves of energy through Komsol's circuits, radiating back into space to the two solar stations. STOP! She pulled energy out of the photovoltaic storage batteries, opened all the relay switches. More. More. The energy surged outward, upward, to full capacity and beyond. STOP! It hurts. I'm going to explode.

Disconnect.

CHAPTER 3

More Excerpts from Selena Menard's *Out of My Father's Seed: A Personal History of the Clone Wars, Vol. I.*

I was with Sven in his small room in the doctor's dormitory. It held a bed, a night table, a comscreen that tapped into the library, a desk and a chair, a bureau for clothes. There was only a small aisle of empty space running the length of the room. An old Terra classical piece of music, by Mozart, was playing. The precise sounds were soothing, leaving room for my thoughts to wander as I lay back in Sven's bed.

Sven had been a medical student at Trattori for four years now and was just finishing up his residency requirement. He had moved fast, jamming three times as many classes into each term as the normal student was able to handle. He was not sure exactly how he could manage this, but he told me he believed his neural pathways were able to grasp and retain information much more efficiently than those of the average human brain. Komsol had done something for him, after all.

But, at age twenty-four, he was getting restless. At

twenty-seven, I felt both younger and older than he, with a completely different life experience from the one he had endured. I looked at him, lying on his side, nude. Sven was leaning on his elbow, his back to me as he gazed out the window. What I saw now was unrecognizable as the emaciated semicorpse that had been delivered to Trattori more than five years ago. Here, before me, transformed largely with my help, was a healthy young male body, dark-complexioned like my father, whom he resembled, with a mop of curly black hair on his head and respectable muscles in his upper arms. After being deprived for so long, he had responded wholeheartedly to my enthusiasm for physical activity, and still saved several hours a day for his workouts. Indeed, with the encouragement of both Marcus and myself, Sven had become fascinated with the intricacies of the physical body to the point of deciding to take his training in the medical profession. He had become a surgeon, being carefully guided and shielded by Marcus along the way.

I thought I could guess what Sven was thinking. All of us of HOFROC—the Human Organization for Rights of Clones—were anxious to be pushing our cause. Now that Sven had acquired the perfect persona, he wanted to be out there doing something. And so did I.

But there was still the question of exactly what it was we were going to do. HOFROC had already begun infiltrating the largest of the clone-comsol centers, trying to organize the average clone-worker. Others of us were gradually slanting the news and literature in a proclone direction. We had even begun bribing Con-Federation officials on Rivolin in order to trigger our first clandestine negotiations with those who held the strings.

More than this was needed, I knew. MedComm would never willingly give up its exploitation of the clones. Some kind of pressure would have to be brought to bear. It was here that our paths began to diverge. The clones, and a few others, believed that only a direct threat to human lives and homes would ever force MedComm to rethink its position. Others, myself included, were reluctant to involve innocent citizens in such an all-out battle.

Luckily, there had been no serious break between the two factions. After all, here were Sven and I, in bed together, each of us representing the opposite viewpoint. I reached over to touch the edge of his left shoulderblade. He winced away from the unexpected physical feeling of my human hand. Sometimes I still forgot that his entire orientation had been cerebral, and that he had only recently begun to allow himself to fully experience the full range of physical possibilities that had been opened to him. That's why I had always felt that this part of our relationship was so important to his normal development. In my role as therapist I had played first nurse and mother to him, and later sister or confidante. These were all relationships he had lacked in his life, as indeed he had lacked all human warmth. That he was able to respond to me as a lover at all was a miracle that I did not entirely credit myself with achieving. There was something in him that drove him forward. It was not an accident that he was the only Komsol clone that had so far been liberated. He had already been reaching outward, beyond the perimeters of his computerized prison, searching for help, when he discovered the small group of revolutionaries on Mivrakki who were also searching for a way to hamstring MedComm.

So now, even if it meant touching me, Sven was willing to do whatever was needed in order to at least give the appearance of a normal human male. I never for once pretended to myself that he might be in love with me.

Unfortunately, my own motives for getting sexually involved with my patient were not so clear. Of course, as I already said, I felt the physical closeness would enhance his emotional development. But what about mine? Was I going backward by entering into a physical relationship with a man that outwardly so closely resembled my father? At first I wrestled with the question of incest. Was Sven actually my father? Or my brother? A little of both, I decided, and yet neither. Only the superficial cell structure was the same. Leaving this question behind as an ethical/philosophical conundrum that had no correct answer, I admitted to myself that I was inevitably drawn to him, just as I was, still, in the deepest part of myself, tied to my father. Perhaps Sven had been sent to me as a means of working out this vestige of my parental attachment. I didn't know, so this speculation I also left behind. In the end, I joined Sven in sexual union because I had no choice. I needed him. Even if the relationship was doomed to be as one-sided as the one with my father had been.

So now, again, thinking that Sven was prepared for my touch, I once more let my hand rest on his shoulder.

"No, not now." He slapped my hand away as if I had been an annoying fly buzzing at his ear. I knew he meant no personal rejection in the action. Nevertheless, I felt as if a thick, black ocean had come between the two of us, and that the distance over to the other shore was eons away.

I leaned back and resigned myself, once more, to waiting. I turned my thoughts away from myself, back to the less painful subject of Sven. I put on my professional mask and once again noted how he carried his head, slightly tilted, as if listening for a voice that was just about to come from around the corner. I had noticed this peculiar characteristic in more than one clone; it was an area I intended to explore one day.

But now Sven spoke, breaking my reverie. I concealed my resentment that when *he* wanted to speak, then we did. I played therapist and catered to him. "Look at all of them scurrying like ants along the sidewalk below." I followed his finger that pointed to the tiny specks of humanity thirty stories down. "Just who do they think they are," he said, "that they dare to assume the power of life and death over us? All those complacent True Borns. They're just as guilty as MedComm. I could kill them all if I wanted. I have the knowledge. And the power. In here." He pointed to his head. "All the facts are stored here. And I've been learning how to use them, without Komsol."

Then he looked at me as if he had forgotten that I was there. "If only you knew what it felt like to be a clone."

"I've known you for five years," I answered. "You've given me a pretty good idea."

"That's what you think," he said, grabbing me by the shoulders and twisting me around until he forced me over on my stomach. He held me securely in this position, not letting me move as he entered me from behind. All the while he gave me a running commentary, something that was unusual for a man unused to freely communicating. He spoke of a bomb, detailing all its intricate parts; he described the corridors and circuits of the Mivrakki Komsol in intimate terms that only he could know; he pictured the minute details as he placed the bomb; slowly, meticulously, he listed the events that triggered the explosion; in slow motion he told how the whole building complex, the circuits, the relays, the consoles, burst into the air in shattered fragments. At the moment of his climax he yelled, "Kill them. Kill them all."

In spite of myself, I, too, burst with the release of layered tension.

But Sven was finished with me. He rolled off my back, turned away, and immediately fell asleep.

I put my arms around myself, holding myself, rocking myself. Soon, I told myself, I had to end this relationship. I had taught him as much as I could. Any more, and I would be the one in need of therapy. Perhaps this was already the case.

But I didn't have long to contemplate my own self-destructive tendencies. There was a knock on the door, and without waiting for a by-your-leave, Sindra was inside the room and prancing in front of the bed. Her blond hair, cut severely short, and her cheeks rosy with excitement, emphasized the strong lean contours of her face. Her body was bony and angular under a tight-fitting brown-and-gold skimpy outfit. When I looked at her I became aware of the few extra pounds of flesh that I carried around my breasts and stomach.

With Sindra's entrance Sven came awake, like a wild animal, skipping the in-between groggy stage. He stood up, stretching his nude limbs and not seeming to mind Sindra's intrusion more than anything else. I reminded myself that, being ensconced in a machine most of his life, he was like a newborn baby proud of its fantastic, maneuverable body. I pulled my robe from off the night table and wrapped it around me as I sat up.

Breathless, Sindra reached out to grab Sven's hand. He jerked his wrist slightly, sliding out from under her touch. I couldn't help noting, with grim satisfaction, that I wasn't the only one he treated that way.

Pretending not to see me sitting on the bed, Sindra caught her breath and began talking to Sven as he pulled a shirt over his head, then leaned down to pick his trousers up off the floor.

"You'll never guess," Sindra said.

"What?" Sven asked.

"Who she really is," Sindra pointed at me, finally acknowledging my presence. I stiffened, afraid of what was to come.

"I'm not in the mood for playing games." Sven finished pulling on his pants and buttoning his shirt.

Sindra frowned for just a moment, then caught up in her message, continued. "Her last name is a fake. She's really Paul Menard's daughter!"

"What!" Sven reached over and grabbed Sindra's shoulders. I stood up, ready with a million different little speeches I had prepared for this eventuality. But Sven didn't look at me.

He pulled Sindra closer to him. "What are you talking about?" he demanded.

"She's a plant," Sindra screamed shrilly. "She's the daughter of the bastard who started all this."

"I don't believe you." Sven pushed Sindra away, stood up and began pacing in the small space of the room. "Why would she go to all this trouble? For all these years?" Finally, he looked straight at me and asked, point-blank, "Is this true?"

There was nothing for me to say but, "Yes."

"No, it can't be," Sven insisted. Tears came to my eyes as I watched the battle reflected in his face. Somewhere, deep down, I had reached him. No matter what happened now, I knew that. It was just too bad it had taken Sindra's disclosure to bring his hidden humanity up to the surface.

The moment passed by. Sindra, knowing when to strike, screeched in his ear, "You're not letting yourself see clearly." She pushed herself in front of him, blocking his line of sight to me. Now I acted by returning the compliment and shoving Sindra back out of my way. Sindra's eyes blazed angrily as she turned to face me, her antagonist.

But Sven walked away from us both, paced another two steps, and came back to face us. "Selena's done more to help us than would be worth her while as a ConFed agent," he stated.

"There's only one thing we need to know," Sindra said, her voice leaving no room for doubt. "She's Paul Menard's daughter and we can't afford to take any chances."

Sven grimaced, abruptly turned away, opened the door of his room and walked out.

Sindra glared at me and said, "You'll see. He'll come over to my side. There's no other choice he can make. He's a clone." And she, too, walked out of the room.

I sat back down on the edge of Sven's bed, clutching the folds of the robe over my breasts. I was afraid to imagine what would happen next.

"How could you? How could you tell them?" I was standing in front of Marcus, practically spitting into his pudgy face.

"If you'd just calm down a minute, you'd be able to hear me say it wasn't me."

"Then who? Nobody else knew," I insisted.

"You weren't all that hard to trace, you know, if someone wanted to backtrack you. And Sindra has been out to get rid of you from the beginning. Number one, she's never comfortable with another woman around. Number two, she was looking for an issue that would help solidify her arguments."

"And I'm that issue?"

"Unfortunately, yes."

"But you went along with them. You never said one word in my defense."

"It wouldn't have done any good. Everyone's mind was already made up, one way or the other."

"You still could have said something, anything," I pleaded.

"It was a matter of expediency," Marcus said. "Nothing personal against you." He tried to pat my cheek. I struck out at him, pushing his hand away from my face. He continued, "By using you as a negative rallying point we were able to convert members to our side. The Clone Organization for Freedom will be more powerful than HOFROC could ever be."

"You're just blindly doing what Sven wants you to do," I said.

"No, I truly believe this is the road we have to follow."

"Don't be so self-righteous." I spat out the angry words. "You were one of them, a MedComm doctor. At least I'm not using any organs stolen from a clone to keep me alive."

"That's hitting below the belt."

"Exactly."

"Turn for turn?" Marcus responded.

"Yes," I said bitterly. "You're proclaiming me guilty by association. I only bear the man's name. You, on the other hand, have actually participated in the atrocities."

"Agreed. I've been there. I've seen the horror up

front. And that's why I need to help them fight Med-Comm with everything I've got," Marcus said.

"At any cost?"

"At any cost," he reiterated firmly.

"Then you and your group are as despicable as MedComm."

"You don't really believe that," Marcus said, returning to his more usual gentle tone of voice. "It's only your reputation, you know. The clones are fighting for the very right to exist."

"I know, I know." I couldn't help myself. I began to cry. "It's just that it means so much to me to be part of that fight. I don't want to be cut out."

Marcus moved close to me, putting an arm around my shoulder. This time I let myself lean against his chest, let myself cry while he held me. "I really cared about Sven," I said. "And I guess, deep inside, I couldn't help hoping that one day he would learn to care about me."

"I don't know if he'll ever be able to love anyone," Marcus said as he held me. My tears had stopped flowing, but I still wanted to feel the warmth of his body close to mine.

I answered Marcus. "The capacity to love is there. Buried deep. But it's there."

"Then first he has to let go of his hate. In the meanwhile," Marcus continued, "consider your sacrifice as your contribution to the cause."

"But I don't agree with violence."

"Each tactic has its place and time."

"I've heard all these arguments before."

"I know that. Still, you have to agree to our right to disagree."

"Not when you're using me as the catalyst to get your way." I pulled myself free of Marcus' arms, drying my eyes with a corner of my sleeve.

"You've got a point there," Marcus had to admit.

"You know I do. And I'm not about to sit still and wait until they decide I pass inspection. I've still got a few friends here. It's my fight, too, whatever you think."

"That's the spirit, woman," Marcus said. "When MedComm learns we're a force to be reckoned with, then we'll be needing your negotiating committees. You'll get the last say, after all."

"I don't want the last say. I just don't want to be excluded."

The litany of my life: Don't leave me out. Recently I'd been paying a high price in order not to be left out. No more, I decided. It was time to do it my way. Not my father's way. Not Sven's way. Not Marcus' way. But Selena Menard's way. My way.

And anyone who wanted to join me would be welcome.

CHAPTER 4

Jeni

Jeni woke up in a small room barely large enough to contain one functional bed, an unadorned rectangular mirror standing over a battered old syntho-chest, a straight-backed chair. The dry wind sent intermittent gusts of sand-filled air bursting through the one window, leaving a layer of yellow dust on the windowsill.

Her body ached all over.

Her nerves felt raw. Pain existed in the muscles of her legs, her arms, her chest. The pain tightened. How was she supposed to breathe? How did air come in and go out? Where was Komsol to help?

She remembered. Komsol was gone forever. Jeni's skin prickled with heat, turning to fire. Burning. It felt as if someone had taken a knife and peeled off a layer of flesh. Her limbs ached with the loss—half of her being had been literally amputated. An empty hole yearned to be filled. Where was Komsol? It was never coming back. She was all alone. She couldn't breathe.

She didn't know how to live by herself. She had been made for Komsol.

A noise escaped from her throat—a sob, a crying sound. She remembered it from her childhood, from that faraway time before she had joined with Komsol. And then she was crying like a little baby. And in between the sobs, her throat gulped deep breaths of air. She was breathing; she was crying. Yes, she was still alive. A gurgling laugh joined the other sounds. And then she was choking and coughing.

From somewhere a human hand slapped her back. Twice. Hard. All the sounds of hysteria were stifled inside her. But she found that the air was going in and out of her body, regularly. She was breathing. Then she noticed an arm around her. Long and warm. Not cold and hard and metallic and safe. Too soft and rubbery. Disgusting. She pulled away from the weak appendage that was encircling her shoulders. She fell over, on her side, in the bed.

A woman's high voice said, "Just let me help you sit up. You'll be all right in a little while."

Jeni wanted to answer, but her voice only gurgled unintelligible baby sounds.

The woman's arms reached over to help Jeni sit up. This time Jeni didn't struggle. She knew she couldn't do it by herself. As she was being helped, Jeni looked at the woman, at her short blond hair, her thin but supple body. The facial features twisted, but the small movements meant nothing to Jeni; the woman's skin had a brilliancy that made it seem like the sun had cast her body in timeless bronze. She wore a short-sleeved red shirt over khaki trousers.

The strange woman turned to a man standing in the doorway and said, "Maybe some of her brain cells were destroyed by the current. She acts retarded."

"That's always a possibility," he answered. The man's appearance was a sharp contrast to the woman's model exterior. Black curly hair framed his dark face, protruded from his short-sleeved brown shirt, and covered his bare arms; his short stocky body emanated an animal vibrancy; his eyes and nose and mouth were sharply etched features on the unwrinkled skin of his face. Jeni found herself studying these abstract configurations while the man continued to speak. "But it's more likely," he said, "that she's been attached to that computer for so long that she doesn't remember how to use her own body. Treat her like a stroke victim. Assume intelligence is still operating and that she'll rehabilitate very quickly. We owe her that much, after what she's done for us."

"Yes," the woman mouthed agreement. "But she's still a chem-slave. Her mind may never clear up. There's no reason to expect that just because you . . ."

"One more patient won't make that much difference," the man responded. "I think she's earned the right to exist."

"Even as a vegetable?"

"Let's wait and see." The man turned abruptly, but spoke over his shoulder. "Remember, we have to start somewhere, or we'll never know what's possible." Then he walked away, out of Jeni's line of sight.

Jeni wanted to call out, "Thank you," but only saliva dribbled out of her open mouth as his silhouette disappeared from the doorway.

The woman propped Jeni's back up against two pillows. "You have no idea how fortunate you are. Not everyone can claim Dr. Sven Soronson's attention. We've just arrived on planet for a few weeks, and lucky for you people, too, with this emergency. I don't know what you'd be doing without us."

The woman's hands pushed and stuck Jeni's back into place.

"My name is Sindra, in case you're interested. And I'll be taking care of you every day. Just behave yourself and we'll get along well enough. But don't expect any extra favors. I'm not Dr. Soronson and I won't cater to your every whim. I just do my job. Now, I'm going to inject this needle into your vein. You can see it's attached to this tube and this bottle which contains liquid nourishment. It's the same way you've been fed all those years while you were attached to that machine. But I guess you never even bothered to notice what was happening to you physically. I've been told you Komsol clones are so drugged and so busy with those computers that you practically forget that you have human bodies. Anyway, you'll be getting your usual drugs, although we'll be gradually diminishing the dosages. In a few days we might even try some solid food. Do you remember how to eat?"

She actually stopped her monologue long enough to glance at Jeni. And Jeni managed to move her head very slowly, back and forth.

"Well," said Sindra, "we'll attack that problem when it comes. But you do seem to understand a little of what I say. Maybe you're not entirely hopeless."

Jeni watched Sindra leave the room. Sindra was tall and her limbs looked strong enough under that soft nonmetallic skin.

Jeni looked down at her own body. Her fingers were misshapen compared to Sindra's. Twisted around each other, they seemed impossible to move. Her legs were too skinny, her knees protruded like deformed lumps.

None of that soft but firm flesh seemed to be covering her bones. Only a paper-thin mottled gray pigment stretched over her skeleton.

Was she supposed to be able to stand up and walk like Sindra? How could she eat if she wasn't able to move her fingers? What was it like to swallow a solid substance? Jeni couldn't remember.

She knew all about the normal actions most people were able to perform. They had been listed in Komsol's tapes. People sat up in chairs. They stood and walked and talked and ate food. Children played games and went to school. Adults worked at jobs in shops and mines and offices and hospitals. Would Jeni have to go to school to learn all these things? Is that how they would rehabilitate her? Always Komsol knew everything Jeni needed to know. Komsol's memory banks had been part of Jeni's own mind. Now all that part of her was gone. Cut off. Destroyed. Jeni felt stupid and useless. Maybe they really should reclone her and let this present self die? But why even bother doing that? Komsol no longer existed. There was no all-powerful computer to fuse with a new Jeni-clone. This new self would also be a useless outcast. Nobody here would care what a clone felt or thought. She would be miserable. Better to let this Jeni die right now. Komsol was gone. What reason was there to keep living?

She sat very still, staring at the needle in her arm. Afraid to move and dislodge the tube, she also imagined jerking her arm away. She could see the clear sugar fluid, filled with drugs, dripping onto the floor, not into her vein. Maybe Sindra wouldn't come back for a long time. Or maybe Sindra would see that the needle had been purposely ripped loose and let Jeni die. Sindra would be glad to see that happen.

Damn Sindra!

That soft weakling. What did she know about Jeni? About Komsol? Together, Jeni and Komsol had been the most powerful entity on Callistra. It was through Jeni's expertise in her own area that Sindra, and all the others like Sindra, had received the energy that enabled them to live on this foreign planet. Yes, that was right, Jeni was the expert. Komsol had supplied the basic facts and stored the data. But it had been Jeni who had directed Komsol, told it what to do and how to do it. Komsol hadn't made Jeni breathe. It was the other way around. Jeni had breathed life into the cold, dead metallic circuits. So what if Komsol no longer existed? There had to be another Komsol on another planet. Or another sort of computer complex where Jeni's knowledge would be needed and admired. There was a reason to live. She'd show these people that she wasn't just another expendable clone. She wasn't just a chem-slave to be stomped on and thrown out when they thought they no longer had any use for her.

Jeni noticed her breath was going in and out, fast

and irregular. Calm yourself. Apply the same techniques now as you used to do. In the past you were so immersed in Komsol you never bothered to notice how your body functioned. But your body knows how to breathe. Just relax and let it happen. Now sit still and wait. Sindra will be back and you will watch very carefully and learn. You will learn how these people do things. You will learn how to force a solid substance down through your throat into your stomach. You will eat and make your body become strong. You will learn how to walk on two feet that will carry you to other planets, other worlds which need you. You will be patient and you will learn.

First you will work on your fingers.

They wouldn't move.

One at a time.

She concentrated on her right index finger.

Nothing.

Okay. Your body is like Komsol. Find the right circuits. Trigger the right neurons. Send an energy message from your brain to your muscle.

Her finger twitched.

I can do it!

She laughed like a three-month baby first learning to wriggle its appendages, and fascinated by the accomplishment.

I really can do it!

Jeni remembered a little now, a vague memory of a before-time when she was a little girl playing with her clone-sisters—before being introduced into Komsol.

Once before she had done this. Yes. This was how. She wriggled all her fingers. Now both hands. And lifted them from the bed and clapped them together. But the sound was barely audible. Harder now. A sharp clap. Good.

She lifted her hands to try once again. But, before she could bring them together, there was another sound, a squeaking sound. Letting her hands drop, she looked up to see that the door had been opened.

Sindra had come back leading a small boy, about

eight years old, by the hand. She pulled the boy into the room. "Look," Sindra said, pointing to Jeni, "she's the one I told you about, the one who caused the feedback."

The boy ignored Sindra, moving forward by himself to stand next to the bed and stare at Jeni. He had red hair and freckles and was wearing a T-shirt over shorts. At first, his face looked bland, unmoving. Slowly, his eyes narrowed, his mouth grimaced, his hands clenched into fists.

He stood, just staring at Jeni. Jeni stared back. Minutes passed. She could feel the hate emanating from the boy, traveling across the small space, constricting every muscle in her own body. He was willing her to die. Again, her breathing became difficult. Gasping, she let out one long breath, and then felt her body holding itself immobile, tensed, waiting for what would happen next.

The boy's eyes opened wider, encompassing her inert figure. He advanced, taking slow steps toward her, his body rigid with his hate. He stood next to her bed, raised his fists to strike.

"No." A voice from the doorway.

Dr. Soronson entered the room.

"No," he said again. "It's not her fault." He reached, from behind the boy, lowering the child's rigid arms. Putting his own arm around the boy's shoulders, he turned the tense figure around, and propelled it toward the door. On his way out he silently reached out and grasped Sindra, forcing her to follow him. Just before closing the door, Dr. Soronson turned toward Jeni.

"Don't let this worry you," he said. "I'll take care of them. And you too. Everything will work out. You'll see."

He closed the door softly.

Jeni felt her muscles relax, felt them once again drawing in long breaths of air. But she had been left with a searing ache in her head. What was that all about? Who was the child? What did he think she had done? No answers. It didn't matter. Jeni had to take care of herself.

She continued to work on her body.

The next day Jeni wriggled her toes and moved her legs a little.

The fourth day she managed, by herself, to push her torso up into a sitting position.

Sindra did what was needed to help. She massaged Jeni's muscles, pumped Jeni's legs and arms back and forth, methodically. Sindra spent exactly so many minutes on one arm, exactly so many minutes on the other. She did only what was prescribed, gave only the minimally required amount of care. Soft human hands pounded on Jeni's calf. But they were uncaring hands, painful hands, maybe even angry hands. Astonishment rose inside Jeni that mere human bones and muscle and flesh could cause and receive such deep throbbing pain.

After more than two weeks Sindra absently patted Jeni's arm. It was not really affection, but an absent pat about a job well done—for Sindra's own diligence and perseverance in a difficult task. Jeni forced herself not to pull away from the touch.

"Okay, clone," Sindra said as she detached tubes from various parts of Jeni's body. "It's time for you to learn to eat like a human being. There's no way you can make it in this world without mastering the basic functions. So here's something we feed the babies. It's mashed banana. I'll put it in your mouth and all you have to do is swallow it."

With a quick upward sweep of her hand Sindra thrust the spoon into Jeni's mouth.

The cold thick stuff on Jeni's tongue was sweet and sickening. It clogged the passageway in Jeni's throat, making it impossible to breathe. Suddenly Jeni was coughing and yellow mashed food was being sprayed all over Sindra's shirt.

"Idiot." Sindra banged the jar of baby food down onto a metal table next to Jeni's bed. The nurse stalked out of the room.

Left alone, Jeni was angry but relieved. Now she would try it by herself. The spoon lay on the table within Jeni's reach. Her twisted fingers grasped the handle. Awkwardly, struggling to keep the muscles in her hand tightly clenched, she dipped the spoon into the food. When she brought the spoon out, it was hard to keep it facing upward. Much of the emulsified banana dripped off. But a little of it did stick to the tip of the spoon. Slowly, carefully, Jeni managed to fit the utensil into the proper orifice. The banana lay on the tip of her tongue. She felt its pulpy texture. She tasted the sweetness and allowed time for her stomach to calm down, to get used to the idea of receiving this foreign matter. While she waited and contemplated this new action, Jeni's saliva mixed with the food, making it smoother, liquefying it. Gradually, of its own accord, some of the watered-down mixture seeped to the back of her tongue, and finally slid down her throat. The esophagus contracted. Jeni followed the contractions from the top of her throat down into her stomach. There, in the center of her body, she felt a cool substance come to rest. It was not entirely unpleasant. More, it was fascinating. Jeni dipped the spoon again, ate some more of the mashed baby food. As she practiced, her hand carried the spoon more steadily, her tongue pushed the food backward more firmly, her esophagus swallowed less hesitantly. Inevitably, much had dripped onto the table and bed covers. But a great deal had descended into Jeni's stomach.

Finally, Jeni relaxed her grip on the spoon, letting it slide off the bed onto the floor. Her hand ached. Now her stomach felt strange, a little heavy. Gurgling noises emerged. Muscles moved and an uncomfortable sensation that was not quite pain slowly descended from her stomach to her intestines and down. Then she could feel stronger contractions and the need to let go. She did. He body felt clear again, relieved. With pride in her accomplishment, Jeni realized she had just undergone the entire cycle, from consumption to digestion to elimination.

Just before dark, Sindra came back into the room. "Ugh. What is that stink? And look at this mess. What in Callistra's name do you think you're doing?" Sindra left the room again, but only for a few minutes. She brought back wet rags, washed Jeni, changed the sheets and blankets. "Damn you," she muttered, more to herself than to Jeni. But then more loudly, "I've got enough shitty work to do around here without you. Next time you just eat when I'm feeding you. And use the call button if you need a bedpan. It'll be easier on both of us." Sindra stormed out of the darkening room.

That night Jeni dreamed. Once again she walked through empty metallic corridors. Once again she felt the energy surging through Komsol's circuits, surging through her own brain cells. Reaching outside herself, leaving behind her miserable physical body, she searched Komsol's memory banks for all the secrets once stored there.

Tell me. I need to know.

The data was hidden somewhere. She just had to find it.

But useless information bombarded her. Ninety percent output from Samson Mine. No problems in silicon extraction. Shipments off-planet bringing in unexpected profit. Not yet one hundred years old, Callistra colony declared a principality of the ConFederation. On and on. Useless information.

She needed to know how to walk. How to get up out of that bed and walk out of that room, out of that hospital, out to a spacefield, onto a ship and away. Get away. Stand up. Walk away. Where was the right circuit? Where was the data?

And then the explosion. The searing white pain filling her brain with fire.

Disconnect.

Jeni awoke in a cold sweat. Shivering, she pulled the blankets up over her shoulders. There was no more heat to warm up the room on a cold desert night. The days were stifling hot and the nights were freezing. There were no air conditioners, Jeni knew. No heating systems were working. No lights. No running water. No longer any silicon output from the Samson Mine. When Komsol had died, so had most of the electricity on Callistra. In that last great thrust against the two power stations Jeni had depleted most of the stored energy in the photovoltaic batteries.

A few domes had makeshift solar collectors that worked only during the day. But mostly there were no emergency backup systems. A pioneer planet couldn't afford the expense. Until recently the Komsol system had been functioning almost perfectly, with only minor mishaps during its more than three hundred years of existence. But over the last three years, more and more malfunctions had been reported. There was even the hint of sabotage. Jeni discounted those reports as irresponsible rumors. Who would dare to harm entire planets full of people? Without Jeni and Komsol, Callistra would be pushed back into a primitive age its people had never dreamed of experiencing. Along with the more immediate destruction, it was doubtful that Callistra's society could survive this upheaval intact.

Now Jeni lay still, cold in an almost totally black night. She realized that part of the pain she was experiencing could be defined as cold. Until now, she had not differentiated separate sensations caused by different stimuli. Pain had been pain. But cold pain was different from sore muscle pain. And loneliness was still another kind of pain.

She clutched the blankets, pulling them around her shoulders. Turning over on her side, she pulled her knees inward and upward, curving her back, bringing her limbs close together to conserve whatever warmth her frail body could generate.

Fitfully, she slept, fully waking only once to find her feet freezing cold. She tucked the blankets close around her feet, curled up and fell asleep again.

The days and weeks passed. Jeni's flesh gradually thickened, grew a little firmer, turned a healthier pink. Her muscles stopped hurting all the time, moved, contracted and expanded as she ordered. Only Sindra came into her bedroom, massaging, feeding, cursing.

Finally, one day, Jeni decided to do it. She slid her legs over the side of the bed. Rolling over on her stomach, she let the soles of her feet rest firmly on the cold tile floor. Pushing with her hands, she straightened her back as much as possible. For one long moment she stood. But her legs were still too weak. They collapsed under her so that she landed in a disheveled heap of bones and flesh. But when she caught her breath, she realized she hadn't been hurt. Just surprised. So she rolled over onto her stomach and pushed herself onto her hands and knees. Crawling, she moved across the small room until she reached the old chest. Now she held the top of the chest and pulled, pulled with all her strength, all her determination, to get out of this detested hospital room. Teeth clenched, sweat pouring down her neck, she pulled.

And then she was actually standing. Unsteadily balanced, leaning on top of the chest, but standing. She looked up from her two legs, which she had been staring at with a determined concentration to keep them erect. Now she looked forward, at the mirror above the chest.

A mutilated image stared back at her. Sunken round large blue eyes set in a bone-thin face. High cheekbones. No eyelashes. No eyebrows. Sporadic patches of uneven dark hair outlined the not-yet-healed scars where the electrodes had been implanted. Grotesque animated skeleton.

Jeni gasped.

No wonder Sindra hated her.

At that moment the door opened and Sindra walked in. With her was Dr. Soronson, whom Jeni had not seen since he had rescued her from the red-haired boy.

Surprise registered on his face. Jeni, shockingly aware of the lack in her own appearance, lowered her head. The man put a hand under her chin and gently forced her face upward until he could look her straight in the eyes.

He said, "It's good to see you standing. You've progressed much further than Sindra has reported." He glared at the nurse, then returned his attention to Jeni. "I want you to know I think you have a tremendous potential for a full recovery. Look what you've done in just these few short weeks."

Jeni's legs had begun to wobble. Dr. Soronson put an arm around her waist and another under her legs. Picking her up, he carried her back to bed. His arms felt confidently powerful around her body, and Jeni realized she did not find the feel of his flesh unpleasant.

Settling her back against her pillows, he said, "I came by today to see if you were well enough to attend a Thanksgiving celebration in your honor. Don't worry, you won't have to walk. Sindra will get you a robot-chair this afternoon so you can accustom yourself to it. It runs on dry-cell battery power, so it still functions. What do you say? Will you be ready in a week?"

The doctor's enthusiasm was catching. Jeni nodded her head, "Yes."

"Good for you." He patted her hand, stood up. "See you in a week." Abruptly he was gone. Sindra had disappeared too.

Jeni was alone again. How long had he been there? Maybe five minutes. But then, like a whirlwind, he was gone.

Something deep inside her body felt pleased, yet uneasy. Stimulated but frustrated. Unfinished. She didn't understand the sensations. Better to ignore them. Too much else to think about. Instead, she stared down at her twisted fingers which would never be straight and strong. Radiation and inactivity had spent years causing her deformities. She could never hope to compete physically with a normal woman like Sindra. She could never hope to appeal as a friend to someone like Dr. Soronson.

She was a physical monstrosity. The doctor's only interest in her had to be purely for the sake of medical curiosity. The good doctor was only playing his proper role—to be kind and supportive, to encourage his patient.

Well, what else did she want? She didn't know. Shrugging her shoulders, she told herself not to complain. His concern was a million times better than Sindra's controlled animosity.

The next week passed quickly. Then it was time. Sindra sponged her down and clothed her in a long blue dress and matching scarf to cover her head. Ready to go.

Suddenly Jeni was scared. Her hands clutched the arms of the ro-chair as Sindra pushed her down the hallway. Turning corners. More hallways. Ramps down stairs. Lights. The noise of many people and other sounds that Jeni couldn't identify. A door opening. Brighter lights. Colors flashing. Eyes and teeth. Hands waving. Looking up from her ro-chair at a mass of torsos, breasts, arms, hair, flowing garments. All moving so fast. Hard to categorize. Who was doing what? Why?

The crowd became quiet. A shuffling of feet. A clink of glass against glass. But mostly silence.

Did they expect her to speak?

A hand landed on her shoulder. Jeni jumped, then relaxed as she heard Sven Soronson's voice.

"Jeni would like to thank all of you for this warm reception. And I'm sure she knows how deeply grateful we are to her. If it hadn't been for her fast action, we wouldn't be here to celebrate tonight. Jeni could have chosen to continue her alliance with Komsol. That's the only world she's known and no one could blame her if she had been unable to destroy it. Instead, she chose to sacrifice herself for the good of all of Callistra. She could have been killed. She knew her action was potentially suicidal. But she did it anyway. For all of us. Let's now give her the accolade she deserves."

He began to clap. The crowd joined him, making a deafening roar resound through the hospital cafeteria, which had been converted into a ballroom for the occasion.

Jeni couldn't help herself. She closed her eyes against the onrush of sights and sounds. She wished she could close her ears, too. Gradually the noise subsided to an ongoing mesh of talking, laughing, rustling skirts, moving furniture. Jeni, her eyes still closed, felt Dr. Soronson pushing her ro-chair.

As she was wheeled through the room, patches of conversation disentangled themselves from the conglomerate noise.

"There's no energy at all. Had to close down my shop."

"Everybody's out of work."

"It'll be another two weeks before the rescue ship arrives."

"Even then, there'll only be enough energy for the vital industries. Basically, we're going to have to start from scratch. Learn how to use manual machinery to mine the silicon, how to sew our own clothes, to cook our own food with real fire."

"Yeah, that damned clone has pushed us back into the dark age."

"It wasn't her fault. She did what had to be done to save us."

"Who knows what really could have been done. Those arrogant clones are inhuman. Can't trust them."

In a whisper. "I've heard that there was a blowup on Folsom just a few months ago. Hushed up, it was. And they never found out why."

"Just like this one. They'll never be able to pin the blame on her. She made sure all the evidence was destroyed."

One more long push. Out of the hot room. A cool evening breeze blew across Jeni's hot cheeks.

"It's all right now. You can open your eyes."

She was seated on a balcony, overlooking a small shrub garden. Two of Callistra's moons hung in the sky, bringing to the darkness a glow that began to compete with the light of day. The balcony itself was made of sandstone, rubbed smooth, with ornaments that were shaped into animals' heads—curving forms, large teeth, and empty eye sockets.

Sven Soronson leaned against a fluted sandstone column. His dark face was illuminated by the moonlight. For a long while the man stared at Jeni. Then, slowly, in a very quiet voice, he said, "You look very beautiful tonight."

What? Was he mocking her?

Before Jeni knew what was happening, Dr. Soronson had leaned over and lightly kissed Jeni's forehead. His lips were a cool caress, brushing her skin quickly. For a moment she looked straight up at him, deep into eyes that captured her, absorbed her.

Then Dr. Soronson pulled himself upright and turned his back on Jeni. He rested against the stone balcony, looking out at the city, the domes pulled back, dark and emptied of its power.

Jeni wished he hadn't moved away from her.

Slowly, the doctor turned back to look at the pathetic figure seated in the ro-chair.

This time it was Jeni who lowered her eyes, away from his piercing gaze.

"Don't look away," he said softly. "I have something to tell you."

But Jeni didn't raise her head. Tears had begun to cloud her vision. Sven Soronson knelt beside Jeni in her ro-chair. He leaned over and pressed Jeni's face against his shoulder. Tears squeezed out of her tightly-shut eyelids.

"It's going to be all right. I promise." He stroked her head, feeling the texture of the scarf over the roughly healed surface of her scalp. "I'm going to take you away from this place. In a few days. To a good hospital on Trattori. You'll get the best of care. They have an excellent psychomotor staff. It's all right."

Away from this place. Did he really mean it?

Jeni pulled away, wanting now to look at his face.

She saw his brow, furrowed with worry, the compassionate searching look in his dark eyes, the questioning tilt of his head, the slight frown his mouth made.

"I promise," he said.

Jeni wanted to believe. Away from here. That was all that mattered.

She lifted her twisted fingers to his face, touched the mouth that had so gently brushed her forehead, and smiled at the soft-skinned human male who was such a complete mystery.

CHAPTER 5

Sven

Each time Sven Soronson saw Jeni he was newly shocked at her physical appearance. He had forgotten how debilitating neural connection with Komsol could be. Lack of an adequate solid diet, lack of any physical awareness, drugs, radiation leakage—these all combined to form the pathetic creature that lay so quietly tied into the web of the ship's cabin bed.

The clone-girl or -woman—he couldn't even guess at her age—was emaciated, with twisted limbs, underdeveloped muscles. Her head was wrapped in a dark blue scarf that covered the healing wounds where the electrodes had been attached. How Jeni had escaped being brain-burned, Sven didn't know. But she had performed a remarkable maneuver, and had come out on the lucky side.

Sven looked down at the sleeping patient. The vital signs were good. He believed that Jeni had recovered enough strength to manage the space/time jumps. But he didn't want her getting overexcited. He had given her a drug that would keep her drowsy and relaxed for the next few days.

Sven bent down now, to check on the second bunk bed in the small ship's cabin. In it lay Nikki, the young clone-boy who had also survived the recent holocaust. His brothers had been killed by the feedback from Jeni's counterattack. No one had seemed to be able to handle the boy's aggressive reaction to their deaths. So, when Sven had heard talk of putting the clone-child out of its misery, he had volunteered to personally take on this second clone-case.

For some unexplainable reason, the red-haired clone-boy immediately began to obey Dr. Soronson. But now that Sven had committed himself to care for the boy, he couldn't wait until they reached Trattori, where someone else could take over. Something strange happened when Sven was near Nikki; something far away seemed to be tugging at the center of the grown man's mind. When Sven chased after this strange feeling, the glimmer disappeared, leaving only a wrenching headache. But the pain of the headache was only a small part of the unease that simmered throughout Sven's body. The eight-year-old clone-boy reminded Sven too much of his own lost brothers.

Rubbing his head, Sven turned away from the two drugged clones, walked out of the cabin and down the ship's corridor. Strapping himself into the passenger seat, he barely noticed when the takeoff pressure of one and a half gravs pushed him back into the webbing.

Why was he getting so many headaches? It must be the tension, Sven thought to himself. He had stayed too long on Callistra and become too involved with the clone-woman and clone-boy. It was better to be out taking direct action. He had already spent too many long years waiting for things to happen. Most recently, there had been the time spent in the ship, waiting for the ripe moment to take action against a Komsol; and before that, all those years on Trattori, waiting to become a doctor; and before that, waiting

for the opportunity to break free of his own Komsol;
and even earlier, waiting, always waiting, to be reunited with his clone-brothers.

Suddenly, a picture of those earliest years came into
Sven's mind. He was unprepared for the clarity of the
vision as the childhood memories marched across his
brain.

A tall heavyset man with a pot belly walked into
the long narrow room. He stood towering over the
nine-year-old clones who were sitting on the floor
with their legs folded underneath them. Each of the
boys had the same dark skin and curly black hair,
drawn lips, and thin nose. Not a sound was uttered by
Sven or his brothers. Not a movement was made by
any one of the silent look-alikes. The tall man, Dr.
Korelli, harumphed to himself, and then said out loud,
"Well, what's new today?" His voice was forced, as if
he expected no answer. Sven and his brothers sat still,
waiting for the man to leave the room. Dr. Korelli
backed toward the door, saying, "We'll soon find out
how much you're really capable of comprehending."

The door was closed. Sven, Soren, and Siven sat on
the floor in a circle. They concentrated on forcing
their awareness of Dr. Korelli's presence to fade from
their minds. These were precious moments, to be held
on to and savored. How very little time the clone-
siblings were given in which to fully commune.

Sven projected a carpet of tiny green blades. Once,
from a window, he had seen such a thing. Carefully,
he led his brothers as they stepped on the grass. It was
so soft. Siven, in a burst of unleashed energy, threw
himself down on the green carpet and began to roll.
He emanated softness and an imagined green smell.
Sven and Soren leaped onto Siven, rolling over him
and onto the grass. Limbs entwined, while sensations
merged of soft grass, silky skin, hard bones, pressure
on a stomach, an elbow covering eyes, an arm around
a waist. There was no absolute borderline between
minds and bodies. Siven's hand was Soren's hand.

Sven's joy was the same joy shared with Siven and Soren. They were one creature, with three separated appendages, bridging the spatial gulf.

The opening of a door focused Sven-Soren-Siven's mind on the present reality. Dr. Korelli walked into the room, put his hand on Siven's shoulder and said, "Come with me." Obediently, Siven rose and followed the tall man out of the room.

Sven and Soren remained motionless. As usual, when one of them was removed, the other two could feel the absent one's lifeline becoming smaller as it faded into the distance. The remaining two boys sorrowed for their brother's loneliness, the unbearable terror of isolation. But there was nothing to do but wait. Soon Siven would be brought back. It always happened that way. The knowledge of always coming together again was what made the rest of it endurable. Besides, they had no choice. They were the property of the Lasari Institute. They had to do what they were told.

Sven and Soren, taking comfort in each other's presence, waited for the third part of themselves to be fulfilled. The minutes and hours that passed by were irrelevant. Time only had meaning to them in terms of whether they were separate or whole. Now they were not whole. They would be whole again, and they would be separate again. There was no way to predict when or for how long. Separateness was a time to endure; wholeness a time for rejoicing.

That was all.

But sometimes the separated member returned with interesting memories to relate. One could also look forward to that.

While Sven and Soren, together in one mind, waited, Sven told a story he had once read.

It was a fairy tale about the ancient days on the home planet of Earth. This story took place very long ago, before the Galactic Era, even before Terra Time. In those days there was a very powerful entity that humans called God. This God decided to create human beings on Earth, just as Paul Menard later had created clones. Both God and Paul Menard were truly powerful. Anyway, back in those very ancient days, there were many tribes of human beings that lived under the rule of God. But most of those tribes had forgotten their Creator and blasphemed Him by worshiping gods they made of stone and gold. Only one last tribe remembered to worship the True God. But, instead of giving rewards to this tribe, God decided it was better to cause them many hardships. God reasoned that if this tribe continued to need His help, they would not turn away and forget Him. Some of the hardships were punishments. This was to remind the tribe of humans that He was all-powerful and could kill them all if that was what He wished to do. God also gave them many laws to keep in order to prove their loyalty to Him. The tribe worshiped their God properly and followed His laws carefully. But still God let them be captured by idol worshipers who made His tribe into slaves. Even in slavery the tribe trusted their God and waited for Him to deliver them from the idol worshipers. Finally, after a very long time, God sent many plagues to weaken the idol worshipers, until they became so frightened they had to let the tribe go free. Thus God led His tribe out of bondage to the Promised Land.

And so, the lesson to be learned is that we clones must continue to honor our Creator, Paul Menard, and wait for Him to deliver us from the other human beings who no longer worship Him. Someday He will know our loyalty and will send a plague to frighten the humans. Then we will be free.

Sven and Soren again pictured the green blades of grass, touched the soft carpet, lay carefully on their backs and looked up into a blue sky which had no walls or mirrors or electrodes or hard-edged teaching machines. It was exhilarating, but a little frightening to lie out there in the open, with no protection.

Then they heard the scream. It was not an audible

noise, but a screeching, wailing sound that turned to fire inside their brains.

Siven!

Something was happening to their brother.

The numbing cold of interspace jarred Sven back to the present. It only lasted for one long moment, and then the ship entered real space/time and Sven's limbs began to tingle as the blood rushed to his fingers and toes. A sudden searing pain crossed from the left to the right side of his head. Undoing the web straps, Sven pushed himself across the null grav space of the control room and down the corridor.

But the pain in his head was too strong for him to continue. He stopped, leaning his back against a wall; he rubbed his head on both sides with the heels of his hands. After a few minutes Sven continued on to Jeni's and Nikki's cabin.

Nikki's eyes were wide open. Dammit, the boy looked at him with such a trusting expression. But, as their eyes made contact, the red-hot pain flashed once again across Sven's forehead. These headaches seemed to be more than coincidentally connected with the boy. There was only one way to test out this theory.

Sven filled the hypospray and administered another dose of sedative to Nikki. Almost immediately, the pain began to recede to a far-distant echo. Relieved, Sven looked at the other bed, where Jeni was still sleeping peacefully.

It was lucky, Sven thought to himself, that the people of Callistra had not been suspicious, but had accepted his and Marcus' medical credentials without questioning their nearness to the vicinity of the catastrophe. Without his intervention, Sven was sure, the good people of Callistra would have conscientiously put Jeni and Nikki out of their misery.

Damn, Sven thought, HOFROC's negotiations on Rivolin were taking forever. And COFF's underground warfare wasn't doing much better. Blowing up Komsols one at a time was too slow. It was a clumsy way to fight. If only they could locate the planet that housed MedComm's hidden military base. Then they could really get somewhere.

In the meantime, while his one tiny comship blew up a Komsol every few months, thousands of clones were being enslaved, tortured, and killed all over the galaxy. But Sven had managed to save these two. Each life was another clone who would one day fight for the cause, he reminded himself.

Silently, Sven bent down and touched the sleeping clone-woman's forehead, lightly, with his fingertips. Whispering to Jeni's unhearing ears, he said, "You're free now. Everything's going to be all right. I promise."

Then he turned away and walked out of the cabin.

CHAPTER 6

Excerpt from Selena Menard's *Out of My Father's Seed: A Personal History of the Clone Wars*, Vol. I.

It was midafternoon. I was in the exercise room, working out in sweatshirt and leg-warmers, when I heard that the ship had landed. After breaking with HOFROC and disappearing over three years ago, Sven Soronson and his crew were back on Trattori. I leaned forward, holding my knees straight, my hands flat on the floor, and the rest of my body loose. I rounded my back. Then, slowly letting myself feel each separate vertebra in my spine, I straightened my torso. Standing, I reached out my arms in one last stretch and let out a gasp of breath as I said "Whew" to the empty room. I lay down flat on my back. Another sigh escaped from between my lips.

I wasn't at all sure I wanted to see Sven or Marcus again. I had made a place for myself in HOFROC without them. I was doing what I believed was right, trying to negotiate for changes in the clone ownership laws, for a relaxing of MedComm's strict hold on the corporation behind the medical front. I was accepted by my friends for myself, Selena Menard, a person who truly wanted to help in the best way she knew how.

I just didn't want to have to deal with Sven's skepticism and Marcus' sticky self-righteousness.

Lying on the cold hard floor, staring at the circling brushstrokes of the white paint on the ceiling, I asked myself, Who am I kidding? I was still scared of them. Scared of what they would think. About what I was doing. About me. A part of me was still living for their approval.

I blinked my eyes, noticing how dry they had become. There was only one way to work this out inside myself, and that was to face the two of them. It was time to go take a shower and find out why Sven and Marcus had returned. Besides, I admitted to myself, I was just plain curious.

Late that same afternoon I knocked on Marcus' door. In spite of my determination, my stomach did a sort of flip-flop. Maybe I shouldn't have come here at all? It was only masochism to place myself in the path of their sneers and accusations. I was safe with my other friends. If Marcus wanted to talk to me he would have come to my office or my room. He knew where I lived.

I was about to turn away when the door opened. Marcus' round face beamed at me as he spread his arms outward in welcome. I leaned against his chest, hugging him, relieved at the warm reception.

But, almost immediately, I pulled back and, half mocking, half serious, said, "I should be furious at you for not contacting me all this time. We've had to depend on unreliable rumors to even guess whether you were alive or dead."

Marcus grinned. "There was no way to transmit any message. We couldn't take the chance that MedComm might be eavesdropping. It was necessary to keep our identity cover solid, and we didn't want to endanger your group either."

"I don't believe anything you have to say. But I am glad to see you." I leaned forward and gave him an affectionate squeeze on his upper arm, then pushed past him, saying, "Let's go in where we can talk."

"Wait a minute . . ." Marcus tried to backstep and block my entrance. But it was too late. I found myself confronting Sven, who was standing in the middle of the small dormitory room.

"Well, look who's here. The All-Powerful Clone, Himself." I couldn't stop the sarcastic words coming out of my mouth. I heard them loud in the otherwise quiet room.

"Shush! Close the door." Sven waved at Marcus, who quickly carried out the order.

"I see you've got your followers well trained," I continued. I could feel the tension building like a knot inside my chest. It was all I could do to keep myself from screaming and hitting out at the clone with my clenched fist.

Sven answered, in a calm, controlled tone. "Military precision is necessary in our work."

"Which is more important than anything else in the galaxy," I answered, baiting him still further.

"Yes. Damn it," Sven said. "Certainly more important than you and your policy of guilt-ridden liberal appeasement. You and your kind fool yourselves into thinking you're working for a good cause. You try to quiet your consciences. But all the while you're playing right into their hands."

"That's not true." My voice was shrill in my ears, and my hands were shaking as I held them in balled fists at my sides. "That's not true and you know it." I turned away from Sven and spoke to Marcus. "I'm leaving now. If you have anything to say to me, come alone to my office." I began to open the door.

"Wait a moment," Marcus said softly.

"What for?"

"For me."

"You hold no claim on me either." I kept my voice level, cold, sharp. "Stay and talk to your friend here who knows everything. He can see inside souls. He has the power to pass judgment on us ordinary human beings, to play with us and then throw us away as if we were rag dolls." Tears had begun to trickle down my cheeks.

Marcus reached his hand out to me. But I shrugged out from under his touch as a shiver ran through my body. "You're so enamored of him. Stay here and follow your messiah." I turned my back on the short, stocky doctor.

Marcus tried one more time. "Please. There's someone else at stake here. Someone who needs your help. Please trust me, Selena. If you don't agree to take on the case, we won't bother you anymore. Just give us one more chance. It's not too much to ask, is it?"

"What are you talking about?" I couldn't help asking as I turned to face Marcus. I was always an easy mark for a patient in need.

"He's just blabbering," Sven said morosely. "I don't need the daughter of Paul Menard to help me."

"Why don't you just shut up for once!" Marcus glared at the clone. "It's not you who needs her help. It's Jeni."

"Who's Jeni?" I looked at Marcus.

"Come with me," the human doctor said. I found myself following, as much in response to Marcus' forceful stand against Sven as in curiosity about the nature of this new case. Marcus turned and called over his shoulder, "You too." Sven put his hands in his trouser pockets, looked noncommittally down at the floor, but soon I heard his footsteps as he walked behind us.

We took the airlift to the ninth floor of the hospital and walked down a maze of corridors. Marcus pushed a door open and ushered me into the small but brightly lit room. Sven followed and stood behind us.

I stared down at the pale wraith of a figure, dressed in a pink hospital gown, that lay propped up against the pillows. The body had no flesh to speak of; the scalp was mottled and partially devoid of hair; the arms that protruded above the pink covers were atrophied, and the fingers grotesquely twisted; the face itself was young and appealing, even in its gauntness; large blue eyes, accented by the bony ridges of the cheeks and hairless eyebrows, stared in surprise and fear at our group of three normal people.

Pushing past Marcus and me, Sven walked to the side of the patient's bed. The girl swiveled her face toward Sven, but it was obviously difficult for her to control the movement and keep her precarious balance. Sven reached out to steady the shaking, fragile frame. She moved her hands upward, grasping Sven's arms above his elbows. I was surprised that the girl, in her deteriorated condition, had even this much muscular coordination.

Sven, meanwhile, leaned down and brushed his lips over the girl's forehead. "It's all right," he whispered. He sat down on the bed and maneuvered the girl's frame back into the encircling safety of his strong left arm. With his other hand, he drew one of her twisted appendages into his own lap. "I want you to meet Jeni," he said softly.

Jealousy took over where my anger had left off. In all the eight years that I had known Sven, never once had he exhibited this much compassion and tenderness toward me.

Sven continued, "Jeni is a Komsol clone. We brought her here for rehabilitation."

I realized my mouth had been hanging open and clamped my jaws tightly shut. Of course. How could I forget what Sven had looked like right after his rescue.

"Do you think you can help her?" Sven asked, looking directly at me.

For a moment our eyes met, and, knowing how hard it had been for Sven to ask that question, I felt my anger and jealousy begin to melt into the background. "Of course," I heard myself answering. "Of course I'll help her."

I pulled my eyes away from Sven's hypnotic gaze and looked down at the pathetic creature at his side. "My name is Selena," I said to the rescued Komsol clone. "Selena Menard." Silently, I swore to myself that this time it would come out differently.

Yes, of course I would help Jeni. I would help Jeni to regain her strength and muscular coordination, to learn to be with people and enjoy her life, to become a full-grown normal human woman. This clone would have a chance to blossom.

I walked over to the bed and gently picked up the hand that lay in Sven's lap. "It's all right," I said, echoing Sven's earlier words. I didn't know if I spoke to the girl in the bed, to Sven, to Marcus standing in the background, or to myself. It didn't matter. It would be all right—for all of us.

For the first time in three years I touched Sven's shoulder without anger. I spoke softly to him, saying, "You can go now. I'll take good care of her."

Sven looked up at me, a grateful expression in his eyes. But he said nothing as he rose and, with Marcus, left the room.

I began to manipulate Jeni's arm, all the while speaking softly to the girl-clone. I explained something about the work we would be doing together. As I spoke to Jeni, who occasionally nodded her head in understanding, I began to know we had been given a second chance. All of us who had come out of my father's seed—his daughter, his identical clone, Jeni (fruit of his experiments), and Marcus (who followed the road my father had chosen not to travel)—had been gifted with one more chance to right my father's wrongs.

And our own mistakes.

CHAPTER 7

Jeni

Eight people of various sizes and shapes formed a circle in the large room. Some stood on the shiny wood-paneled floor; others sat; one was lying down. Mirrors lining the four walls reflected countless images.

Jeni sat, hunched over, her legs crisscrossed, her arms encircling her stomach. The clone-girl furtively watched the psychomotor therapist who was dressed like the others in loose workout clothes. How very different, Jeni thought, this person was from Sindra, who had first been assigned to her case. This new therapist really cared about her work. And how beautifully long and silky was Selena's soft black hair. And her gentle round face. Although buxom, Selena's muscles were tight, her stomach flat, her legs long and graceful. Jeni wondered if her own body could ever be made to reach such a peak physical condition.

Selena stood up and began to speak. "Caren, how's your leg feeling today?"

"It's still stiff, Selena. But much better, thank you,"

Caren said. She was a woman about fifty years old, slightly plump but not fat. ·

"And you, Jon? What about your back?" Selena asked.

"I can bend forward a few more degrees." Jon, about twenty-five years old, muscular, bent over to il-lustrate his point.

"That's fine. And you, Devra?"

Devra, who was seventeen and overweight, stared down at her toes. "Oh, I had a fight with my mother last night. So she wouldn't let me out of the house. I just watched the tri-dee and ate cookies all night and now I have a terrible stomachache."

"I hope it gets better soon. But you know you're supposed to bring your angry feelings here instead of fighting with your mother or eating cookies?"

"Yes," Devra answered in a small voice.

"Okay," Selena said. "Now I wonder how Felipe is doing?" She looked over at the teen-aged boy who was lying on his back. Felipe's body was inert and silent. "Well, maybe we'll hear from him later. In the mean-while, I'd like to say hello to Sven, who is joining us today. Sven, how are you?"

Sven stretched. "I'm ready for a good workout."

"Good. And you, Jeni. You're looking very healthy this morning. Your cheeks are so rosy."

Jeni peeked up at the psychomotor therapist, ten-tatively smiling across the circle at Selena. Then Jeni nodded her head in one quick acknowledgment and finished by lowering her eyes slightly so she wouldn't have to look at anyone.

"Well, it's good to have you with us today, Jeni. And you too, Nikki."

Jeni looked up again. It was the red-haired boy who had burst into her hospital room on Callistra. He glared at Selena. But then his eyes began to dart from one group member to another, lingering too long in Jeni's direction, then continuing their nervous search. The eight-year-old boy shifted his weight from one foot

to the other, clenched his fists, loosened and clenched
them again.

Jeni looked at the boy, feeling his tension from
across the room. Her head began to throb with a dull
pain. Why did Sven have to bring Nikki to today's
session? Sven would end up spending all his time
watching out for that boy. It was obvious that Nikki
wasn't really ready to participate.

Jeni remembered the first time she had come to
Selena's group. Selena had spent many months working
with Jeni privately when one day the therapist told
Jeni that she was progressing physically very rapidly
but that some socialization was indicated. Jeni had
shaken her head, violently, *no*. But Selena had insisted,
and Sven had backed her up by forcefully propelling
Jeni into this room. She had been just like Nikki, who
was now so restless, looking for some way to escape.

But now, after almost two months, Jeni had to
admit to herself that she actually looked forward to
these communal exercises. She liked being with these
people, and with Selena. The psychomotor therapist
knew when to inspire movement and when to let you
alone.

Jeni realized that Selena had started the music tape
and that everybody was already seated on the floor,
bending and stretching from the waist. As the deep bass
notes of the classical music flowed, Jeni moved to its
regular beat, and to the higher sound of Selena's voice.
It all blended into comforting multiple tones. It reminded Jeni of other times.

She had forgotten. It had happened so long ago; the
memories almost seemed to belong to another person.
Jeni could see that other woman, self-confident like
Selena, towering over herself and her three clone-
sisters. Jeni must have been about two years old. The
woman had neck-length light brown hair, the same
color as Jeni and her sisters. Somehow, even then,
Jeni knew this was the clone-mother, and that the
Jeni sisters would grow up to look just like this
woman. The adult Jeni had turned baby Jeni over on

her stomach and spanked her bottom. Simultaneously, the other three sisters chorused Jeni's cries of pain. But even so, they could feel the thread of love emanating from the clone-mother's mind. Grown-up Jeni cared about her children. But they had to learn to behave. You weren't supposed to rip the wires out of the teaching game. You could hurt yourself. The spanking meant you weren't ever supposed to do that again. It didn't matter which one of the clone-sisters got punished. All four of them learned the lesson.

After the spanking, the clone-mother picked up Janie and cuddled her. Gradually, all four sisters stopped crying and began rolling around on the floor, gurgling with laughter because the clone-mother was tickling Janie.

"Stretch out your legs and reach to one side, to the other side. Reach outward." Selena's voice was rhythmic, keeping stride with the beat of the music.

Jeni did as she was told, reaching out. The air was empty, but her fingertips tingled with the presence of other people.

Clone-sisters, on either side, held Jeni's hands, each other's hands. Jeni/Jenine/Jinny/Janie—all four bodies were the same, all four minds were one. They reached out to one another, through one another. One being with four separate appendages played the age-old children's game of ring-around-a-rosy. The clone-mother's voice rang out, "All fall down." Simultaneously, always together, never alone, they plopped down onto the floor.

"Turn the head. Feel the neck muscles."

My muscles. Your muscles. Our muscles.

"Now sit still, straight, feel the spine stretching down to the floor, stretching up to the ceiling."

Up and out. Muscles and minds strained to reach the clone-mother. Where had she gone? Why was she crying when the men came to take her away? And then Jenine and Jinny and Janie were taken away, too. They became distant presences, hard to reach, but still there. Jeni's head throbbed as she clung to the now tenuous mind-links.

Standing: "Swing one foot. The other. Bend from the waist. Twist. Stand on tiptoe." It was all good training for muscle tone and coordination.

Training with small comsol units. In isolation. Longer and longer sessions. The sisters' minds drew even further apart, until they finally disappeared. Only the teaching machines remained.

"Jump in place. Push up. Higher."

Exhilaration the first time Jeni felt the current run through her body, felt the power to reach out beyond her own small self, beyond her sisters, into circuits and memory banks that held so many fascinating facts.

"Sit still. Breathe in deeply. Expand your lungs."

Draw in the current. Send it out. Reach out, become part of the current, trigger the relays, send your thoughts into mechanized arms, out to the moons. See how big and powerful you can be. This is your world now. Join with Komsol. Forget your physical body. Forget the sisters. Forget the clone-mother. The drugs will soothe your sleep.

Another music tape began to play. Electronic. Staccato. Startled, Jeni was brought back to the large room filled with people who were separate beings, condemned to isolation from each other, from Jeni.

Felipe began to writhe on the floor. Devra waved her arms in circles. Gradually, the girl's whole body began to circle, faster and faster, as the music gained speed. Jon crouched and leaped into the air, crouched and leaped. Caren was sensuously pulling in her stomach, pushing out her breasts, exaggerating these movements into a sort of belly dance.

In spite of herself, Jeni's attention was attracted to Nikki. So much angry energy seemed to be contained in the small boy's limbs. His hands made short spastic movements away from his body. His arms and chin began to jerk outward. Soon he was bending his knees to the staccato rhythm. The energy couldn't be contained. He began jumping in place. Nikki's arms wildly flailed out as the child ran around the room. Hoarse shouts emerged from his throat. In order to avoid a crash encounter, other dancers were forced to sidestep out of the way. Suddenly Nikki dropped to the floor, his chest heaving with silent sobs.

Selena knelt beside the boy, tentatively touching his shoulder. Nikki shrugged out from under her hand. Selena stood up and said, "I won't touch you if you don't want me to." She waited while the boy's heaving was reduced to a quivering which finally slowed down until the boy lay curled up on the floor, entirely exhausted from his exertions.

Jeni turned away from Selena and Nikki. She looked down at the floor, felt her abdomen contract, her back curve, her shoulders fold downward. Letting her body curl in on itself, Jeni closed her eyes and rocked. Rolling over onto her elbows and knees, she tried to make herself into a tight ball. Then, slowly, she began to unravel. Gradually, in the darkness of her closed eyelids, Jeni began to open and rise. Put the sole of one foot on the floor. Push up from the other knee. Keep the back curved downward. Then unroll the whole body, reaching out and up.

Jeni could feel her pelvic bones jutting out around the flat stretchiness of her stomach. She could feel the skin tightening on the back of her neck, behind her knees, being pulled thinly over her bones; she felt her muscles tighten and contract.

Open the eyes. A white flash of light quickly receded to a normal frequency. Now see the mirrors reflecting hundreds of Jenis, standing on tiptoe, arms raised to the ceiling. Her hair was grown now, into short silky brown strands. Her body had straightened out, looking almost normal. Even her twisted fingers no longer appeared quite so monstrous. Taking a step forward, Jeni reached out to her new reflection. To another image and again another self. Without realizing it, she was gliding around the room. This is Jeni. That's Janie. And Jenine and Jinny. Look at all of me. Twirling. Jumping. Smiling at all her sisters.

Free. To be with herself. To feel how well the muscles worked, how her legs and arms could move. To yell out her joy in this new-grown woman's body. To laugh. To cry. To laugh again. To hold her stomach so it wouldn't burst.

To feel Selena's cool hand on Jeni's warm sweating shoulder. To feel Selena touching one of Jeni's hands, pulling her forward.

The two women raised their arms and began a three-step. They waltzed together, in a wide circle. Other group members, in twos and threes, joined the dance. Some danced smoothly; others stumbled over their own or partner's feet. But all were smiling.

Devra's voice: "I can dance."

Felipe's voice: "I'm alive."

Jon's voice: "I can do it."

Caren's answer: "Yes, I can feel you."

The dancers moved closer together, switching partners. Now Jeni was dancing with Jon. His strong arms propelled her across the floor. With a wide smile, his face beaming down at her, he said, "You really are looking very pretty today."

For one moment, riding high on the music and the dance, Jeni believed him. She smiled back at him. But then she remembered her twisted fingers, the scars on her scalp, her body still too bone-thin. Her muscles tightened. Why did everyone have to lie to her? It would be better to let her alone, to let her learn to live with her deformities, her ugliness.

Jon continued. "I've been watching you ever since you came here. You've really changed a lot."

Jeni shook her head, *no.*

"I really mean it," Jon said.

He was so insistent. Would he keep pushing it if he didn't really mean it? Jeni remembered the images that had been reflected in the mirrors. Her short brown hair flowing softly around her face; her body that could now move with ease. But hadn't that only been an illusion brought on by the ecstasy of the dance? Or was she really changing?

Jeni wasn't sure about anything anymore. She looked down at her feet, embarrassed.

And a new pair of strong arms encircled her waist. A vibrancy ran from these fingers, down her back. She looked up to see that her new partner was Sven. Relaxing in his arms, Jeni let him guide her around the floor.

They circled past the other dancers, past Nikki, who was standing alone in a corner of the room. Jeni watched as Selena danced over to the small figure. The therapist reached for Nikki, who let her put her hands down on his shoulders and guide him into the dance.

Following Jeni's gaze, Sven, his arms around Jeni's waist, asked, "Do you want to hear about Nikki?"

Jeni looked up at Sven and shook her head, *yes*.

"As you know, he also used to live on Callistra. He was part of a five-clone group, and since they were only eight they still had two more years before being conditioned for separation. But he and his brothers were already training with the simplest comsol units. Four of them were plugged in at the time of the malfunction. Of course, they weren't as experienced as you and didn't know how to disconnect themselves. They were killed by the feedback, instantly. Nikki was on a rest period in the adjoining room. He says he saw a white flash and heard his brothers screaming. His siblings died instantly, and Nikki was the only one left alive. He went into shock."

Poor Nikki. Jeni hadn't realized the ordeal he had so recently endured. They both had much in common. They had been bred for the same purpose, were second-class persons, and had lost parts of themselves. And Sven, for whatever reason, seemed to care about each of them.

Jeni looked up at Sven. His head was centered on his strong neck, his shoulders were relaxed, his arms held her firmly and his fingers were lightly sensitive on her back.

Abruptly, Sven stopped dancing. He looked straight at Jeni. "I've been doing all the talking. I have no idea what you're feeling. Don't you think it's about time you crawled out of that shell and began to speak?"

Jeni opened her mouth, but only a gargled sound came out. *See, I don't know how,* Jeni thought at him.

"Come with me," Sven pulled her by the arm. "I'm going to teach you right now."

No, Jeni thought. *I'm not ready. You're pushing me too fast.* She jerked her arm out of Sven's grasp and ran away. She had to be by herself—to think. Quickly, she looked back over her shoulder. Sven was standing still, a startled look on his face. He raised his hands and began to rub at his temples, as if to push away some kind of pain. Good, he was making no attempt to follow.

Down the intricate maze of hallways she ran. For a clone who had been used to traversing an entire planet, the hospital corridors had been easy enough to memorize. Jeni found the airlift and rode it down to the main lobby. Now, don't look too conspicuous. She forced her pace down to a casual walk, crossed the wide foyer, and exited the building.

Strong sunlight made her stop and blink her eyes. Refocusing, she moved slowly down the walkway. Jeni took deep breaths of the crisp invigorating air. Her arms ached to be let loose, to flap wildly with joy. This was the first time she had ever dared to venture alone out of the safe confines of the hospital walls. But she forced herself to contain her physical exuberance. There were too many people out here. She would be noticed.

Jeni walked slowly, letting the sunlight quietly fill her body with its strength. Now that she was out here alone, the surroundings looked very different. There were many low buildings whose concrete strength was comforting. They spread out many miles across the landscape, making up one of the galaxy's largest medical complexes. Patients, with rare or hard-to-treat diseases, were brought here from all the many worlds of ConFed. Doctors came to train and experiment at Trattori's well-equipped laboratories. Sven had even brought her from faraway Callistra to be treated by Trattori's renowned medical staff.

But now, between the buildings, Jeni noticed the wide courtyards with manicured lawns, benches, and tables. Patients strolled along paved pathways in hospital robes, or pushed the little buttons that gave directions to their ro-chairs. How wonderful it was to be standing on her own two feet. Jeni felt again her ever-renewed wonder at the miracle of physical freedom. She had never imagined it could be like this.

She took a few hesitant running steps, then let herself go as she flew down one of the narrow paths. She kept going, feeling the air pumping in her lungs, her muscles gaining confidence as they grew used to the movement, the sweat beginning to coat her skin, the warm sunlight streaming benevolently down on her body. The people and the buildings became a blur as her legs gathered momentum, carrying her from one pathway to another.

Finally, it became harder to catch her breath, and her muscles began yelling complaints at this unusual exertion. She slowed down, and then found she just had to stop. Perspiration dripped over her eyes. Her body was shaking with exhaustion. She rubbed her fists across her eyes to clear them of moisture, smiling to herself.

Jeni looked around and saw that she was in a wide grassy area not too close to any of the buildings. The low greenery spread over the flat ground. There were few people out this far away from the main concourse. As Jeni stood still, she felt herself more and more alone. There was only the wide-open sky and flat ground. In the distance the windows from the hospital buildings glared, sending reflected sunlight outward.

Jeni was truly alone. This was what she had wanted. But, no, she couldn't think out here, with no strong walls for protection. It was too far away. Her body, which had been shaking with exertion, began to quiver with fear. She had to get back. Anything could happen out here. It was too wide open. She was too vulnerable.

Panicking, she turned around and began to take the first running steps back in the direction she had come. But her muscles protested, and she collapsed to the ground on her knees. Bending her head down to the ground, Jeni cried softly. She was lost. Now she desperately wanted Selena or Sven to find her. But they had no idea where she had gone. There was no way they could help her.

Someone had to help her. She raised her eyes to look around. Nobody was near. Partly, she realized, she felt relieved that no one had seen her fall to the ground. Okay then, she would have to help herself. That was the answer. That was why she had come out here in the first place.

The first step—she had to let her physical being regain its strength. It wasn't like Komsol, she had learned that much in the past months. Komsol never needed to sleep, but Jeni, alone, did. And after a session with Selena, Jeni had often succumbed to her body's desire to take a nap. Maybe that was what was needed now.

She stretched out on the cool, soft grass. The dirt carried an aroma of growing things. The sun was warm on her face. Yes, this was good. She closed her eyes and felt herself begin to drift into a light sleep.

When she awoke, the sun was no longer at its height in the sky. The air carried a chill breeze. Her feet were cold and she was hungry. Her skin felt sticky from dried sweat. Jeni stretched and stood up. Her body felt a little cramped, but as she flexed her muscles she knew energy had returned to her limbs and that she was perfectly capable of walking back to her hospital building. It didn't even look so far away any longer. She laughed lightly to herself as she slowly began to retrace her steps. What a silly little girl she had been to let herself get so frightened. But not really silly, she corrected herself. The outdoors, and, yes, even her own physical body, were still strange to her. She had not been brought up like the True Borns, who never gave these things a second thought. She could not be expected to know automatically how her mind and body would react in each different situation. But now she knew: you could not run too far without expecting to get tired. She had learned this lesson. There would be many more to learn, but Jeni was no longer afraid. Each occasion could be conquered by a careful survey of the elements. The important point was to remember not to panic. This, indeed, was the most important lesson to be gained from today's escapade. Do not be afraid. Fear was more dangerous than anything else. Without fear, she would conquer this new world.

While she walked, Jeni held her head high and watched the sun's rays turning red and orange as Trattori's star slowly dipped below the horizon.

CHAPTER 8

Jeni

The next day Jeni walked, by herself, across several courtyards to Sven's office. She knocked on his door.

"Who's there?" Sven's voice asked.

Jeni waited until he opened his door.

"Oh, it's you." Sven's dark face lit up in a smile. "I was hoping you would change your mind. Come in." He put his hand under Jeni's elbow, guiding her.

"Sit down," he said as he offered her a chair. "You're beginning to fill out very nicely." Jeni saw his eyes travel up and down the length of her body. She was embarrassed about the tight-fitting white summer outfit that she was wearing. Too much of her awkward shape was showing.

Jeni blushed and shook her head, *no*. But she knew she was pleased with the compliment.

Without any more preliminaries, Sven began his lesson.

"First, it's a matter of directing the outgoing airflow

81

through your larynx and making the vocal cords vibrate. You'll get a rough sound. Try it."

Jeni grunted.

"That's right. Next, you have to learn how to manipulate your tongue, your lips, your lower jaw. Now put your hand on my throat, right here." He placed her fingers. Although engrossed in the mechanics of the lesson, Jeni was aware of a slight thrill passing from her fingertips through her body as she touched the smooth skin of his throat.

Sven continued, "Can you feel the change in frequency when the vocal cords vibrate?" Jeni nodded her head. "Now, at the same time, watch me." He pronounced the vowels. "You keep your tongue in the center of the mouth and move your lips. Copy me."

Jeni followed his orders, trying to push her lips into the subtle positions he was showing her.

And then there was a bang as the door was pushed open to slam against the wall. Nikki was standing in the hall, his fists clenched, his face screwed in angry lines.

"Nikki," Sven said in an exasperated tone, "I thought I told you not to follow me everywhere." Sven walked toward the boy.

Choking, then forcing the words out, Nikki said, "I want to be with you."

"You can't stay with me every minute of the day," Sven said, laying his hand gently on Nikki's shoulder. "And anyway, how do you always manage to find me?"

"I already told you that," the boy said. "I just know where you are. I can feel you in my mind."

Sven rubbed the side of his forehead with the heel of his hand. "We'll have to talk more about this some other time. Right now I'm busy."

"Why are you with *her* so much?"

"Nikki, please, run along to your room. I'll come and talk to you later."

"Right away," Nikki insisted.

"I'll be there when I'm ready. Now go."

As the boy turned away, Sven shut the door. He

sat down again near Jeni, his mouth grimacing with held-in pain. Jeni's head, too, began to vibrate in sympathy with Sven's discomfort. Sven said, "I'm sorry, but so far I'm the only one he really talks to. He follows me everywhere."

Jeni nodded her head to show she understood, that it was all right. She raised her fingers, gently touching his forehead.

For a moment Sven closed his eyes and relaxed against the soft touch. He murmured, "It'll go away in a few minutes. It always does."

Jeni stroked his brow with her other hand, thinking, *feel better.*

Sven opened his eyes. "What? Did you say something?"

Jeni shook her head, *no.*

"Well, then, let's get back to business," he said.

During the next few days they covered the whole alphabet and began to work on simple words. In less than two weeks Jeni was speaking.

"I did it so fast," Jeni said.

"Not so fast," Sven answered. "It was really only a matter of remembering. You should have been speaking months ago."

"It didn't seem so important to me."

"You mean, you were afraid."

"I guess so."

"You're not afraid now?" Sven placed his hand on her cheek.

"I'm still afraid. But not as much."

"Good for you." He bent over to kiss her, his lips touching her mouth.

Jeni jumped backward.

"What's wrong?" Sven asked.

"I don't understand," Jeni said in a small voice.

"What don't you understand?" Sven placed his hands on his hips, patiently waiting.

"I don't understand you. Why are you so interested in me? I'll never be as pretty as Selena. Or any other woman." Jeni had covered her cheeks with her hands. But, realizing this action exposed her twisted fingers, she quickly thrust them behind her back.

"Is that what you think about yourself?" Sven smiled. "In that case it's time someone set you straight. You have round, sad, deep-blue eyes that give your face a mysterious quality. Your lips are small but, especially when you pout, they are truly inviting. Your hair, now that it's grown in, is so silky that I want to rub it and feel its smooth texture."

"But I'm so thin. And these." Jeni held up her mis-shapen fingers.

"Your muscles are growing stronger every day. And your fingers will straighten. You'll see," he said softly. "You may not believe me now, but miracles can happen." Sven reached for her again.

"No, I don't want you to touch me."

"Why not?"

"I'm so confused. I never felt like this before."

"Of course not. You've been cloistered away with a metal god-machine. Don't you think it's time you deigned to rejoin the human race?"

"What can you know about it?" Jeni turned her back to him.

Quietly, almost in a whisper, Sven said, "I'm a clone, too."

Jeni turned around to face him. "What!"

"I also have known the power of the Komsol con-nection," Sven said. And almost too quietly to hear, "And the loneliness that comes when it is gone."

"Oh." Jeni's eyes widened. And then, "That explains why you've been watching me, making sure everybody took proper care of me."

"Yes, and Nikki, too."

"But how"—Jeni waved her arm in a wide arc—"did you get to be a doctor? How did you become so much a part of their world?"

Sven motioned for Jeni to be seated as he lowered himself into his desk chair. "Only a few people know I'm a clone," he said, and went on to tell Jeni the story of his escape from Komsol, and how Marcus had helped him to become a doctor.

But Jeni was confused. "You wanted to escape from Komsol? But it's so lonely out here."

"I know." Sven pulled Jeni out of her chair and into his arms. "I've been waiting for someone like you. Someone else who could beat the odds."

This time Jeni didn't resist. She let Sven hold her, kiss her, stroke her breasts. Part of her mind noted these actions with objectivity, to be examined more fully at her leisure. Another part was in turmoil about Sven's revelation. He was a clone, too! He had wanted to escape! Now he wanted her!

Gently, Sven lowered Jeni to the floor. He kept touching her body, obviously expecting some sort of physical response from her. It was true, she felt strange sensations deep inside her body. But she didn't know what to do with them.

"I don't know what to do," she told Sven.

"Don't worry about it," he said, while stroking her cheek and kissing her ear. "Just relax and let it happen."

"Okay." She would take his advice. She had already learned that it did her no good to be afraid. And now he was trying to introduce her to a whole new set of physical sensations. Actually, it was very exciting. Each day seemed to bring on undreamed-of adventures. Well, she did trust Sven. She would go along with him and see what would happen.

Jeni felt Sven's hands taking off her clothes, caressing her nipples, kissing her mouth, touching her skin. Suddenly, she knew. "Yes. More. Touch me here." Jeni guided his hand back to a breast. It did feel good. "Yes. More."

She moved her body closer to his, rubbing her flesh against his flesh. Every bit of her skin seemed to come alive, tingling with—what should she call it—desire. She wanted him. She wanted him closer and closer, to become part of her. Like clone-sisters. Yes. He was a clone, too. Her mind reached out toward his mind.

But there was a heavy darkness in the way. It shimmered with pain. Oh, how could he stand it? Her own head began throbbing. Stubbornly, Jeni pushed on. She sent her thoughts out to soothe the ripples of anguish, all the while slowly penetrating the sea of blackness that kept her apart from him.

Sven had stopped caressing her body. Now, he gripped her shoulders tightly; his eyes were squeezed shut; his breath came in long drawn-out gasps.

Suddenly Jeni was through, into his pain and terror, his loneliness. And beyond, to that part of him still living with his lost brothers.

Sven heard the scream. It was not an audible noise, but a screeching, wailing sound that turned to fire inside his brain.

Siven!

Something was happening to his brother!

Sven stood up and tried to open the door. It was locked. He banged on the metal casing. *Open up,* he screamed inside his head. *Siven, where are you?*

Soren lay on the floor, banging the door with Sven, but also crying helplessly.

Suddenly, Sven was thrown backward by the force of the door being pushed open into the room. Soren, on the floor, gasped as if his breath had been knocked out of him.

Siven's pain in the distance still reached their minds. Twisted and illogical thought sequences interrupted their own sequential flow.

Although Sven could see, through his distorted vision, the face of fat Dr. Korelli looking down at him, the boy could only stand mute near the door, his mouth hanging open. Sven was unable to separate himself from Siven's sporadic bursts of pain, or from Soren, who was lying curled on the floor, his face hidden under his arms.

Dr. Korelli shook his head and muttered to a colleague who peered over his shoulder, "You see how they are? Dumb. And we couldn't make that one speak, not even with the surgical probe. If this doesn't prove that normal brain function is disrupted in clones, I don't know what will."

Abruptly, Dr. Korelli shut the door.

Sven and Soren sat very, very close to each other. Their minds interlocked, refusing to look outward. Long nightmares full of pain, terror, and distorted visions bombarded their innermost beings. They knew it was what was left of Siven. But Siven was too far gone to help. They knew that, too.

The terror and confusion made its last giant thrust toward them, and then receded backward until it disappeared. Now there was nothing but an empty hole where Siven used to live. Sven and Soren merged even more closely, each looking to the other, and blinding himself to the third part of themselves that was empty space.

The next day Dr. Korelli erected a simple wire barrier between the two clones. Sven and Soren sat on each side, immobile as usual, reassuring each other that they were still together. When Dr. Korelli put up a cardboard barrier, they still felt no need to change their behavior. They sat very still, their arms hanging loosely by their sides. Next, the scientist took Soren out of the room. Sven could still feel his brother's presence nearby, in the next room, and walked over to the adjoining wall where he quietly sat down to wait. The clone brothers could sense each other's presence almost as acutely as when they occupied the same visible space. The material wall barely inhibited their mind-fusion.

Suddenly, Sven jerked his hand away; but he was unable to stop the pain that was being transmitted from Soren's mind.

The shocks grew stronger. Involuntarily, Sven pulled back his thoughts, disconnecting from Soren. But the loneliness was too great. And, far away, he could hear Soren shouting. Sven let his mind rejoin Soren, let himself feel the pain as he told Soren he was still there.

But the voltage grew stronger and more painful.

Sven couldn't help himself. For longer and longer periods of time he withdrew into his own personal shell. Soren was screaming for help, for Sven to make them stop the pain. Sven began banging on the wall. Then, determinedly, he cut Soren from his mind and turned his attention on the metal door. He tried the pressure lock, and found that it had not been sealed. Sven pushed open the door, ran out of the room and began pounding on the neighboring door.

It was Dr. Korelli who unlocked the door that led into Soren's torture chamber. All of Sven's energy was centered on keeping his own mind free of Soren's pain so Sven could concentrate on the physical attack. The door opened and Sven pushed into the room to see his brother's body arched in agony as the current ran up and down the spine. There was one long piercing scream inside Sven's head before he put up a last impenetrable barrier against the pain that threatened to engulf his own mind and body.

Soren's body still writhed on the hard table where it was pinioned. But the eyes were glazed and the life was gone.

For a moment Jeni still felt the deep, throbbing, pounding pain inside her/Sven's head. With an effort, she pulled her consciousness away from Sven's center, and thought to him, *Yes, they're gone. And my sisters are gone, too. But we're together now*. Jeni felt his surprise at her thoughts as they appeared in his mind, then a snapping release as the old hurting memory fell into a black bottomless pit.

I love you, Sven thought to Jeni. She was aware of his hands loosening his grip on her shoulders, once again touching her mouth, her neck, her breasts. *I want you,* Sven thought. His hands felt less gentle against her skin, more demanding, desperately needing.

He inserted something between Jeni's legs, moving up and down. Outside her. Now he pushed it inside her. Deep. "Ouch!" It was hurting. "No. Wait a minute. Stop."

Sven stopped. "It'll be all right in a few minutes. I'll go slowly," Sven reassured her. She felt in his mind that he was telling the truth.

"Okay," Jeni said. *Go ahead.*

Sven began moving again. The pain between her legs grew stronger, even though Sven was trying to be careful. But there was another new feeling, a rippling, pleasurable sensation. It became stronger, magnified, until the pain seemed to recede. Sven was moving faster, thrusting deeper inside Jeni, as if he wanted to penetrate to the very depths of her physical being. And all the while, now, their thoughts entwined more closely. She could feel his pleasure in her body, the sensations that soared in his groin. And she knew that he knew her pain and shared her excitement as she discovered the possibilities inherent in her own body.

Together, they moved. They were two parts of a whole, joined again. His circuits and hers, vibrating on the same level. Oh, the ecstasy of it, as the waves broke, as the unbearable tension exploded magnificently in her/his loins. And then quieted, spreading its echoes from her toes to the roots in her scalp. Now, such a delicious warm lethargy. So good to feel his warm sweaty body pressed against her. So good to hear her heavy breathing in his ear. So good to doze, just for a moment. To dream of belonging again. To sleep.

Inside Komsol. Larger than her own frail body. To feel the power of the current as it passed through open relays, as it picked up information, carried out her orders, as the results came back along other pathways and were recorded on magnetic tapes and disks in the memory bank. Facts preserved on microdots:

In a computer—high-frequency electrical pulses, or bits, carry information through copper coils; in a human—electrical impulses, or messages, travel along nerves; in a computer—open relays form pathways for the electrical pulses; in a human—when a motor neuron fires there is a resultant change in electrical potential. This nerve impulse is then transmitted, through other neurons, to a muscle cell. Although there is a great deal more electrical leakage from the human neuron, both systems are essentially similar.

Jeni awoke, lying quietly on the floor while Sven snored. Staring at the blank ceiling, she realized she could potentially control her own nervous system in the same manner she had directed Komsol's mechanical functions. She just needed to learn where everything was located, and to practice. But all the information was available. On Komsol's tapes that were stored in her own memory!

Jeni envisioned Komsol's core tapes. Here was the one she wanted: The human brain has 14 billion cells. It contains the cerebrum, the midbrain, the pons, medulla oblongata, and cerebellum. Each part is specialized for voluntary or involuntary functions—including motor movement, speech, the five senses. The hypothalamus is the center of the autonomic nervous system. Through this Jeni could control her metabolism, her mood, her appetite, her reproductive cycles. Just set up her own circuits, cause her own neurons to fire (or not to fire), direct the impulses along conscious chosen paths.

To have power again. It felt so wonderful. And this, too. She looked at Sven, gingerly patting his black wavy hair. Such an amazing experience. It was because of him she had awakened so completely.

It was good to be alive. And, yes, at this moment she could even believe she was pretty. She knew that Sven saw her that way. Her body felt so delicious. Maybe Sven was right. Maybe there was much out in this world that could surpass Komsol. This experience had been one. Perhaps there would be others.

In the meanwhile, she looked again at her own still twisted fingers. Maybe she could program the bones to straighten themselves, program the tissues and ligaments into greater strength and elasticity. She would work on the problem. Look inside herself. Find the appropriate mechanisms.

She felt gentle fingertips gliding over her chin and

neck. Sven was awake. He kissed her, smiling, looking into her eyes. She reached out to touch his mind. But the dark barrier had returned, blocking her efforts. Well, she thought, there would be plenty of time for them to commune now that she knew it was possible. Gradually, Sven would learn not to be frightened. Jeni would help him to heal the old hurts.

Sven stood up, rubbing his forehead. He had something he had to do, he said. He had to get going. They both dressed. Jeni didn't know what to say. She had many questions, but Sven was in a hurry. He kissed her again, on the cheek, and hurried out of the room.

Jeni was left with a dull, throbbing pain where Sven had penetrated. What to do? She decided to find Selena.

Selena was in her own office, dictating notes into her dicta-type machine.

Jeni knocked on the open door and stood there, uncertainly, waiting.

Selena looked up. "Hi, Jeni. Come on in. I'll be done in a minute."

Gingerly, Jeni sat on the edge of a chair while Selena rearranged some papers. The therapist looked up. "What can I do for you?"

Jeni found it hard to begin. She didn't know the right words or the proper questions. But she had to start somewhere. "I need to talk to someone."

"About what?" Selena asked.

"About what happened," Jeni said.

"Oh, on Callistra. Yes, that was absolutely incredible. I've been fighting all along against using clones inside comsol units. There are laws against mistreating animals, yet they persist in torturing you clones." Selena sighed. "Don't they realize it makes no difference whether a person is hatched from her mother's womb or duplicated from a single cell. You and I, we're both human creatures."

Jeni didn't know whether to laugh or cry. Yes, they were both human. But this one needed some lessons. "I'm sorry," Jeni said. "I didn't mean about that. It's something else."

"Oh," Selena blushed. "I didn't mean to sound off like a pompous idiot." Selena laughed self-consciously, then asked, "What do you want to talk about?"

"Sex," Jeni said. "I just had sex with Sven and I have some questions."

Selena was silent for a minute, then, in a sober voice, said, "He finally got to you. I was wondering how long it would take."

"What are you talking about?" Jeni asked.

"Oh, nothing." Selena averted her eyes.

"Please be honest with me," Jeni said. "I read the tapes on reproduction in Komsol, but they couldn't explain what it would really feel like. How can I learn to live with people if you won't tell me what's going on?"

"Okay." Selena got up and put her arms around Jeni's shoulders. "The same thing happened between Sven and me. But it was a long time ago."

"Then you know what he feels like?" Jeni looked up at Selena, smiling a little, happy to be sharing this experience.

Selena struggled for a moment, feeling her own hurt at Sven's rejection of her in the past, and now, her jealousy of Jeni combined with her fear that Jeni would be hurt, too. But the clone-woman had to jump into the water sometime. "Yes," Selena said noncommittally, "I know how good sex can feel with someone you care about."

"But it also hurt a little. Will it always do that?"

Selena knelt by Jeni's chair, holding Jeni's face level with her own. "He should have been gentler with you. But it hurts some women that way the first time. He had to rip through a thin membrane that blocks the opening. But it won't hurt like that again."

"But I feel so lonely now. Like something's gone away from me. I can't explain."

"That'll go away. And it won't always happen either. It's a good idea to just hold one another. Both before and afterward. Sometimes I think that's more important than the actual sex act. Did Sven hold you?"

"For a little while. But then he had to go away."

"Well, I'm holding you now. Does that feel better?"

"Yes. Much. Thanks." Jeni took a tissue from Selena's desk and wiped her eyes. "I feel so silly now, like I should have known all these things. But I never knew what to ask."

"Don't feel silly," Selena said. "We all have our first time." She walked around to the back of her desk. "But I think you should start taking these." In her hand was a small vial of pills. "Once a month."

"What are they for?" Jeni asked.

"To keep you from getting pregnant," Selena answered.

"I still don't understand," Jeni said.

"If an egg becomes impregnated, they abort the cycle."

"But I can do that by myself," Jeni said.

"It's my turn now," Selena said. Her head was tilted slightly to the left. "I don't understand."

"Can't everybody do it?" Jeni was wide-eyed. "I thought I was just learning what everybody else already knew."

"Dear Jeni," Selena smiled strangely, "It seems you know a few things to teach us."

"But it's just a matter of changing the chemical balance in the hypothalamus. So the body isn't prepared to conceive. Then the egg just keeps on going."

"Jeni," Selena sighed. "You make it sound so simple."

"It isn't?"

"No. I can't do that without these pills. And neither can anybody else."

"But . . ."

"Can you do other things like that?"

"I think so. I'm just beginning to learn."

"We'll have to find out . . . Hey, what's going on?"

The lights were blinking on and off. Selena punched a code on her viscom. No response. The two women ran into the hallway. Some of the servo-mechs were stopped in midtrack. Others were turning in circles.

Fear tightened in Jeni's stomach. It couldn't be. Not the same thing that had happened on Callistra. She had never been able to figure out what had gone wrong. If something similar was happening here, the clone immersed in Trattori's comsol might be unconscious. Or even dead. Maybe Jeni could help.

"Take me to Komsol's control unit," Jeni said.

Selena just stared up and down the hall. Patients and staff were all running in haphazard directions, stumbling over each other in the blinking lights.

"Hurry up. I can help."

Selena began moving. "It's not far. We can get there in about ten minutes."

They hurried out of their wing of the hospital, across several grassy parks. Selena guided them onward until they reached a paved roadway. Across it was a large complex of square silver buildings connected to each other by long rectangular extensions. They ran inside the nearest door.

Jeni found that the corridors and rooms were built along the same lines as her own now defunct Komsol. Unerringly, she ran to the seat of power, the central room where Trattori's clone would be contained. As she hurried, she noted the familiar surroundings that looked the same but different. Now she was seeing with human eyes, not through abstract data directly transmitted to her brain.

When they reached the main room Jeni could tell that the clone was not conscious; vital signs were low. She switched the controls on the console to manual, turned on the optical scanner and the voice-response units. Static appeared on the screen. That meant Komsol itself was not entirely dead. She punched keys, fed questions to the input unit. Waiting for the answers, she fidgeted. Used to instantaneous feedback, it seemed years before the data finally appeared. A picture of Selena and herself appeared on one of the screens. Okay. She had a start. Trattori's solar power stations were still functioning. It was not the same situation as on Callistra. The people here had a better chance. First order of business: to get the hospital units working properly, to divert power to the life-and-death areas. Next, find out what had gone wrong. Where? Circling out from her central position, she sent power through concentric relays, trying to find the weak point in the system. There it was. In the logic element. The data was all scrambled. One and one added up to three. How could this be? With shock, she realized that the only possible answer was sabotage. It had to be someone who knew how to dull the clone's senses while this person erased and reprogrammed the computer. She didn't carry the thought any further. It was imperative she reprogram Komsol, immediately. Sweat gathering on her brow, she worked at the task. After many hours, she finally breathed a sigh of relief. She set the scanners in motion, watching as different scenes flashed by. Life was returning to normal. Not too much harm had been done.

A call for more power here. Jeni pressed the proper key sequence. Watch the overload in sector six. She was too engrossed in her work to hear footsteps. But then a hand touched her shoulder.

"I'll take over now."

Jeni looked up to see a young man in a white coat with the Komsol insignia, a sun contained within a computer, on the lapel. She moved aside.

And her legs felt like water. Selena's arms supported her as they walked back across the small parks into her wing.

"It's been almost twenty hours." Selena told her as she tucked Jeni into bed. "We were afraid to disturb you during the emergency. But now that it's all almost routine you had better get some sleep."

"Where's Sven?" Jeni asked dreamily.

"I haven't seen him since this began. But don't worry about it. You go to sleep now."

And Jeni slept. A deep sleep. Everything was right in the world. She was a human being with flesh and nerves and muscle. She knew how to manipulate these now. And more. She was needed. She could work

Komsol from the outside. Without the implants. Without the isolation. Everyone was safe. Selena. Nikki. Sven.

Where was Sven?

Jeni awakened. The curtains were drawn, but she could see light sneaking in between the windowsill and the edge of the material. It must be day. Time to get up. She tried to move. Her limbs felt heavy, leaden. Her feet were cold. Just lie here for a minute more. And then she was asleep again.

Selena was sitting next to her bed when she awoke the second time.

"How are you feeling?" Selena asked.

"My feet are cold." Jeni stretched and yawned. "What time is it?"

"Three o'clock in the afternoon. You've been asleep for eighteen hours."

"Where's Sven?" Jeni sat up in bed.

Selena's face looked serious. Hesitating, she finally said, "Melanie, Trattori's clone, saw him a day and a half ago."

"She saw him?"

"Yes. Sven told her he was going to check her chem balance. That's the last thing she knew before she woke up in hospital. Then when we got her attached again to Komsol she printed out what had happened."

Jeni lay back against her pillow, remembering the last time she had seen Sven, lying under his warm sweaty body. It couldn't be just coincidence. He had been on Callistra, too, right after it happened. And now he had been identified by Melanie. He must really hate Komsol.

But how could he dare! He was not only cutting off vital power, he was letting people get randomly killed and maimed. And other clones could be killed, too.

Jeni turned over on her side, crying soundlessly into her pillow. And now he was gone. Leaving her all alone, like before.

She felt Selena's arm surround her. Jeni let herself feel the comfort of the therapist's bodily warmth, and murmured something about her feet being cold. Through her haze she felt warm socks being pulled over her feet. Finally, Jeni fell asleep again.

For the next few days Jeni stayed in her room, staring at the walls, sleeping, eating only meager amounts of food. Once in a while she aimlessly paced up and down the hospital corridor outside her door. She didn't talk to anyone or see anyone except Selena, who stopped by each morning.

One day Selena said, "That's enough of this. It's not the end of the world. Get yourself dressed in your workout clothes and come with me."

They entered the therapy room, the one with wood floors and mirrors on all the walls.

"No, I don't want to do this today," Jeni decided, beginning to back out.

"Stay. As a favor to me. Please, Jeni," Selena asked, touching Jeni's arm gently.

Jeni looked in Selena's eyes. Could she still trust the therapist? Well, one out of two was better than nothing.

"Okay, I'll stay." Jeni said as she pulled off her socks. Bare feet were less likely to slip on the wood floor. But it was chilly. She curled up her toes as she took her place in the circle. Selena led the exercises. Jeni felt her body stretching, tightening, exerting itself. It felt good. In spite of herself, Jeni felt alive.

Then it was time for the improvisation. Music was playing. A high melody overlaying a low thread of tension. People were moving in their own private spaces, then joining with others.

And there was Nikki. Jumping up and down. Poor boy. He had been deserted, too. By his dead clone-brothers. By Sven. By the world that didn't care.

Jeni walked over to him, reaching toward him with her hands, palms upward. Nikki punched out at her, just barely missing. Jeni stepped backward, feigning fright, covering her eyes with her hands. She peeked between her fingers. Falling to the floor, Jeni lay exposed, helpless. Nikki lifted his foot. Would he really

kick her? She rolled away. Then crouched. Rising from
the floor, very slowly, she opened her arms, welcoming
the red-haired boy. He stool still, perplexed. Jeni stood
erect, firmly planting her feet. Her arms were still wide
open. She began circling. Nikki circled also. They were
two animals, sniffing each other out at a distance, moving closer, not knowing if they would fight or rub up
against each other. Closer still, and then Jeni put her
hands on his shoulders. Nikki pushed, but Jeni wouldn't
loosen her grip. He pushed. She pushed him. Back and
forth, to the rhythm of the music. Now stomping, leaping together, rolling on the floor until both were breathless, lying in each other's arms in an exhausted heap.
Jeni could feel the boy's breathing rhythm, synchronized
with her own. As her chest heaved in and out, her head
began to throb. Behind the pulsing Jeni realized she
could feel a faraway thread from Nikki's mind. Their
separate bodies relaxed into each other. The boy spoke
aloud, "You didn't mean to do it, did you."

"No," Jeni said, "I couldn't help it. Something up
in the sky went wrong. I just tried to stop it."

Nikki breathed deep, letting his breath out in one
long sob. Then he was crying in her arms. She held
him close, soothing the hurt that emanated from his
mind.

*Don't let them put me back in that machine. I'm
scared. I don't want to die.* Jeni heard the boy's thought
clearly in her own mind.

Sven, at age eight. "Shush," Jeni said out loud. "It's
all right. I promise. You won't ever have to go back
in." *I promise.* She rocked the boy until his tears
stopped flowing.

That night she helped Selena put Nikki to bed. The
two women kissed the boy good night and closed his
door.

"Selena," Jeni said. "I made Nikki a promise. I told
him he would never again have to be attached to a
comsol unit. Can you help me keep that promise?"

"Yes," Selena held Jeni's hand. "I can. I've already

recommended to the board that he's no longer psy-chologically suited for that kind of work."

"If they decide against him, I'll take him away myself," Jeni said vehemently.

"And I'll help you. From now on, it's my promise, too."

The two women walked down the corridor, quiet now as the lights dimmed for the night.

But a clone was behind those lights. Melanie was still enslaved to Komsol. Sven was right, Jeni thought, we have as much right to walk freely as they do.

But how could he? How could he be so purposefully destructive? Didn't he realize he was maiming and killing his own people? He was defeating his own purpose with this wanton sabotage.

No, she couldn't forgive him. But for a little quick thinking and much good luck, she, too, could be lying dead, with Nikki's brothers, on Callistra.

CHAPTER 9

Sven

I really botched that up, Sven was thinking just before the anesthetic hit. If I hadn't been so careless the Melanie-clone never would have been able to identify me. I wouldn't have had to run away from Trattori. And Jeni. Sven once again touched Jeni's soft skin as his mind drifted into the warm, all-embracing sea of unconsciousness.

When Sven awoke, there was a new name and new papers to go with his new face: Dr. Lenny Markovan, traveling surgeon from Sansarra. Coming from a sparsely populated arm of the galaxy, Dr. Markovan was on an odessy in search of the latest medical techniques. Thus went the rationalization for his exodus from Sansarra and for his arrival on whatever planet was the next target.

Reaching over to the table next to his berth, Sven picked up a hand mirror and held it close to his face. The blue lenses effectively masked his brown pupils and his bleached hair was now straight instead of black and curly. The scar lines on his face were almost invisible. In a few days they would disappear entirely. His regeneration message was exactly on schedule. Nobody would ever see Sven Soronson again.

Not even Jeni.

Sven leaned back against a pillow. What was wrong with him? He had never messed up like that before. Komsol hadn't even been fully destroyed, just temporarily put out of action. Well, it didn't do any good to chew over his failure. He shook his head and sat up in bed. Immediately, he was dizzy and nauseated. The anesthetic was still affecting him. He slowly let his body fall back to a supine position. There, that felt better.

Maybe he should get some more sleep. He closed his eyes. A picture of a woman slowly materialized. It was Jeni. Sven saw her as she looked when they had made love—short and thin, but beginning to round out in breasts and hips. Her silky brown hair brushed against his face. Her blue eyes gazed at him with passion and trust. She seemed so fragile, so in need of protection. He reached out to hold her.

No. It was only a drug-induced mirage. Jeni wasn't here. Sven had left her behind, on Trattori. And that image of her as fragile was only his masculine conceit. Jeni didn't need his help anymore. She was really quite a remarkable clone. Who knew how far she would be able to go? All the signs were there—fast regeneration of body tissues; an almost impossible recovery of her physical abilities; intelligence; an intense survival instinct. And her body. Yes, she was really beginning to blossom into a full-grown woman.

Jeni would be able to manage very well. She didn't need Sven any longer. And he didn't need her.

He had already sacrificed too much for this whimsical attraction. He had waited a little too long on Trattori, and would have continued blindly waiting, if it hadn't been for Sindra, who had reminded him of his responsibilities. "Time is running out," Sindra had said. "We have to get back into action. Selena can take care of the clone-girl. That's what the therapist is good for, being a nursemaid." Sindra had egged Sven on, claiming he was the only one who could coordinate the attacks. As usual, Sven could come up with no convincing argument to refute Sindra's rationale. Sindra was right. He had to disregard his personal inclinations and get on with the job. Later, he could think about himself.

Sven turned over on his side, gingerly adjusting his face on the edge of the pillow. This was where he belonged, right here on his comship. Jeni was really no good for him. Her emotional needs were too great, too demanding. And those constant headaches, whenever he was near her or Nikki, were driving him mad. He had actually been imagining she could read his thoughts! That was impossible, he knew. Years ago he had had to resign himself to live only within the prison of his own mind. He had forced himself to accept the incontrovertible fact that no one other than his dead clone-brothers could be capable of breaching normal thought barriers. No one, not even Jeni, could tear a passage through such concrete walls. And even if she could, what right had she? Who was she to think she could enter into his private places, to unearth the memory of his brothers, to bring forward that pain-filled time? No! He only wanted to forget. He didn't want to be disturbed by those memories. Let them rest. Let him rest.

Sven knew that if he hadn't been upset by Jeni's interfering presence he would never have acted so hastily, never would have left the job only half finished. And that was what was most important. Sindra was right. His first responsibility was the cause. Nothing else was important. As Sven lay quietly in his bed, he thought that he had done a good job in clearing a pathway to the truth. After a while he fell asleep.

A few hours later, when he awoke, Sven was aware of a gnawing emptiness. Probably he was hungry. He sat up and flexed his muscles. They were cramped from staying in bed so long. It was time to get up.

Sven climbed out of the bunk where he had been

sleeping off the anesthetic for the last twelve hours. He dialed himself a sandwich, ate it too quickly, and then wondered if he was going to be able to hold down the food. Better put his mind on other things and find out what was happening.

Sven found Marcus in his cabin, going over the latest model microsurgery kit. The human doctor, who had given up his chance at immortality when he had chosen to rebel against MedComm, was hunched over the machine, drawing diagrams, making notes. Although Marcus was a bit heavy, his pudgy fingers manipulated a surgical knife almost as well as Sven's own. Even though Sven knew this human had once been part of MedComm, the years the doctor had spent with Sven since Sven's escape from Mivrakki's Komsol had brought Sven to trust completely the man's ability with the cosmetic knife.

Marcus looked up from his work. "How're you feeling?"

"Fit as a fiddle," Sven gingerly touched a spot on his face which was still swollen. "Hell, I don't know why we still use these archaic phrases. I haven't the faintest idea what that means."

Marcus chuckled. "Archaisms are what hold humanity together."

"Then damn archaisms," Sven said. "And damn humanity."

"You might as well damn yourself," Marcus said. "You know, you are human, too!"

"Not according to your laws, I'm not." Sven bit down on his bottom lip.

"They're not my laws. You know that," Marcus said.

"You're human, aren't you?" Sven shot back.

"Damn it, what's got into you today? You sound like you're itching to pick a fight."

"Nothing's the matter. It's just your damned insistence that I have to belong to a race of beings who specialize in torture. And if I choose to refute your opinion, you get your hackles up. You're just too sensitive about being human. You can't forget where you come from."

"It's you who can't forget your origins. You're haunted by your heritage as a clone."

"Sometimes I don't know what you're doing here with us," Sven said.

"Look, this is getting us nowhere. I don't even know what we're arguing about." Marcus was quiet for a moment. Then, "It's that clone-girl back on Trattori, isn't it? Want to turn around and pick her up?"

"You know that's out of the question. We're nine jumps out of that space/time. And besides, she wouldn't recognize me." Sven stomped out of the small cabin. Better go see how the rest of the crew was faring.

Entering the pilot's room he saw Toby hunched over the map, plotting a course. The tall bony mathematician, an escaped comsol clone, was the exact opposite of Marcus.

"Where to?" Sven asked.

"How about Whitsun? They've got three solar stations, two main clones, and a slew of lesser ones. It would be a real kudo for the cause, huh?"

"Yeah, I guess so. Only I don't want to go planetside this time. One of you can do it."

"Aw. You know we're no good at the pretty talk. You're the one who knows how to fool those True Borns."

"Well, I don't feel up to it this time. So we have to do it another way."

"We can hit 'em from space. Like we did to the Callistra Komsol."

"But that's so drastic. I'd rather just destroy the machines, not the clones. After all, we're supposed to be liberating our brothers and sisters. Not killing them."

"Your girl friend from Callistra survived."

"She is the only full-Komsol clone that's ever survived such an extreme attack. At least four eight-years-old died."

"Well, you've got the option. You can always go down-planet."

"I know. I know. I'll think about it." Sven began to stalk out of the pilot's cabin, then turned around and asked, "Where's Sindra?"

"Just went back to her cabin."

Sven peeked in the door. Tall, straight, and lithe, with no breasts or ass to speak of, Sindra's reactions were quick like a cornered animal. Whirling toward him, she looked ready to spring. "Oh, it's you."

"Who'd you expect? The way you jumped you'd think you were living in a nest of vipers."

"Maybe I am."

"Everybody's in a real sweet mood today," Sven said sarcastically.

"Did you ever think it might be you? Not the rest of us. The way you're skulking around . . ."

"Aw, shut up already."

"Well, if you don't like it here," Sindra said, "why don't you go back to your sweetheart on Trattori? You certainly stayed with her long enough."

"Will everyone stop with that already?" Sven answered. "I only came here to find out what you had in mind for Whitsun."

"I'm working on it. You can't expect to pop in on any culture, just walk right in and blow up their power source. Give me a little time to psych out the people. I'll tell you when I'm ready. Now get out." She practically slammed the door on his face.

Whew. Sometimes I'd like to quit this business. Who am I, anyway, to go around playing God? Deciding who lives and dies. Dammit. But who are they, those True Borns, to design us according to their whim, to own us, to kill our souls, to treat us like puppets? Why don't they dig holes in their own brains, stick electrodes in their own heads, drug themselves into insensibility, isolate themselves so the only company they ever know is Komsol? Damn them. Look what they did to me. To Jeni. To Toby and Sindra. To every other clone in ConFed. Treated us like dispensable bits of ma-

chinery. This one's not working properly. Well, just make another Sven-clone. Or another Paul Menard-clone for his daughter. A savior-clone for Jeni and Nikki. A military genius for Sindra. A murderer for all those murdering True Borns.

Damn them. I'm me.

He turned back to Sindra's cabin, pushed the door open. "Forget about their lousy culture," he shouted. "We'll hit them from space this time. I don't want to dirty my little toe on their shitty world."

Without waiting for Sindra's response, Sven turned around and began pacing the corridor, fuming.

Wasn't there any damned space on this ship where he could be alone?

CHAPTER 10

Excerpt from Selena Menard's *Out of My Father's Seed: A Personal History of the Clone Wars, Vol. I.*

Rivolin, in the Orion Arm, is the birthplace of Anselm Gabrol, and since the Year One of the Galactic Era has remained the seat of the loosely knit Confederation. As each new planet sends its emissaries to negotiate trade agreements, Rivolin builds additional housing for the officials and provides facilities for the interminable discussions. As the centuries have passed, the planet's surface has become covered with government installations, built in architectural styles from over three hundred worlds, as well as with art and science museums that are repositories for treasures from all over the galaxy. There is no more land to be farmed, and mining of Rivolin's depleted resources is no longer profitable. Government has become Rivolin's vital industry, and the people who live and work on the planet are supported by representative taxation from all the member worlds.

I walked alone in the precisely manicured garden. Roses from Old Terra bloomed under the late-afternoon sun. A Japanese bonsai sanctuary stood across from an Irellian crollus aviatory. Piretta's magnificent midea vines were just up ahead. I stopped to pull one of the grapes from a vine and found myself looking around to see if anybody had noticed me committing this terrible violation. Then I laughed. It was only one grape. I was letting my anxieties about other matters overhelm my sense of proportion. Fingering the grape as I continued my walk, I thought how wonderful this trip would have been if it wasn't for the trouble that had drawn me to Rivolin.

But the inequity still existed. That was the only reason I had come here, to this planet. My HOFROC delegation had only arrived on-planet a few hours ago. But Willis and Vera had flopped wearily into their beds, saying they couldn't move another inch. I had left them behind at the hotel, carrying a light jacket against Rivolin's chill summer night. I was too upset to sleep. Almost immediately upon disembarking I had received a disquieting message. Paul Menard was on Rivolin and hoped his daughter would be able to meet with him. Only two more hours remained until six o'clock, when I was supposed to rendezvous with my father. It was now thirteen years since I had last seen him.

But why was he on Rivolin? Did he intend to appear as a MedComm witness against clones' rights at the Joint Council?

I hadn't counted on this additional complication. After years of subterfuge, of pro-clone propaganda, of behind-the-scenes negotiations, one word from my father, Paul Menard, and all would be lost.

But maybe my father, with MedComm, was planning to make a few token concessions with the hope of appeasing the clone terrorists? So far, MedComm's private fleet had not had any luck in its attempts to capture Sven Soronson and his crew. MedComm had not even been able to discover the aliases that the clones were using.

It seemed that both HOFROC and MedComm hoped to eliminate Sven's terrorist violence. Yet it was for the purpose of freeing the clones, not enslaving them, that I had come to Rivolin.

But there was another reason I had finally decided to apply for a leave of absence from the hospital and make this trip. With all of HOFROC's years of searching, we had never been able to discover MedComm's main base of operations. Even Marcus, once a practicing MedComm surgeon, had never been made privy to their inner circle. MedComm could be right here on Rivolin, ensconced in some innocuous building in front of my eyes. Their secret was that well guarded.

All this cloak-and-dagger was very exciting. I was finally right smack in the center of the action. But I felt a twinge of guilt as I thought of Jeni, who was back on Trattori impatiently waiting for news. The clone-girl was growing rapidly, physically, emotionally, and intellectually. Before leaving the hospital planet I had gotten Jeni a position in a computer lab working on a more foolproof mechanism for the solar transmitters. Jeni still harbored feelings of responsibility over her failure to prevent immediately the Callistra disaster, and this research seemed to help relieve the guilt. Of course, because Jeni was a clone, she was not being paid for her work. I think I resented this discrimination even more than Jeni, who was not yet fully aware of the ways of the human galaxy.

Well, this was why I had come to Rivolin—to rectify such inequalities, as well as to put a stop to the more horrible atrocities.

But how much could I hope to accomplish with this audience before the Joint Council? I didn't know. I wished my brain would stop running at high speed. It seemed as if I had not had a moment of rest for weeks. If only I could achieve a few minutes of quiet, of peace. Here I was, walking in the famous Rivolin Gardens, and I could just as well have been sitting in a prison cell.

I forced myself to become aware of my surroundings, to bring myself back to the present. Straight ahead of me, in the midst of all the greenery, was a paved circle. In the center was the statue of a thin man, his face looking toward the sky, his palms spread upward in entreaty out in front of his body. I walked closer, to read the inscription:

ANSELM GABROL—
YEAR ONE OF THE GALACTIC ERA
"LET ALL PEOPLE ENJOY PEACE"

Everyone knew those famous words said by the Peacemaker. After the plague had swept through the Orion sector in 2191 A.D.T.T., Earth, still weakened by the disease, had sent its tired space fleet out in a foolish attempt to regain its lost supremacy. Other small planet-states had begun to fight among themselves. But no world had been strong enough to obtain a lasting victory. Finally, Anselm Gabrol from the Altair System had managed to negotiate a trade agreement encompassing a loosely knit corporate body whose purpose was to oversee the resumption of trade between the isolated worlds, as well as to settle any disagreements that might arise. Over the next years the organization had grown to include more than three hundred separate planets. Anselm Gabrol had been hailed as the Peacemaker, and the year 2240 A.D.T.T. had been changed to Year One of the Galactic Era.

Suddenly I realized I was ruminating in terms of centuries, avoiding the minutes that had been given me to live right now. I looked at my watch. The time had passed too quickly. My mind was racing, but my body was standing still. I knew I had to hurry if I intended to meet my father for dinner. Where was the nearest exit?

I spotted the red arrows that pointed the way out, found the street map and dialed my desired place of arrival. The electronics whirred for a minute, and then emitted a printed sheet with the fastest route marked in red. Welcoming this practical diversion, I concentrated on following the directions. I entered the fastest-moving ro-way lane with some trepidation. I was no longer used to big-city travel systems.

When I finally arrived in the restaurant section my heartbeat felt like one continuous stream of water pounding over the side of a cliff. It was good to feel, once again, the firm, unmoving ground under my feet.

I walked along the sidewalk, still following my street map. Restaurant signs boasted exotic foods from the farthest reaches of the galaxy. Ah, this should be the turn. That was it. Alixandro's Café. The sign said spicy Pirretan food.

Now that I had gotten here, I stood silently outside the restaurant door. The urge rose in me to run away, bolt down the street and lose myself among the millions of people who were not Paul Menard's daughter. But that had always been my tendency—to run away and avoid confrontations. I had done that once before when I left my father's house. And I had been fighting this tendency ever since.

Well, I was my own woman now. There was nothing he could do to me. He had no more influence over my life, I told myself, standing alone out in the middle of the busy street.

Did I really believe that? No, but it sounded good. Nevertheless, I had to admit I had grown stronger in all these years away from him. I could hold my own in a verbal battle. It was deep inside me where I still felt vulnerable.

Well, I was on guard, and that was the best I could do. Whatever was going to be, let it happen.

So I pushed open the door and entered the dimly lit restaurant. A waiter directed me to my father's table.

The man dressed in a dark gray cloth suit who turned around to face me looked too old. Could it have only been thirteen years since I had last seen him? What about the organ transplants? Hadn't he been using them? The tired look I had seen in his eyes that last time was now reflected in the bent-over way he held his body, in the wrinkles on his forehead, in the loose skin under his jaws, in the liver-yellow look of his skin, in the thinning gray hair on his head. He shouldn't have aged this quickly, even without the transplants. Had he stopped taking the hormone shots, too?

Observing from an emotional distance, I watched as Paul Menard spoke, his voice wavering not only with age but with emotion. "Selena. I'm glad you came." He rose to greet his daughter. Me.

Suddenly, without thinking, I was flinging my arms around this old, vulnerable man who was my father. No more words were spoken for a while as we held each other.

Finally, I gently loosened my father's arms from around my waist, and said, "Let's sit down and talk." My father took a napkin and poked at the corners of his eyes, coughed to clear his throat, and then looked up at me as I finished blotting the tears from my own cheeks.

"I mean it," he said. "I'm really glad you came."

"So am I," I answered.

"I just wish it hadn't required such circumstances to bring us together."

Quietly, I said, "The clone question is what drove us apart. It seems fitting it should bring us together."

"I want you to know," Paul Menard said, taking my hand, "that I was never really angry at you."

"It seemed like you were, at the time."

"No. I was angry with myself, for sitting back and letting it get out of hand. And I guess I was a little angry at you because you were the one who kept reminding me that I was avoiding my responsibilities."

"But I don't understand," I said. "If you felt I was right all along, why didn't you do anything about it?"

"Daughter, three hundred and sixty-three years is a long time to be alive. I've lived almost four full lifetimes. I felt I had made my contribution to society, and now it was up to society to figure out what to do with it. I had stopped caring about anything. Nothing was exciting to me anymore. Some mornings I could barely get up enough interest in life to get out of bed. What else did society want from me? I was too tired. I only wanted to be left alone."

"And now"—the words seemed to stick in my throat—"have you changed your mind?"

"I'm still tired," my father said. "But I've decided that four lifetimes is more than any man should be allowed to live. One starts to stagnate, you see. And if all humankind became like me, pretty soon we would die out."

"Is that why"—I touched the top of his hand with my free hand—"you've let yourself go like this?"

"Immortality is not what it's made out to be. I've decided that it's time to let nature take its course."

"But it's only been thirteen years and you look so, so . . ." I couldn't finish.

"Shush, dear. I know what I'm doing. When you stop the hormones after such a long time, the body, used to its dependence, begins to break down very quickly."

"Are you sick?"

"No. Just getting old."

I rubbed my father's hand, brought it up to my mouth and kissed it lightly. Then I looked up at the wrinkled face and said, "But you still haven't answered my question. Have you changed your mind about the clones?"

"I'll answer you soon. Don't worry. Just humor me and let me go at my own pace."

"Okay."

"Well, after you left I sank deeper into my depression. I retreated almost completely from the world. You see, I had no one with whom to argue anymore. In my state of mind I was no good for anyone. After three more years of this wallowing in self-pity, your mother decided to leave me. She said that if immortality meant complete stagnation, she didn't want any part of it. She'd rather be alive now, even if it meant dying young.

"So there I was, completely alone. Somehow, your

mother's words reached me. 'I'd rather be alive now.' They made sense to my old ears. Here I was, the oldest human being in existence, sitting around in a senile stupor. What was the point of it all?

"There was no point. I made the decision right then to stop any further treatments. I was tired. I would let myself die.

"And then something remarkable happened. Since I knew I was going to die, I began wanting to do things, for one last time. I wanted to go to the theater, to concerts, to the tri-dee. Even a simple walk in my garden or down to the shopping vista became pleasurable. I kept thinking to myself, this might be the last time. I felt as if every minute of the day might be my last.

"I thought about never seeing you again. I thought about what you had said before you left. And I knew you were right. I did have to accept responsibility for my actions. I did have to try to do something about it. There wasn't much time left for me. I had to hurry.

"But nobody can rush MedComm. Or cause a revolution to happen before the time is exactly ripe. If I pushed it too fast, I would have predestined myself to fail. I had to go slow, first making casual references to old friends. I published a few papers that subtly hinted at the unknown capabilities inherent in clones. I pointed out to some younger scientists that it might be possible to quicken the growth of a single cloned organ to full term. Then it would no longer be necessary for members of MedComm to have several reproductions of themselves waiting around to supply spare parts. In fact, it would be cheaper to do only one organ at a time.

"As I did all this, I noticed the underground literature that could be found on occasional street corners. The pamphlets spoke of the dangers of power centralization in Komsol and the lack of jobs for honest workers. They spoke of the exploitation of a slave labor force instead of a free, paid working class. They described the atrocities performed on clones in the name of science.

"I knew you had had a part in all this, and I felt closer to you, knowing I was doing my bit. Even if I never saw you again, I was content.

"The poison of the dream of immortality was gone from my system. In working toward freedom for clones, I found that I had freed myself."

My father took a drink from the glass of wine, made from the midea grape, and was silent. He closed his eyes, as if the long explanation had completely drained him.

"Are you all right?" I asked.

Paul Menard slowly opened his eyes. "Yes, I'm fine. Sometimes I forget that this body can no longer race through time. I must go slowly."

"Should you go back to your hotel?" I was worried about him, but also wanted to keep talking.

"No," he reassured me. "I'll have dinner with you. But I can't stay out too late. I need my rest. And tomorrow I want you to join me at the Joint Council. I want you to see how it works before you lock horns with MedComm. And there are a few people you should meet. But for now, let's enjoy the food and each other's company." He waved a waiter over to take our dinner order.

I watched as my father enthusiastically questioned the waiter regarding the choicest dishes. Yes, tonight was a time to celebrate. I was glad I had not run away from this encounter.

CHAPTER 11

Excerpt from Selena Menard's *Out of My Father's Seed: A Personal History of the Clone Wars, Vol. I.*

The Forum is a gigantic round room designed on the order of a Roman arena, but much bigger. Down below, in the center, stands the Speaker of the Council. Surrounding him, in concentric circles gradually rising higher and higher, are first the permanent committees, and then the planetary delegations.

Today, all the seats were occupied. A vote was on the agenda. The Speaker called the meeting to order.

I was sitting, with Vera and Willis, in one of the balcony tiers reserved for visitors and unrecognized delegations. In two days, when it was HOFROC's turn to speak, my delegation would be invited down to a temporary circle reserved for just such occasions. In the meanwhile, we were only spectators.

Watching the heated discussion below, I was awed by the idea that soon I would be speaking in front of all those people. Transmissions of my speech would be sent to all the member planets. Would my throat muscles constrict at the critical point? Would my voice be able to drown out all those objections and angry rebuttals?

I listened now as the Speaker, a large man whose massive figure carried his presence throughout the great hall, rapped his sonic gavel; a high, piercing sound caused me to clap my hands over my ears.

Then it was quiet.

The Speaker said, "The delegate from Solstice is recognized."

"Sir, the Eastern Periphery demands immediate embargo of trade goods from Mivrakki. We cannot condone the assassination of President Parma Condolli and the takeover of Mivrakki by a military junta. Furthermore, it is known that they have begun manufacturing armaments, and those of us in Mivrakki's sector fear an outward push of aggression in line with the show of force that has already been made. I demand a vote for censure and embargo, along with the promise that ConFed will take all possible steps to keep this aggression contained within the confines of Mivrakki." The delegate from Solstice sat down.

A voice from under my own balcony yelled, "That's not enough."

The Speaker rapped his electronic gavel and said, "You have not been recognized."

"Then recognize me," the voice said. "I am Lista Colman, from President Parma Condolli's cabinet." A surge of joy rose in me as I recognized Lista's name and remembered the warm presence of the revolutionary woman.

Another voice rang out. "We are now Mivrakki's official delegation. That person is out of order."

The Speaker tried to outshout the tumult that ensued. Again, he was forced to send out the electronic hum that vibrated painfully inside my head. He spoke. "We recognize the minister from the deposed government. Come to the podium and speak."

I looked down and saw Lista Colman, now about sixty years old, striding purposefully down an aisle.

Once at the dais, Lista grasped the edges of the podium, leaned forward, and spoke in deep and earnest tones.

"Good people," she said. "I have information that will shock and dismay some of you. Others may already know what I am about to say."

"I protest," shouted the official delegate from Mivrakki. "We are the government. She should not be allowed to speak. Her defamations will . . ."

"You are out of order." It was the Speaker. "That question has already been decided. Sit down and be quiet or you will be evacuated from the premises." The Speaker turned toward Lista. "Go ahead."

The middle-aged woman continued. "I have a truth to tell. I was present during the coup that took the president's life. I saw what happened and know who was responsible." She paused. "The men who took over were led by outsiders. They were led by privateers from MedComm's fleet."

A murmur rose in the hall from the shock of this revelation.

The Speaker asked, "Can you tell me what Med-Comm would have to gain from such a venture?"

"Yes," Lista answered. "Mivrakki is a sparsely populated planet, pioneered by people who had believed God never intended humans to live longer than their natural span of years. We hold to our own ways, we do our own manual labor, and wish only to be left alone. For the last nine years, ever since we freed ourselves from Komsol, our Workers' Union has obtained the majority vote. But MedComm, watching our progression away from technology and toward humanity, considers us a threat. I believe they plan to carry out a program of total extermination against our people. And, since Mivrakki is located at a distance from any of the major trade lanes, they hoped they would be able to complete their coup unnoticed."

I leaned forward in my seat. It was fascinating how supposedly separate seeds came to fruition around the same time. It had to be more than coincidence. People all over the galaxy were moving toward change. And

Lista Colman of Mivrakki had always been in the fore-front. Now I wondered how much this turn of events could directly help my cause.

Someone tapped me on the shoulder. I looked around to see my father sit down behind me. He smiled and motioned to pay attention to the drama unfolding in the arena below.

The Speaker asked, "If your planet is so unimportant, why would MedComm put itself out on a limb by such alleged activities?"

"Because," said Lista, "they know that a small idea can grow into a much larger one. They have calculated that, although our ideas are ahead of our time, our small world is the vanguard for the future. And, since they take a long view of the future, they hoped to stamp out the nucleus of discontent at its core. Besides," she concluded, "they have such a superior view of themselves that they believe themselves exempt from the usual laws that govern humankind."

"Do you have any proof of these allegations?" the Speaker asked.

"Only my testimony and that of other eyewitnesses."

"We need something more tangible," the Speaker said.

Irate voices were raised in anger all over the Forum. Delegates were leaping to their feet, yelling. As the Speaker rapped once again for silence, I heard one last protest. "MedComm thinks it can get away with anything!"

"SILENCE," the Speaker boomed. "There will be silence." He leaned toward Lista Colman. "Although we do not usually interfere in the private affairs of any world, it seems that this case warrents the attention of the Council. Are you ready to call for a vote of censure and embargo?"

"Isn't there anything more that can be done?" Lista Colman asked.

"The ConFederation is not a ruling state. We abide together through mutual agreements and cooperation.

We can only recommend economic and social sanctions. We can take no military action."

"But what good will an embargo do?"

"We can hope that this, and if needed, more widespread economic sanctions, will cause aggressors to reconsider their actions."

"It's not enough," Lista said. "But if it's all we can have, then Mivrakki's people call for a vote of censure and embargo."

"There will be a short recess in which delegations may confer. The vote will be taken in one hour." The Speaker stepped from the raised platform on which he had been standing.

My former elation dropped to bleak depression as I turned to my father. I said, "What can we hope to gain, if the Joint Council can't even stop human genocide?"

"Don't worry, dear," my father said. "The vote hasn't been taken yet, and MedComm concerns itself more with public opinion than you might realize. All these years they've had a virtual stranglehold on the Con-Federation's population through their monopoly on Komsols, clones, and the promise of immortality. But more and more worlds are becoming self-sufficient, and although many still are frightened of being forced to do without the Komsol system, a large minority have begun to join Mivrakki in their views. Resentment is growing against MedComm's privileges. Why should only a handful have access to immortality? MedComm may still have power today, but they are becoming afraid for their future." He grinned. "The timing of this issue will most definitely benefit our cause." Paul Menard stood up. "Come. I want you to meet some people."

I followed my father, motioning Willis and Vera to join me. As we entered the hall, my father turned toward me and whispered, "Remember that the fact that they have not been able to protect planets from the clone attacks on Komsols is not favorable to this issue." He jerked his thumb back toward the Forum. "It's our main bargaining point."

I was not so sure I liked the idea that Sven's warfare against MedComm was turning out so advantageously. But if this was the reality, then I would have to work with it.

Out in the curving hallway tight-knit groups of people spoke in excited, but hushed, tones. Runners ran from one delegation to another, carrying messages, making bargains. Leaning over the railing, I could see hundreds of delegates conferring, waving their arms, intensely trying to convince one another that right was on their side.

"Over here." My father drew me by the arm. Willis and Vera followed behind us. Paul Menard introduced his daughter and her delegation to two men. "This is Bertil Renson, a scientist who agrees with my views. And Bob Kelty, a representative of MedComm, who, I believe, is ready to negotiate."

What, now? Already? This was happening too fast.

Bertil Renson, young, only in his mid-twenties, spoke first. "Mr. Kelty already knows my views on this matter. I think he is convinced that some laxity toward the clones will not lessen MedComm's profits."

Had they done all the work for me?

Kelty spoke now, in a self-important tone. "It's not a matter of profit, Dr. Renson. I want you all to understand that we do not believe we have been engaging in any actions that are morally unacceptable. But we are willing, for the sake of good public relations, to make a few concessions."

I looked at Kelty, a man with young features obviously obtained from cloned organs. But his shoulders stooped and his eyes carried the same tired expression that I had seen in my father. Maybe it was only a matter of time, and then the young could take over by default. That is, if a new generation of false immortals could be prevented from rising. So far, it seemed that the old guard had been very jealous of their status.

"What concessions?" I asked.

"What is it you want?" Kelty asked.

"We want complete freedom for all clones and their rights as citizens of the ConFederation."

"That is out of the question." Kelty shook his head vehemently. "They are little more than animals and could not fend for themselves."

Bullshit, I thought to myself.

Kelty continued. "But we are willing to let you people supervise any teaching programs you might care to implement. Then you'll find out for yourselves how stupid they are."

"What else?" I asked.

"You've complained about health conditions. We're willing to negotiate a set of medical standards and will allow your own medical staff to do a yearly checkup. We are also willing to phase out our clone farms as we step up research into quick organ-growth techniques. Our terms are nonnegotiable. We will concede no more than this."

"It's not all that we want. But we will consider it," I heard myself saying.

"One more thing. We want something in return."

This was the clincher. "What?"

"We want Sven Soronson, or whatever name he uses now, to be stopped. We insist you bring him in as a prisoner and turn him over to us. If you don't agree, we will begin executing ten clone-children a day until you comply with our request. What is your decision?"

I felt as if a load of bricks had been dropped on my head. Realizing that I had been staring wordlessly at the MedComm representative, I composed myself and forced myself to speak calmly. "Will you excuse us while we discuss your proposition?"

"Surely."

The three of us from the Human Organization for Rights of Clones turned away and formed our own group. We spoke in whispers.

"How can he dare?" I voiced my shock.

"He can dare whatever he wants," Willis said. "He knows the majority of the ConFederation would prefer to sacrifice a few clones in return for the life of Sven Soronson."

"But we can't let that happen," Vera said. "Can we?" She looked at me as if I knew all the answers.

"The choice seems to be between two evils," I said hesitantly. "I've had my disagreements with Sven in the past, but I never thought it would come to this."

"MedComm's left us no choice," Willis said. "It's either Sven or hundreds, perhaps thousands, of innocent children."

"I wish we had never come to Rivolin," I said. "We pushed MedComm too far."

"No," Willis said. "If we back away now, nothing will ever change. We have to accept their terms. It's war, and in war there are casualties. Soronson knows that."

"I suppose you're right," I agreed. I smiled at the irony of it. We were using the same logic Sven had used when he had made the decision to turn against me, using who my father was as the catalyst to help form the splinter group of COFF. In Sven's eyes, the sacrifice of one person for the greater cause was justifiable. Now, here I was doing the same thing.

"It's a good beginning," Willis insisted. "MedComm's concessions may seem too small, but it's a sign the tide is turning. We've got our foot in the door."

"But how are we supposed to capture Sven?" Vera asked, getting practical.

"I know someone who might be able to contact him," I heard myself saying. There was no point in going with the theory but not the action. If we delayed too long in delivering Sven, there was no doubt that MedComm would carry out its threat against the clone-children. "You remember Jeni, the clone from Callistra? She's the only one he's likely to let come near him. They were very close on Trattori."

"But will she do it?" Willis asked.

"She is very much against Sven's violent tactics. And I don't think she would be able to let all those children be killed."

"Maybe she can contact him," Willis said doubtfully, "but can she capture him?"

"We'll have to ask MedComm for help with that aspect," I said. "And I don't like that idea either."

"Neither do I," Vera said. "But I think we have to try it."

"Then we're agreed," Willis said.

"Agreed," Vera said.

"Agreed."

We returned to Kelty and negotiated two last points: a ConFed commission to ensure MedComm's fidelity, and professional help to aid HOFROC's representative in capturing Sven Soronson.

Kelty said, "Then after you've spoken to this Jeniclone, we'll expect you to bring her to meet us."

"Oh," I said, feeling as if I wanted to sink into the floor. What had I gotten Jeni involved in? "Do you have to meet her?"

"Of course. We want to check her out for ourselves."

"I suppose that's acceptable." I didn't know what else to say. MedComm was pulling all the strings.

"It's the only way," Kelty said.

"Where should we meet you?"

"On your planet. On Trattori."

"What?"

"Here is our code." Kelty handed me a piece of paper. "Contact us when you're ready." He turned around abruptly, and walked away.

"Well, that's it," Dr. Renson said. "Nice meeting you." He, too, strode away.

I stood still for a moment, my thoughts hovering in a sort of blanked-out space. I asked my father, "Is that all?" The words were hard to enunciate. My lips felt stiff and unworkable.

"That's it. You've completed your mission."

"But what about the Forum?" I was just realizing that I had committed not only myself but all of HOFROC, and Jeni, too, to follow this road of desperation. And doomed Sven to probable death.

"Oh, you can still speak there," my father answered lightly. "It's good timing with all the rest of this going on." He waved his hands at the other delegates who were beginning to shuffle back toward their seats. "But, you know, almost everything is settled like this before the issue is spotlighted. And MedComm was anxious not to have another scene in the Forum. They want this to blow over as quickly as possible. You were in a good bargaining position."

In shock, I looked at my father. Didn't he realize that MedComm had had us over a barrel? That my group had been manipulated into a corner? I shook my head, perplexed. Well, my father didn't know how much I was connected to Sven and Jeni. Maybe Paul Menard really did think it was a good deal?

I considered that idea. After all, the concessions MedComm had made were not really so minor. For a moment I felt a surge of elation at how much we had accomplished. MedComm must really be running scared to have had to resort to such dire threats. They had offered a package deal that couldn't be refused. And, although the thought of turning over any person to MedComm was repulsive, the loss of Sven would not be too tragic. His mad rampaging was killing clones as well as humans and, in the end, would certainly work against the cause.

I noticed that my father was urging Willis and Vera back to the balcony. "It's time for the voting," I heard him say to them.

I walked slowly back to my seat. The momentary elation was beginning to ebb. Was I asking too much of Jeni? True, the clone-woman had grown in physical strength and was intellectually many times quicker than the average human. True, Jeni would be able to confront Sven on his own level—and reach him emotionally. I remembered the first time I had seen Sven with Jeni, how his hard exterior had melted before the clone-woman. Yes, Jeni was the only one who stood a chance of getting anywhere near Sven. It had to be tried.

But there were still Jeni's naïve feelings toward

Sven—first the infatuation and then the hurt at his rejection. Was Jeni really ready to handle such feelings, when I, Selena, could barely manage them myself? Well, the clone-woman had to grow up sooner or later. Jeni would just have to decide for herself what to do.

The Speaker called the meeting to order and began to ask for a roll call. A two-thirds majority was needed to vote for censure.

Interrupting, a MedComm representative asked to take the podium. He was recognized. He offered the committee's apologies, said a few members of Med-Comm's fleet had acted without the knowledge of their superiors in this matter, and would be severely reprimanded. They would be ordered to leave Mivrakki as soon as a democratic government could be instated. Once again, he hoped the Council would accept Med-Comm's sincere apologies.

The delegates rose to their feet, screaming and clapping.

What double-talk, I thought. On the surface it sounded so civilized, but who could tell what was really going on underneath the veneer.

A great dissatisfaction rose up inside me, and then a feeling of claustrophobia. I couldn't bear another moment of this bedlam. I pushed my way past the close-packed bodies gathered on the balcony. Then I was out the door, into empty space. I could breathe again.

I leaned against a wall, my eyes squeezed tightly shut. But a few tears still managed to escape.

I jumped, startled, as a hand touched my shoulder. Opening my eyes, I saw a short, thin man looking at me with a concerned expression on his face. It was Daven Migdal, Lista Colman's co-worker. Everyone seemed to be converging on Rivolin for the Mivrakki issue.

For one long minute he looked through his thick-rimmed glasses, directly into my eyes. "Are you all right?" Daven asked me, his fingers ever so gently caressing my cheek.

"No." The word burst out of my mouth, the tears out of my eyes. Without thinking, I leaned against this almost-stranger from the past. I felt his arms encircle me, hold me, stroke my back, cradle my head against his chest. His touch was firm, yet deep and caring. I let myself sink into his physical presence.

When the tears were gone, I gently stepped backward, and with a low, embarrassed laugh, said, "I don't usually throw myself into someone's arms like that."

"Don't worry about it," Daven answered, not letting go of my hand. "I like holding you."

After another long moment I felt the need to draw my hand away, but said, "You certainly have a knack for being in the right place at the right time."

"I try to be where I'm needed," Daven answered. He leaned up against the wall where I was standing. "I was in the next box with the rest of Lista's delegation, and saw you go off by yourself. I had been meaning to say hello to you, and this seemed like my chance."

"I'm flattered." I felt myself blushing like a schoolgirl.

"I've always liked you," Daven continued, disarming me completely. "But back then I never really had time to get to know you. Too much was in flux, like now."

Smiling, I said, "We're like planets circling the same star, but crossing orbits only once every ten years."

"I would hope to see you more often than that," he said. "But in the end we each need to follow our own path."

"And yours is?"

"Tied right into yours. I've been following Sven's explosive tour of the galaxy. Not that I condone what he's doing, you understand. But the fact is, each time he destroys a Komsol he leaves a world ripe for the picking. All those people, suddenly without their superpowerful technology, need someone to teach them how to really live. To teach them how to work with their own hands. To teach them how to organize them-selves, to fight for their survival."

"Sounds like a dream come true for you," I said, remembering back when Daven had chosen not to re-turn to Mivrakki. "It's just what you said you wanted to be doing."

"Yes," Daven said, but his face muscles tightened. "Although not at the cost of so many lives. However, that part of it all is out of my hands." He turned his palms upward in illustration.

"Unfortunately," I answered, "not out of mine."

"Is that what the problem is?" he asked solicitously.

"Yes," I answered, and explained my dilemma.

"It sounds like you're stalemated, for the moment anyhow," Daven said, with sympathy. "I'm sorry I can't give you any brilliant strategy to use against Med-Comm. I don't think you have any choice but to do what they ask. You'll just have to wait for an open-ing, and be ready to leap."

"Yes," I agreed. "I know there's no quick-and-easy solution. But I do feel better about it now that I've talked with you. And cried," I added, laughing more easily now.

"Glad to have been of service, gentle lady," Daven said, smiling as he pushed the glasses back up the bridge of his nose. "Perhaps you would be interested in taking a walk with me, away from all this confu-sion. Methinks the lady would benefit from a further diversion." As Daven leaned forward, making an elabo-rate bow at my feet, his glasses slid off and rattled noisily onto the floor.

I couldn't help laughing, as I had been meant to do, holding my side as I leaned against the wall and watched Daven make a show of extreme blindness as he groped along the floor.

"Yes," I gasped, almost out of breath. "Yes, I'd love to take a walk with you." I stretched out my hand to-ward him. "Lead on."

Daven grasped my hand, kissing it in a formal gesture from bygone days. But this time he was careful to keep one finger poised on his glasses, holding them in place, as he made the slight bow over my outstretched hand.

Then, throwing formality to the winds, he grasped my hand firmly and began running down the hallway. Our footsteps echoed, filling the empty air behind us with the sounds of our rapid departure.

It was good just to feel my body moving, to feel my legs pumping, to feel Daven's fingers around my hand, to reach out to him, to feel his life force so close to mine.

Everything else could wait. Tomorrow there would be enough time to deal with all my problems.

Today, all I wanted to do was run. To let my body live and feel. To love and be loved.

To forget.

CHAPTER 12

Jeni

Jeni walked into Complex D. Two rows of desks faced each other in the center of the room, back to back, with their data outlets directly connected to Komsol. One blond man studied his fingernails as Jeni passed his desk. A second person swiveled her chair, turning away from the clone, and another glared at Jeni with open hostility. Stiffening her back, Jeni continued to walk past the technicians.

Having had relatively little contact with the True Borns, Jeni was still unused to such treatment. From her childhood she could only clearly remember her clone-mother and clone-sisters. Afterward, interred inside Komsol, she had had no connections with the feeble human world, and had desired nothing more than what Komsol could give. Then had come the catastrophe, and Sindra's angry ministrations. Sindra was the only antagonistic contact Jeni could remember. Since that time, first Sven and then Selena had kept Jeni in a sort of protective, loving custody.

It had been after the near disaster Sven had precipitated that Selena had found Jeni this job. Although anti-clone resentment had been stirred up by Sven's action, Jeni still hoped to show the humans that not all clones were bent on sabotaging Komsols. With Selena's urging, Jeni had agreed to become part of a task force involved in redesigning the Komsol-clone system in order to make it foolproof against attack. At first, Jeni had been enthusiastic. She didn't want any more people, human or clone, to be injured or killed. She was glad to be needed, glad to be able to use her expertise in this vital area. Her assignment revolved around the refinement of the solar transmitter. It was a crucial mechanism, and several scientists were involved in this one aspect.

Jeni finished walking the gauntlet of averted faces and hostile stares. Sitting down at her own computer outlet, she composed herself until she felt the heated flush disappear from her cheeks. At first she had tried sharing her ideas with the other technicians working on the project. One person had muttered a few words about being too busy to talk. Another had not even been that civil, turning his back on her, pointedly ignoring her presence. Finally, the project chief had told her to submit her findings in a written report. Otherwise, stick to her own business and don't bother the other workers.

Then she had understood. To these humans, the idea of being helped by a clone was appalling. It might be possible that they would accept her scientific contributions, otherwise why would they have agreed to let her work here? But it was obvious she would never receive proper credit or gratitude for her diligence.

Not only was she almost totally ignored in the laboratory, but at lunch, in the cafeteria, people made a point of avoiding her table. Even in the corridors, the True Borns gave her a wide berth. Everywhere, by their obvious avoidance, she was marked a clone—a pariah.

Jeni looked down at her hands, covered in white gloves, and rubbed her slightly twisted finger joints.

"Prejudice doesn't need a good explanation," was what Selena had said. "Society feels better when it has a scapegoat, it works more harmoniously when it can band together against a common enemy, when it can vent its dissatisfaction and anger on one group." Selena had also said, Jeni remembered, that the one group that became the scapegoat was, on the surface, the most dissimilar and the weakest of all the groups that made up a society. This configuration could be seen throughout history. The weakest and the strangest groups were always the ones that became the focal points for society's hatred.

This analysis exactly described the position of the clones within the ConFederation. They were too different from the True Borns, not considered real human beings since they were artificially contrived. Scattered throughout the galaxy, they were too weak to form a cohesive, strong group. Especially the Komsol clones, who were so completely divorced from the mainstream.

Yes, clones were the perfect scapegoat.

Jeni sat still, wondering if anything would ever change. When would Selena get back from the meeting of the Joint Council on Rivolin? At least Selena proved that some humans were decent. But if most of them were like these others here, how could Selena hope to gain anything for clones' rights from the Council? Jeni didn't know. But Selena knew so much more about the world of humans than Jeni did. If Selena was out there, trying, maybe there was reason to hope.

Okay, then, I'll do my part.

Jeni ran over yesterday's calculations, and fed a new set of possibilities into the computer. In this area she was completely sure of herself. She knew what she was doing. If the problem was solved by the time Selena returned, Selena could continue to act as spokeswoman for the clones by presenting Jeni's accomplishment to the human scientists. Then they would have to recognize Jeni's abilities. It would be one more tiny step toward convincing the galaxy that clones were human, too.

She set herself to her task with renewed determination. *I'll show them. Clones are as smart as humans, maybe more so. I'll force them to recognize me.*

And all the other clones. With this thought Jeni realized that one clone alone could not hope to change a galaxy full of people. It would take a concerted effort, by all clones, to give a show of strength. That's what COFF and HOFROC had been doing—organizing clones and human supporters. When Selena returned, Jeni would offer her help. She would go to as many planets as possible and contact the Komsol clones. They were the ones who needed help the most, Jeni knew. They were the ones who needed to be guided back to self-knowledge. Once aware, the Komsol clones had enormous power at their fingertips. They would no longer be considered weak, inhuman misfits. They could demand respect. They controlled entire planets. They could not be ignored.

Jeni was excited at this idea. True, it was an enormous project, but, she knew, she was the one to do it. And there was no better time to start than right now. She would start with Melanie, Trattori's clone.

This was easy enough to conceive, but more difficult to carry out as a real action. Jeni, better than most, knew the egocentric world of the Komsol clone. Each was a withdrawn entity, with a strong emotional barrier against an awareness of other personalities. This was a result of, first, the childhood self-contained unity between the clone and its siblings. Later, the immense power behind Komsol became all-fulfilling. To the Komsol clone there was only his or her planet—and Komsol. Nothing mattered beyond this immediate territory where the clone's power could achieve almost godlike proportions.

Jeni knew that, in her previously encapsulated state, she would never have been interested in communicating on a personal level with a freely moving individual.

The problem, then, was how to sufficiently provoke

Melanie's interest. Jeni began by working through the laboratory's computer outlet.

Hunching her shoulders over her console, she began punching keys. Starting with mathematical equations, ones that Melanie would normally answer without paying any attention, Jeni began to add harder and harder problems. Finally she keypunched one insoluble problem after another. Pressing the keys rapidly, firing her questions at a rate no normal human brain could comprehend, she knew she would gain the Komsol clone's attention. Only someone like a Komsol clone, could work this quickly. Melanie had to notice the difference. Yes, the computer stopped printing out the contradictions inherent in the multiple problems. The screen blanked out for a second and then, in printed words, asked, "Who's there?"

Jeni identified herself as the former Komsol clone who had saved Melanie's life a few months ago. She continued, saying she was in need of intellectual stimulation. Could they play a game of mini-stats?

Melanie said yes, that it would be a diversion.

That day and the next, they played. On the third day Jeni began to insert questions about the planet. "How long ago was it pioneered?"

"More than three hundred years ago."

"By whom?"

"By doctors and scientists who wanted to establish a medical refuge."

"What is the population?"

"Three million, if you include average number of patients from off-planet and clones."

"Clones?" Jeni asked. "I haven't seen any clones."

"They are situated on the second continent."

Clones? On the other side of the world? Jeni would have to ask Selena about that. But right now she had a more immediate purpose.

"Melanie, how long have you been on Trattori?"

"Eleven years."

"How old are you?"

"Twenty-one years."

"How many sisters did you have?"

There was a pause before Melanie responded. "Two." And then Melanie began to ask the same questions of Jeni until, "Is it terrible out there?"

"No," Jeni answered, "It's not terrible. It's beautiful. There's a whole world of sky and grass, rough and smooth textures, heat and cold, of tactile sensations. Oh, so many things."

"But weren't you scared?" Melanie asked. "I wouldn't know how to begin living without Komsol or how to exist only in a physical body."

"Yes," Jeni admitted. "I was scared. But I wasn't given any choice. You know what happened?"

"Yes. Sven did to you what he tried to do to me."

"That's right," Jeni said, rubbing her fingers. "But now I'm kind of glad that it happened. There's so much here that I never knew existed."

"But what about Komsol? How can you bear to live without it?"

"At first it was like my body had been chopped in half." Jeni winced at the memory. "But then I discovered that my own neural pathways were imprinted with much of Komsol's data. I can actually reproduce in my mind a data printout including information almost as complete as that which Komsol stored in its memory banks."

"That's amazing," Melanie said. "But I'm still not sure I would like to live out there with the True Borns, without the power of Komsol for protection."

"That's the only problem," Jeni admitted. "They treat me like a low-born animal. But," Jeni continued, "there are people out here fighting for us. Even now, there's a delegation on Rivolin bringing up the question of clone citizenship before the Forum."

"Is there anything I can do to help?" Melanie wanted to know.

"I don't know," Jeni answered. "But be ready. Who knows what can happen. Right now, the most important thing is for clones to open up the lines of communication, like we're doing right now, to contact other

Komsol clones and show the True Borns what we're capable of doing." Jeni continued, explaining about the solar transmitter project she was working on.

Together, the two clones combined forces to solve the problem. Working for a day and a half, they designed a small anti-force–shield that could not be triggered by any stimulus other than the specific wavelength to which it was cued. Only its own Komsol would be able to contact the solar satellite without triggering the protective field. It was a good piece of work.

Melanie printed out the computations on a sheet of paper. Jeni ripped it out of its slot and excitedly ran over to the project chief. Forgetting herself, she said, "I've got it. Here's the answer." And pushed the piece of paper in front of his eyes.

The project chief glared at Jeni. "What the hell do you think you're doing? Stop shoving that piece of dribble at my nose." He grabbed the paper and began to crumple it.

Jeni's chest heaved. She wanted to cry. But no, she wouldn't give him the satisfaction. No more weakness. Standing up straight, she spoke in a loud voice for everyone to hear. "I am telling you that this is the solution you've been trying to find. If you do not look at it and use it, I will go to your superiors and show them that you don't really want to find the correct answer. That you have chosen to plead that it can't be done rather than admit a clone has bettered you. I will show you up for the incompetent fool that you are. If you have any sense at all you will study that piece of paper and submit those findings. It's entirely up to you whether you get credit as project chief or whether I am singled out as the sole innovator. It's up to you."

The project chief stared at the clone with eyes filled with hatred. But he smoothed out the crumpled sheet and said, "I'll look at it when I get a chance."

"You'd better," Jeni said as she walked out of the room. Holding her head high, she marched down the corridor. Her body emanated an air of determination and urgency. She would not be stopped. People stepped aside to let her pass. They stared at her as she strode down the middle of the hallway.

She was not ignored.

When she got back to her own room, she closed the door, took a deep breath. Tears of anger welled up in her eyes. No. I won't let them make me cry. I won't be weak. But her body quivered as she held back the tears.

After a few minutes, calmness returned. Jeni sent orders through her neural pathways: muscles—relax; adrenalin production—slow down; diaphragm—contract regularly; heart muscles—stop racing. Okay, that was better.

It would be even better after she found Nikki. That was the answer—for clones to stick together. She buttoned up her sweater and went over to Nikki's room.

"Get on your jacket," Jeni told the boy. "We're going for a little walk."

"Where to?" Nikki asked.

"To visit another clone. To see Melanie."

They arrived in the large room where Jeni had taken over control of Komsol when Melanie had been disabled. This time, Jeni punched out a request to Melanie on the manual console.

The door to the smaller room slid open. This was the sacred sanctuary where Melanie's body was encased in her life-supporting system, where the clone's brain was physically connected to Komsol's circuits.

Gingerly, Jeni touched the switch that would light up the opaque coffin-shaped machine in which Melanie lay.

Jeni leaned over and looked down, gasped, turned away, and then forced herself to look again.

The other clone-woman's body was shriveled to a tiny size, almost fetuslike as it floated in a nutrient-liquid bath. The limbs were twisted, the body a caricature of the human shape. This was what Jeni had once looked like—a tiny malformed female body with electrodes growing out of puckered sores from her hairless scalp.

No wonder Komsol clones had such a short life expectancy!

Jeni wanted to reach out and touch the sad-looking body that lay in front of her. But she knew it wouldn't be a good idea, that her hand would only introduce unwanted bacteria into the nutrient bath. Instead, Jeni reached out for Nikki's hand. The boy had been staring with horrified fascination at Melanie's floating body.

Nikki responded to Jeni's touch by tearing his gaze away from Melanie and looking up at Jeni. There was a strange glassy look in his eyes. "Melanie says she doesn't really understand why you had to see her with your physical eyes, but she's happy if it gives you satisfaction."

"What?"

"Melanie says . . ." Nikki began again.

"I heard you. I meant, how do you know what she's thinking?"

"She spoke to me the way my brothers used to talk, the way I can sometimes talk to you."

"Can you do that with anyone?"

"No. Just with you and Melanie. And I could feel Sven, but he wouldn't answer."

"Clones, then," Jeni was really talking to herself. "You can communicate with other clones?"

"I guess so," Nikki answered, wondering why this seemed so important. He had done this all his life with his brothers.

"Do you think," Jeni continued, "that you could talk to me and to Melanie at the same time? Could you help us to talk to each other?"

"I don't know," Nikki said, "I never tried to do that."

"Well, go ahead and try now," Jeni said. She patted the boy's cheek and looked down at him, staring in tensely. Nothing happened.

Nikki squirmed under her touch, restlessly shifting

his feet. "I can't think when you're looking at me so hard," the boy complained.

"Oh, I'm sorry," Jeni said. "I'll look at Melanie instead. Is that okay?"

"Sure," Nikki answered, grinning. "Just not at me. And don't think so hard. It's easier when you're not so busy inside your head."

Jeni let herself relax, let her mind focus on imagining a bright candle flame. Concentrate on the small flicker of light. Then forget to concentrate. Relax.

A sharp pain stabbed through her forehead. Relax, she told herself, sending the message to all the muscles in her body. Then the pain was gone and she heard Nikki. *I'm here.* She could feel Melanie's presence, too, even before the other clone-woman announced, *So am I. Isn't it wonderful? I had forgotten what it could be like.*

So had I. Jeni. *Until Nikki. But I can't do it all the time. Nikki seems to have more control over it.*

Melanie. *That's because he hasn't spent years away from his clone-siblings. You and I have been separated too long.*

That's true enough. Jeni. She gave Melanie the equivalent of a mental hug. *We've been too long away from our own kind.*

Now that I can feel you in my mind, I can remember what it used to be like. Melanie's thought had a wistful feel to it.

And can be again. I hope that one day we can all be together, whether inside or outside Komsol. Jeni.

I don't think I would ever want to live in the human world, Melanie thought to Jeni.

Not even if it was all clones? Jeni answered.

Melanie. *No. Especially if I can do this with you and still have Komsol.*

Jeni. *I used to be happy with only one world, just like you. Now we've just rediscovered this mind-world. But there's a third world, the physical one. We're physical beings, too.*

No! Melanie's thought was vehement in its tone of denial.

Jeni listened to the essence of horror and decided to let go of that direction. But she had another idea. *Do you suppose that the mind-world is limited by physical space? Nikki, how close do you have to be to someone to hear their thoughts?*

I could only hear my brothers real good when they were in the same room with me, or maybe right next door. But I could still feel them when they were in the same building. The worst was when they went too far away. It was just like . . .

That's okay, Nikki. We're here with you, now. Jeni.

Nikki. *I know.* He squeezed Jeni's hand, which he was still holding, and moved against her so he could feel her body next to his.

Is that what it's like? Melanie wondered. *I guess it does feel nice.*

Yes, Jeni admitted, *it took me a while, but now I really like the softness. And you can feel it with us now. You don't have to come out of Komsol.*

Thank you. Melanie's thoughts snuggled up close to Jeni and Nikki.

Jeni could feel the clone-boy's mixture of pain-being-soothed and joy in his newfound friends; she could feel Melanie's mixed-up feelings and gradual opening up to new experiences; and beyond that, Jeni could feel the power of Komsol, the strength of its metallic walls, the surge of its energy through its circuits. It was like coming home again.

But it took Melanie to come up with the idea. *Yes, I have all this power. Maybe we can use it.*

How? Jeni asked.

Melanie. *As I see it, Nikki is the conductor for the mind-link—he directs the energy and makes the connection. But maybe Komsol can amplify the signal, make it strong enough to carry across a wide distance.*

Let's try it. Jeni's thoughts were excited. She could feel Melanie feeding the mind-energy into Komsol's circuits, could feel the buildup of power, could feel the beams reaching outward, traveling in those familiar concentric circles, searching. Jeni rode with the power, joining her mind with Melanie's brain as together they directed Komsol. They pushed on, outward, beyond the limited barriers of their physical space. Finally, in the distance, Jeni thought she could sense a fuzzy presence. But it was amorphous, amoebalike in its indistinct form. They needed to find a more concentrated focal point.

Just then, Melanie broke the link, and, with her distinct thought pattern, announced, *they're looking for you. They've been told you came here. I don't think they should find you inside my room.*

Jeni agreed and quickly, with Nikki, exited from Melanie's sanctuary. They were about to leave the main console room, when two guards stomped into the room. They wore the Komsol insignia—an ideogram of a sun inside a computer—on their jacket collars.

"What're you doing here, clone?" one of the guards asked Jeni.

When she started to answer, he waved her quiet and continued, "They've been looking for the boy. Got some tests to do." The Komsol guard grabbed Nikki by the shoulder. "And nobody's allowed in here without permission." He began to push Nikki toward the door.

No! The boy's thought reached Jeni; his eyes pleaded with her to save him.

"No!" Jeni said aloud. "You're supposed to wait for Selena Menard to get back."

"She's not here. We are." The guard jerked his thumb back the way he had come. "That's the way it goes."

"No." Jeni tried to pull the guard's hand away from Nikki. The second guard stepped over and forcefully held her back while Nikki was pulled out of the room.

"Let me go." Jeni struggled with the man.

"I don't talk to clones," the second guard said. True to his word, he marched Jeni out of Komsol's corridors, past several hospital buildings, and back to her own room, in complete silence.

When Jeni awoke the next day, her first thought was for Nikki.

Pulling on some clothes, she ran through the hallways, not trying to slow her pulse that was racing along with her feet. When she arrived at Nikki's room she found the door ajar. Pushing it all the way open, she was horrified to see that the small bedroom had been emptied of all its personal contents. An unmade mattress lay rolled up on the box springs. The floor had just been washed, and little puddles of soapy water were still apparent. When she sent out a mind-probe, searching for an aura of Nikki's presence, she could find no sign of him in the immediate vicinity.

Nikki was gone!

They had taken him away. Selena had promised to keep him safe. Jeni began to run toward Selena's office, but after a few steps remembered that the therapist was still off-planet. Frantically, pacing up and down the floor in front of Nikki's room, Jeni thought, *where can they have taken the boy? Is there anybody who can tell me where to find Nikki? No, the officials would only sneer at the idea of answering a question from a clone. They won't tell me anything.*

There was nothing to do but wait for Selena to get back. *Dammit, I feel so helpless.*

Suddenly she realized people were looking at her strangely as she paced back and forth in the hallway. *I have to get out of here.*

Forcefully, pushing her way past any people that blocked her route, Jeni made her way out of the hospital wing. Once outside, she ran down the now familiar paths that led to the meadow that had become her favorite thinking place.

She knelt in the grass, hugging her arms around herself. There was a knot in her stomach, building, growing larger, pushing upward. Putting her hands down on the stony dirt, she arched her back, raised her face to the sky, squeezed her eyes shut, and let out one long agonized scream.

When her body emptied itself of all the frustration and anger, Jeni pushed herself into a standing position. Her feet were firm on the ground. The warm breeze blew the grass gently against her knees; the sun beamed its rays down on the lone woman standing in the meadow. Jeni raised her arms to the shining star, lifted her head to the sky, and shouted, "I am a clone. And I'm a human being, too."

And then more quietly, she added, "I'll find Nikki. One day we'll live free, just like all of you."

CHAPTER 13

Excerpt from Selena Menard's *Out of My Father's Seed: A Personal History of the Clone Wars,* Vol. I.

I had just gotten back from Rivolin and was only still unpacking when I heard footsteps running down the hall. The door was pushed open and Jeni burst into my room. Gasping for breath, Jeni could barely get the words out of her mouth. "Nikki's gone."

"Calm down," I tried to reassure the clone-woman. "I'll get his file right away. He's probably just over at Complex R."

"Why would they take him there?"

"They must have decided it was time to finish up his comsol training," I said sarcastically, "completely ignoring my recommendations against it. But don't worry. I'll tell them that I haven't completed my own research delving into clone psychology. That I need to continue observing the boy before I can write up my own paper on the effects of separation and displacement on the clone mind. I'll get him back into my custody. He'll be safe—for a while."

With a sigh of relief, Jeni sank into one of the office chairs. "I was afraid I'd lost him."

I was leaning over a drawer of my chest, putting away one of my titeskins. "I won't let this happen again," I said. My voice was tense, and I didn't try to hide my anger.

"I have a plan," Jeni was saying. "But first tell me what happened at the Forum."

I walked across the room and sat down on the edge of my bed, facing Jeni. I could feel my shoulders slump as I lowered myself down to the mattress. "Some of it is good, and some of it is very bad," I said. I continued, explaining to Jeni that, yes, MedComm was willing to give clones better education and medical treatment. But not freedom. The clones were still to be enslaved to MedComm's greedy desire for profit and immortality. However, it was a good beginning and would give our own agents a better chance to infiltrate and organize the clones. HOFROC was already making plans for an underground that would spirit clones away from the masters, give them false identity papers, and help them adjust to the human world.

But there was a price to pay for this, a very expensive price. In return for their concessions, MedComm wanted Sven Soronson. If Sven Soronson was not delivered, they would begin to kill ten clone-children a day.

I described the situation to Jeni, explaining that Jeni's close relationship with Sven made her the necessary candidate for the unpleasant task of locating Sven.

"But what will they do with Sven?" Jeni asked.

"Question him. Probably kill him." I shook my head. "I didn't want to have to ask you to do this, Jeni. But they left us no choice."

"I don't know if I can do that to Sven," Jeni said, rubbing the fingers of her left hand with the other, unconsciously trying to straighten out the joints.

"It's up to you to decide," I said. "It's hard enough for me to even ask you."

"How can I let all those children die? Or let Sven kill all those other clones with his crazy attacks?"

"It sounds like you've decided."

"I guess so. I've never agreed with Sven's tactics. He's killing our own people. He killed Nikki's brothers. He could have killed me." I could hear Jeni trying to convince herself.

"I've never agreed with him either," I said. "But I wouldn't go against him like this if we didn't have to."

"Why do they have to make it so hard for us?" Jeni lamented, sounding like a little child.

"Life isn't fair." I was talking as much to myself as to Jeni. "You have to fight for what you want, sometimes against the people you love best, sometimes even against yourself." My voice was very low.

"I intend to fight," Jeni said loudly, breaking the ribbon of tension that had been growing between us. "But after we're done with this, I'm going against them. They won't ever be able to do anything like this to us again." Jeni went on to tell me about her plan to contact and organize the Komsol clones, to control the power on hundreds of Komsol worlds. "And when everything is ready, we won't take any lives, we won't kill anybody, but we will shut down all services until they give us our freedom."

"It sounds good," I agreed. "But it will take a long time." Maybe too long. But I didn't say that out loud.

"I have nothing else to do with my life," Jeni said. "I'll do it, no matter how long it takes."

"I'm with you," I told her. Which was true enough, even if I felt discouraged for the moment.

"Then," Jeni said, "when this thing with Sven is all over, you'll help me and Nikki get True-Born identity papers?"

"Of course," I said. At least this was something I could do. Then I had an idea. "Didn't you tell me Nikki has a sort of mental radar that he uses to track down Sven?"

"Yes," Jeni answered. It seemed to me Jeni had

something else to say, but when she didn't elaborate, I continued talking.

"Then I think we could convince MedComm to let you take Nikki with you. He'd be safer away from all the vultures here. And maybe you could find a safe place to leave him until you can go back for him when all this is finished?"

"Yes," Jeni responded to my suggestion with enthusiasm. "Let's do that. But will MedComm agree?"

"We'll just have to insist on one of our own conditions," I said, straightening up my back as I stood up. "I'll make it sound good to them." It was the least I could do, to save one clone-child after sacrificing Sven.

I knocked and entered Jeni's bedroom and waited while she finished getting dressed.

"How do I look?" Jeni asked, twirling around on one foot.

"Absolutely stunning," I said, smiling to myself at the difference between this human woman and the wraith of a being I had first encountered.

Jeni stood still and looked into her bedroom mirror. I watched her marveling over the change in her body. She was straight and tall, with a slim but not too thin figure. Her face was framed by an aurora of brown hair with red highlights that had come from all the time she had been spending under the sun in her meadow. Her body curved in and out in the right places, and even her fingers were practically straight. Their slight degree of imperfection was not noticeable under the black gloves.

"We better hurry if we want to be on time to the MedComm meeting," I forced myself to say. Jeni smoothed down the red-and-black outfit she was wearing, took one last look at herself in the mirror, and turned toward me.

"I'm ready," Jeni announced.

"Let's get going," I said, but my voice sounded reluctant even to my own ears.

Jeni looked down at her hands, then shyly up at me.

"You know, Selena," Jeni said, "I've never attended something like this before, I'm not really sure how I'm supposed to act."

"Just wait and watch. Then take your cues from them." I took Jeni's hand. "And most importantly, don't try to change any of their hardcore prejudices. This isn't the time or place."

Holding our overnight bags, we left the hospital building, took one of Trattori's rare ro-ways to the landing field, and in the early-morning light boarded MedComm's aircar that was waiting to take us halfway round the world. The trip took five hours, at high speed. Jeni and I relaxed back in our seats, but spoke only a few words about the fluffy white clouds, the expanse of ocean below, the smooth flight without turbulence. Although we were the only passengers in the eight-seater, I was worried that a spy-recorder might have been installed. It was better just to be quiet and enjoy the trip.

Losing two hours during the trip due to different time sectors, we arrived at Trattori's second continent at late afternoon. Unnamed and supposedly uninhabited, the terrain looked barren and rocky, desolate under the waning sun. Suddenly, a white light shone from the ground, spreading gradually over the whole surface. It was almost too bright to watch. Blinking our eyes, we saw the rocks and dry dust shimmer and disappear. Where a few moments before had only been desolation, there was now a large landing field surrounded by a complex of low buildings that stretched to the far horizon.

"I had no idea this existed," I said in shock. "I think we may have stumbled onto something big."

"Melanie told me that there was a large population of clones on Trattori," Jeni said softly. "They must all be here."

"This must be MedComm's headquarters," I said, astounded at the realization. "We've been searching for it for years, and it's been right here on Trattori all this time." Then I shut my mouth tightly and motioned Jeni to be quiet.

There was nothing to do but watch as the aircar landed vertically in an open area between the parked comships. Silently, we followed the pilot who guided us across the field into a maze of underground tunnels, and finally to a small room. Our guide left us to ourselves, telling us that we had only ten minutes to freshen up before he would be back to pick us up.

Jeni and I entered the large meeting room, decorated with red velvet curtains and a plush darker red carpet. Around the oval mahogany table sat the members of the Medical Committee, dressed in dark suits made of rich silks and velvets. As we seated ourselves, I recognized the round-shouldered man named Kelty who was calling the meeting to order.

Kelty continued, "Now that everyone is here, I think Proctor Girot is ready to speak." He looked to his left at an overweight but solid man with short blond hair that emphasized the harsh folds of flesh in his face. Girot, I thought, has that ageless appearance. His skin grafts gave him a thirtyish look, but his eyes peered out on the world with a mixture of ruthless determination, paranoia, and weariness.

"Thank you, Kelty." Girot nodded his head vaguely in his assistant's direction, then, with a quick sweep of his eyes, surveyed the people seated around the table. "Okay. You all know the problem. Over the past few years there have been an increasing number of breakdowns in the Komsol systems throughout the Confederation. These, as you know, have not been haphazard accidents. We are now sure that at least one man has embarked upon a determined effort of sabotage. We don't know how many others are working with him. It is imperative that we catch him and find out. If he is not stopped soon, he will become a definite threat to the peace and prosperity of our entire galactic community. We, of MedComm, cannot allow this to continue." Proctor Girot paused for breath, at the same time looking around the room with an expression that invited comments.

"But how can we stop them?" This question came from a small man, peering across the table.

"Mr. Solen," Proctor Girot said, "as you know, we have, during our own recent brush with catastrophe, been able to secure the name of the ringleader. He is a clone going under the name of Dr. Sven Soronson, and has been passing himself off as a human surgeon. He is also traveling with one Dr. Marcus Kasur, who was, I regret to say, once one of us. We must now be suspicious of any traveling medically-outfitted comship with a crew that might include these two so-called doctors, among others. Their presence in the vicinity of a recent explosion should further confirm their identity. Don't you all agree?"

The group nodded assent. I watched their automatic reaction, coming slowly to the conclusion that something was wrong with these people.

"The problem," Proctor Girot continued, "is that the computer can chart no regular pattern in this destruction. There's no way to tell where these maniacs will strike next. And MedComm's fleet is too visible a force to go rampaging across the galaxy. We wouldn't stand a chance of getting anywhere near the rebels."

"Then how can we possibly find Soronson?" Mr. Solen asked in his timid voice.

"That's what I'm here to tell you," Proctor Girot said, his tone crisp with impatience. "We have made a deal with HOFROC. You all know about that organization?"

Once again the heads nodded up and down. Watching, I decided that they were all so old and tired inside that they had stopped thinking for themselves. They did what was easy, obeying Girot without too many questions as long as the Proctor pushed his case forcefully. Just like my father had once done, they had almost stopped caring.

Proctor Girot continued, "In return for certain concessions on our part, HOFROC has agreed to help us

in this endeavor. Soronson's wanton sabotage hurts
their cause as much as it hurts us. Selena Menard, the
great Paul Menard's daughter, has consented to speak
to you about this problem." Proctor Girot turned toward me, motioning for me to begin.

"You've heard about the clone who saved Callistra
from being completely destroyed?" I asked the group.

The ten members of the committee nodded.

I saw that they reacted to me as blindly as they had
listened to Girot. "Well," I continued, "that same
clone, Jeni, has offered her services. She is well qualified, probably having more knowledge of Komsol than
any computer technician who has never been attached
to a unit. Jeni has proven her capability in dealing
with emergency situations, not only on Callistra but,
recently, here on Trattori. It is our belief that one
lone, harmless-seeming comship would have the best
chance of approaching the rebels. And since Sven Soronson was personally attached to Jeni, I believe she
is the only one who could infiltrate his defenses."

"But she's only a clone." This came from stoop-
shouldered Kelly. "A soulless automaton."

Kelly seemed to be the only one besides Girot who
had any real fight left in him. "If that is the case," I
said, "it would only ensure her efficiency." The sound
of my voice rang loud in the room. "And there is another advantage that only she can supply."

"What is that?" Proctor Girot asked.

"As I've already told you, she's developed strong
emotional ties with a clone-boy named Nikki who has
achieved a close mental rapport with the man calling
himself Sven Soronson. In the months that Soronson
was here on Trattori, I have seen demonstrated, time
and again, the boy's uncanny ability to hone in on
Soronson's mind. Nikki could follow the man anywhere. So, with the boy's radarlike ability, and with
Jeni's personal appeal to Soronson's emotions, I think
we have a good chance of finding him."

"What about Jeni's loyalties?" Proctor Girot said.
"They are both clones. What reason do I have to be-

lieve that she might not also have a stake in seeing the Komsol system destroyed?"

Until now Jeni had sat silently next to me. Now, it seemed, Jeni had decided it was time to speak out. "Excuse me." Everyone's eyes turned to the chem-slave who dared to utter a sound. "As you say, yes, I am a clone. And as a clone I abhor the deaths of my fellow-clones that this person is causing. I might, even now, be dead because of him. In addition, all my training has been geared toward the welfare of the True-Born population under my care. If, as you seem to be, you are willing to put entire planets under the supervision and total care of a clone, I can see no reason why you should now doubt either my ability or my loyalty."

"Well spoken, clone," Proctor Girot responded. "But I am not entirely convinced. At any rate, as previously agreed, you will, of course, be accompanied by one of our human technicians who will both pilot your ship and effect the final capture."

"I am perfectly capable of piloting a comsol ship by myself," Jeni said calmly.

"I begin to think you protest too much," Proctor Girot said, staring straight at Jeni.

"No," Jeni answered, modulating her vocal cords to an emotionless pitch. "It's just that I am not used to the company of humans. Also, I believe that Sven Soronson would be more likely to trust me if I came alone."

"We," Proctor Girot spoke slowly, "are not likely to trust you at all if you continue to insist on this point."

"I accede to your request," Jeni said, almost too quickly.

"It is not a request," Proctor Girot said. "It is an order."

Jeni lowered her eyes.

"Prepare to leave within forty-eight hours. You are dismissed." Proctor Girot nodded his head at both Jeni and myself.

We stood up and left the room. As the door was closing behind us, Proctor Girot's laughter broke the silence. Then the words, "If she thinks she's going to get away with anything, wait until she meets Jorge Vallik."

And Kelty asking, "Why even let her think she has any say at all in the mission?"

"She's more likely to find Soronson," Proctor Girot responded, "if she feels she's working out of her own initiative. Give them enough rope and they'll hang themselves."

The door clicked into its slot. The corridor was silent.

"Whew," Jeni said. "I wasn't sure I could carry it off." She manipulated her fingers, as always, trying to push them into straighter configurations. "Damn them. But I did what I had to do."

"Yes," I encouraged her. "You did it very well."

"Thank you," Jeni responded. "But I wish I could have convinced them to let me go by myself."

"But that would have been impossible. You knew it was part of the agreement before we came here," I said.

"Yes, but somehow I hoped . . ."

"Why is it so important?" I asked.

Jeni looked at me. "It's a matter of independence. I'm tired of taking orders from humans all the time."

"I was only wondering if that's all there is to it."

"What do you mean?"

"I mean, are you absolutely sure you can trust yourself?"

Jeni looked away from me, down at her hands, at the floor, at the ceiling.

"I think your silence just answered me," I said to Jeni.

"But," Jeni whispered, "I do love him."

"And can you let this man you love stop progress while he blindly continues to kill both innocent people and clones?" Something in me said I should push Jeni to this final determination.

"You know I can't." Jeni sighed. "But I wish they could get someone else to do their dirty work."

"But you and I know you're the only mobile clone who can equal Sven's extensive knowledge of Komsol, the only one who can find him. And the only one he's likely to let come anywhere near him."

"I know. I know." Jeni wrapped her arms across her chest. "But can't they at least let me do this with a little dignity? Can't they let me be alone with what I have to do?"

I wanted to touch Jeni, to hold her and rock her in my arms. But I did nothing. There was a time to let go, and this was that time. Over the next few months, Jeni would have to walk without me. I had to let my child-patient grow up.

I remembered back to that first day I had seen Jeni, and I knew that this time I had succeeded. Jeni was a woman now, a human woman living in the human world. All the joys and sorrows that came with her humanness would now be hers. I could only sit back and let her live her life.

And go on with my own. I was still a therapist, a good one, and I had other patients who needed me. And work to do with HOFROC while we waited for the outcome of Jeni's mission.

CHAPTER 14

Jeni

Jeni relaxed back into the web seat. The comship had just taken off and was being well handled by the MedComm technician. Nikki sat, tied down in the other passenger seat next to Jeni. He had a big grin on his face as he watched first Jeni, then the tech, and finally became riveted to the small porthole that looked outside the ship. As Jeni watched the boy, she recognized in herself the mixed sensations of thrill and fear. This was it. She was really going out into the galaxy for the first time, on her own. Would she be able to play her part well enough to pass in the human world? What was going to happen? It was both frightening and wonderful. With Nikki, Jeni stared out of the porthole, watched the surface of the planet recede, watched as the blackness of space enveloped them.

Finally, after a half hour, Jeni drew her attention back inside the comship. This vessel, like all the others, contained the standard four double-occupancy cabins: one for her and Nikki, another for the tech, and two more for whatever prisoners they might capture. The ship's small size made the jumps through space/time quite safe. A larger ship risked the danger of physical dispersal when reentering space/time because its size was greater than the specific area encompassed by the galactic coordinates. In this small regulation-size ship, they were just an ordinary tech team coming to check out Komsol's circuits. Supposedly, Sven Soronson would not be alerted by such an innocuous repair ship.

As the takeoff pressure of one and a half gravs continued to push her deeper into the web, Jeni let her mind return to her last moments on Trattori.

There had been Selena. Jeni felt confused about her feelings toward the psychomotor therapist, wondering why she hadn't told Selena about her own tenuous mind-link with Sven. And with Nikki and Melanie, too. Accustomed to telling Selena everything, somehow this had seemed too private to share. Maybe it was a thing to be kept only among clones?

Jeni couldn't decide. But there was one thing she did know—she loved Selena and was both sorry and a little bit afraid of leaving her mentor behind. They had spent the entire morning walking together, in the meadow, talking. But at the end, Jeni had insisted that Selena had to stay behind at the hospital. The women had hugged each other, holding tightly. Too bad the therapist didn't know how to pilot a ship. But Med-Comm wouldn't have chosen her anyway. They knew Selena's sympathies were pro-clone. They needed a stricter watchdog.

And they had found one. In this tech sitting in front of Jeni. She stared at his back, a big broad back, then watched the muscles rippling down his neck as he bent over the ship's console, concentrating on the next maneuver. She figured they were far enough away from Trattori by this time to be ready for the first space/time jump.

Yes. Now. Her fingers grasped at a cold emptiness. Then her fingers, her entire body, was a cold emptiness. Only a split second, but forever. And then they were back in real time, light-years away from their starting point.

Nikki uttered only one word. "Wow!"

The tech leaned back, untied his safety straps, stood up and stretched. Turning toward Jeni, he said, "It's about three hours before the next intersection."

"I know," Jeni answered. Immediately, she regretted the quality of annoyance that had manifested itself in her voice. She might have to live with this man for many months. It paid to be on polite terms with someone, especially an unwanted companion, when forced to inhabit such tight quarters as these.

Reddening, the tech said, "I just thought you might want to stretch your legs a bit. Or catch a nap."

"Thanks for telling me," Jeni said. "I'm sorry I was a bit brusque, just then. But with all the last-minute rushing and the goodbyes, I'm not in the best of tempers. I hope you'll excuse me."

"Oh, it wasn't anything." The tech smiled. "Can I help you unstrap?"

"Yes, thanks." Jeni let him undo a buckle that she was perfectly capable of handling by herself. "You'll have to forgive me for something else. I've forgotten your name."

"It's Jorge Vallik," the tech said. "And I'm looking forward to spending the next few months with you." He beamed down at her.

"Yes, we should get along." He was acting too friendly. Jeni knew that this man knew that she was a clone. Well, maybe he had been given orders to play up to her. "Right now I think I'll take that nap you suggested." She pushed herself up and out of the web before Jorge could extend his hand. The ship was on half-grav now, so Jeni bounced in a gentle arc into the air from the slight force of her push up from the web seat. Landing easily on her feet, she took two steps over to Nikki and helped him to unstrap. Holding on to the boy with one hand, she used the support handles jutting out of the wall to guide them back toward the cabin.

"You'll get used to the half-weight soon enough, kiddo." Jorge called after her departing form.

Jeni didn't bother to turn around or answer. Let him think she needed all her attention to maneuver herself and the wide-eyed Nikki down the short hallway.

Not soon enough, she stepped behind the closed door of her cabin, into her own private space. Here was where she and Nikki would be spending most of their time.

About five feet by eight feet, it would have to do. The lower and upper bunk beds were still closed. When opened, they would take over most of the available space. Additionally, there was a small console that hooked into the ship's library and computer. Although she couldn't control the ship from this outlet, she would be able to watch the tech's maneuvers. She planned to use the excuse that the space/time jumps exhausted her and spend as much time as possible in her cabin "resting."

Pushing the button that released the lower bunk bed, Jeni sat down, sighing. For a moment the cold metallic interior had been comforting, the nonflesh of the ship's indiscriminate walls bearing a kinship with Komsol's inhuman corridors. But, quickly, following that initial comfort, had come a wave of homesickness —for Trattori's meadows, the grass and sunlight and green-smelling air that she had lately become used to breathing. She felt herself divided, parts of two people coexisting within one flesh-and-blood body—the cerebral Komsol clone and the newly awakened human woman.

Nikki tugged on her shirtsleeve. "How long a ride is it going to be, Jen?" he asked.

"At least a week," Jeni answered.

"Oh boy!" Nikki jumped up in slow motion. As he floated down in the light grav, he waved his hands excitedly.

During the next week Jeni convinced Jorge Vallik to let her practice piloting the comship. After all, he was always around to oversee her actions in case she made any mistakes. Jeni knew the theory perfectly, but had not had any practical experience. It was possible, she told Jorge, that in an emergency a second pilot would be needed. Jorge reluctantly agreed that it was a reasonable precaution to take, but at no time was Jeni to forget that he was in charge on this ship.

When she wasn't practicing at the ship's console, Jeni occupied herself by viewing culture tapes. Nikki watched with her. Both were able to learn much about how people lived on the different planets of the Con-Federation.

"Look at this one," Jeni said to Nikki. It was a log-cabin society, purposefully rejecting the use of modern science. Theirs was a religious return to the soil, an attempt to develop their own "spirits" rather than a technology.

And another. A world where people had been genetically altered to fit the environment. Running on four short legs, close to the ground, they were able to sustain the pressure of their new planet's heavy gravity. They still had two arms, with hands with opposable thumbs, six limbs in all. Their furniture was long and low, strangely articulated into shapes to fit their bizarre bodies.

Still another group, living on five low-grav moons, had surgically implanted wings that carried them quickly across miles of their hilly terrain.

Some of the cultures, such as these, had chosen rural life styles. But the majority were strongly industrialized, making full use of the Komsol system. Although each planet had its own individual government, they were all loosely associated with ConFed, even those worlds not based on Komsol. Looking up founding dates, graphing the Komsol planets versus the rural ones, Jeni noticed that the last seventy-five years showed an increasing drop in the creation of new Komsol-dependent planets. A hopeful sign, she thought, of growing dissatisfaction with MedComm.

She hunched over the library outlet, searching for a

particular piece of information relating to something Selena had spoken about. Yes, here it was. A news release bringing events on Mivrakki up to date. That was the planet which had openly defied MedComm at the Joint Council. What happened on Mivrakki would be a crucial indication of the Council's effectiveness as well as a barometer of ConFed's general attitudes.

The answer was clear. MedComm had capitulated, completely evacuating its troops from the sparsely populated world. Galaxy-wide opinion did make some difference to MedComm's actions. Jeni filed this important information away for later use.

In the meanwhile, they were only a day away from their first destination, Whitsun, the last planet Sven had hit. A large, overpopulated planet that depended on three solar stations for all its energy, it had been a perfect target. While the robo-techs managed all the menial and semiskilled tasks, a large artist class had spent much of its time creating escape environments for its own use and for export. The complex fantasies that had been created had attracted the disenchanted of other worlds. Some of the immigrants came with high ambitions of achieving artistic success, while many others simply wanted to lose themselves in the make-believe environments.

Now, all the magnificent pictures had faded from the screens. The too-real imaginary worlds no longer left imprints on human neurons. The electro-orgasmic machines did not vibrate. The robo-techs had stopped dead in their tracks. No food was being produced or distributed.

Although the solar stations had exploded, there had been no deadly beam, as on Callistra, to scourge the cities. Here, it was not needed. The people, incapable of finding their way out of their automatic metropolis, completely unaware of how to plant, harvest, or even cook their own food, were literally starving to death. At first there had been looting, of course, but very soon the obviously available supplies had been used up. And, after the first mad killings, the people had become too weak to continue fighting each other. They were dying of their own ignorance. Some, whose minds were completely befuddled, didn't even realize that this wasn't just a bad viddyscope.

The rescue ship had arrived two weeks before Jeni's comship landed. The carnage and destruction were overwhelming. The cities were being abandoned. Survivors were being lifted off-planet to undergo rehabilitation therapy. Those who wanted to remain artists would have to start again somewhere else.

After they landed, Jeni walked into rescue headquarters, with Nikki trailing on her hand and Jorge following close behind.

They spoke to a small bald-headed man, a bureaucratic official guiding the rescue operation, showing him their "repair" papers as well as the classified document that revealed their true purpose. None of the documents revealed Jeni's identity as a clone. Stamped by MedComm, these papers were supposed to gain complete cooperation from any operating unit or planet connected with Komsol.

"Does anyone know how this happened?" Jeni asked.

"Are you kidding?" the official said. "These people wouldn't know their ass from their elbow. All they know is that everything was suddenly turned off. Stopped cold."

"What about the Whitsun clones?"

"One is dead. We have the other in hospital, here. She is in such an extreme state of shock we haven't decided yet whether to destroy her or send her out for repair."

Jeni winced, felt Nikki's hand squeezing her own, very tightly.

"Can I see her?" Jeni asked.

"If you like," said the bald-headed man. "But I don't think it'll do you any good."

He led the way down a corridor bustling with doctors, nurses, patients on wheeled stretchers, auxiliary self-powered comsols, and on into a small, badly-lit room. A tiny shriveled-up body lay attached to an emergency life-support system.

Jeni asked everybody ·to wait outside. But Nikki wouldn't let go of her hand. "Okay," she said, "but just stand quietly."

Jeni examined the clone. The inert figure was about Jeni's own age. The eyelids fluttered open; blue eyes stared at Jeni. It was hard to know that intelligence existed behind those eyes.

"Can you speak?" Jeni asked.

There was no answer, only the mindless stare. Jeni touched the other's hand gently.

"She says her name is Jenine," Nikki's voice whispered.

"What?" Jeni looked at Nikki. "You can reach her mind, too?"

Nikki didn't answer. The boy let go of Jeni's hand, inched past her and laid his head down next to Jenine's arm. Touching the helpless clone's arm, he said, "She feels like you."

Could this be true? "Is your name Jenine?"

The eyelids flickered in response.

"My name is Jeni." She knelt, next to Nikki, grasped the other woman's hand. "Sister?"

Yes, my sister. Jeni heard the answer, without exact words, like an echo far in the distance. But she knew it was Jenine speaking. Her clone-sister.

But with this echo was another echo. A deep feeling of despair. Of failure. Of pain. Of slipping away.

Come back, Jeni thought. *Please don't give up.*

It happened so quickly. I had no warning. I should have stopped it. Jenine.

No. You couldn't. It's not your fault, Jeni thought back to her sister.

But the echo was receding now, going further away. *Come back. You can be free. Like me.* Desperately.

But there was only emptiness where her mind reached out. Jenine's eyes were glassy, staring, now truly mindless. Nikki was sobbing. Jeni pulled the boy into her own arms. Together, they rocked. Jeni's eyes burned, but no tears came. Anger tensed her limbs. Nikki stopped crying, looking up at Jeni's face.

Wordlessly, Jeni said, *She's gone.*

Nikki nodded. *I know.*

Don't worry. From now on we'll always be together. I'm not going to lose you, too.

They rose from the floor and walked out the door. The tech and the bureaucrat looked at her, questioning.

"She's dead," Jeni said curtly. And stalked away, back to the comship.

If she had been unsure of her mission when they had started out, Jeni had no doubts now. Sven had killed Jenine, her clone-sister. He was as bad as the humans, maybe even worse than MedComm. He was a clone killing other clones.

He had to be stopped.

CHAPTER 15

Jeni

During the next month and a half, Jeni's small comship visited other planets in Whitsun's sector of space. It was a haphazard search, with no particular leads to follow. So far, Nikki had not been able to sense even a remote trace of Sven's presence. But then, as Melanie had said, Nikki was the conductor, not the amplifier, and was limited by physical space. It was too bad that their mind-link experiment, with Komsol as backup, had been so rudely interrupted on Trattori. If only she and Melanie had had the time to further explore their capabilities. Jeni might, even now, be able to contact Melanie, and possibly other Komsol clones, and make a more systematic search for the clone killer, Sven Soronson.

But there was no point crying over spilled midea wine. All they could do was to contact those worlds which were highly developed and overly dependent on the Komsol system, as these were the type that were always hit. Jeni would check out each planet's Komsol, and punch into the computer a warning against unknown doctors or comtechs, and an advisory to keep a careful watch on their solar stations. When that first order of business was taken care of, Jeni would ask Nikki's help and try to breach the clone's emotional barriers through the mind-link. She hoped that by identifying herself as a former Komsol clone she could quickly gain the new clone's attention and sympathy. But she was not given too much time to follow through on her contacts as Jorge Vallick would send for her as soon as he had finished his part of the investigation. It was his job to question the stuffed-shirt governing officials, asking them if they knew of any itinerant doctors or techs who might fit Sven's or Marcus' description.

When Jeni and Jorge left each planet, instructions were given to inform them of any news of this sort.

Finally, over the viscom, came the report that Palaster had been hit. It was a planet only partially industrialized, with one main city, Palas, other smaller cities of varying sizes, and rural farming communities. The government, seated in Palas, was run by Premier Bas Kolka, who ruled his people with an iron police force and was supported by an elite group of rich landowners called Harmins. In fact, this world was strictly divided into three social castes. There were the rich Harmins, whose genealogy could be traced back to the financial backer who had initiated the colonizing of this planet; there were the tenant farmers who tithed most of their produce to the Harmins, barely eking a living for themselves out of the earth; and the Bassils, the lower caste menial workers and unemployed. The name Bassil was derived from a leader who had unsuccessfully tried to organize the farmers and workers against the Harmins in a revolt that had taken place over two hundred years ago.

Always walking on a thin line between peace and civil war, when the Komsol complex went up in a burst of flames Palaster's social structure had also blown sky-high. As automatic services ceased in the Upper City, the Bassils in the Lower City, who had never known the luxury of Komsol's mechanization, began to riot, burn, and loot. A growing unruly force of underfed, angry workers moved up toward the supposedly unprotected rich section. Premier Bas Kolka, assuming that the Bassils had been responsible for the sabotage of Komsol, sent his Special Police Force, a misnomer for what was in fact his army, out to squash the rebellion. At first squads of the SPF had indiscriminately shot down any and all Bassils they encountered, whether man, woman, or child. It didn't take long for Barak, the present-day leader of the Bassils, to organize the workers' resistance, a thing that had been long in the planning stages. With the SPF kept from entering the core of the Lower City, the premier ordered his forces to cordon off the whole section. No person was allowed in or out. All stragglers were killed without question. The Lower City was literally under siege. For three days they had been unable to replenish food or medical supplies. Part of the section was still in flames set off by the misguided masses. With the Lower City besieged and with nonexistent Komsol services in the Upper City, it was as if Palas was a dead city trying to kill off its inhabitants. A rescue ship had been called for, but, because of its large size, and therefore its inability to jump through space/time, it would take at least a month to arrive. In the meanwhile, the warring population was finishing off the destruction that Sven had begun.

All this information was broadcast by ConFed to Jeni's comship. It seemed likely that Sven's group might still be on Palaster, as he often liked to stay and assess the damage, simultaneously protecting whatever cover he was using by not suspiciously disappearing. Of course, he would not be using the name Jeni had known him by. She would have to look for an off-world medical team, going under an alias.

Jorge Vallik contacted the officials at the Palas comship field, receiving permission to land. Jeni asked the tech if he was sure it was safe, since the planet below was so tumultuous. He assured the clone that their MedComm papers would protect them anywhere in the galaxy. But, as they approached the planet's surface, Jeni still felt uneasy. However, Jorge was human and had lived among humans all his life. She supposed, in these matters of human politics, he would know best.

Upon landing, Jeni, Jorge, and Nikki left their ship, and, as they walked toward the nearest building, saw, in the dusk of early evening, a delegation coming to meet them. Good, Jeni thought. Jorge could explain their mission and they could get down to business. Already too much time had been spent aimlessly searching the starways.

But then Jeni realized that the delegation was armed. It looked more like a police escort, dressed in black-and-silver military uniforms, than a diplomatic one. Perhaps the violence was so widespread that such protection was needed?

The armed escort of ten police reached Jeni's small group. Before they knew what was happening, weapons were raised and the three visitors were ordered to march along. Jorge tried to protest, asking what was going on. He was told to shut up and save it for the high officer.

Jorge said, "But we're from MedComm." He reached inside his jacket pocket, but before he could pull out the papers, he was kicked from behind and sent sprawling, face down in the dirt.

Jeni leaned over to help him up. The blond, muscular tech shook off her hand, muttering, "I don't need your help."

Jeni turned her back on him, took Nikki's hand, and continued walking. Behind her, she heard Jorge muttering unintelligible words under his breath.

They came to a barbed-wire fence and followed it a few yards to the gate where two more stiff-faced, uniformed men waved them through.

They were marched along until they reached the entrance to the ro-way system. The guards pushed them up the stairs and onto the still, unmoving path

that should have been rolling toward the heart of
Palas' Upper City. Everything was so still, quiet,
empty. Jeni assumed that all the people were hiding
behind locked doors in the safety of their homes.

When the first intersection was reached the guards
ordered Jeni, Nikki, and Jorge down a ramp. Jeni
stumbled, but regained her footing quickly, not wanting
to be the cause of any further incidents. As they were
about to step onto another one of the nonfunctioning
pathways, footsteps could be heard ringing on the
metal steps below. The long lines of ribboning ro-ways
obscured vision below the platform on which they
were standing. The guards pushed their prisoners onto
the ro-way, hurrying them forward.

But they were not quick enough. Men, with bearded
faces and ragged clothing, ran up the stairs, closing in
on Jeni's group. As two guards pushed the prisoners
forward, the other eight turned to fight. Jeni heard the
hissing sound of the laser guns behind her, but couldn't
turn around to see.

There was no time to dwell on the battle at her rear.
Hands appeared on the sides of the ro-way, followed
immediately by bodies being hoisted onto the path.
Three men surged forward, overcame the closest two
guards who were staring in shock at this unexpected
source of attack. These ragged men grabbed Jeni
around the waist, lowering her off the edge of the ro-
way into someone else's arms. She tried to struggle
free, thinking only that she couldn't be separated from
Nikki. But then she saw that they had gotten Nikki,
and Jorge, too.

The process of lowering her over the edge was
repeated down several layers of ro-ways until they
reached solid ground. Then one of the bearded men
looked around at the others, said, "Everyone here?"
With the answer affirmative, he said, "Throw the
switch!" Jeni was pushed unceremoniously flat on the
ground as she heard an ear-splitting explosion. When
the sound died away, she raised her head tentatively,
saw the band of ragged men rising to their feet and

brushing themselves off. She, too, stood up, looked around, and saw the concrete and metal rubble that lay scattered in all directions. Looking up, she found that a piece of purple sky gleamed brightly through a jagged hole in the ro-way system.

Turning to the man nearest her, who seemed to be the leader, she asked, "What's going on? Who are you?"

"No time to talk now, lady," the man said gruffly, but not unkindly. "They're stupid, but there are lots of them. We better get going."

Hesitating only a moment, she decided to follow these people. They weren't forcing her to go along. They were rescuing her. Grabbing hold of Nikki's hand, she pulled the boy along. He seemed to sense that Jeni trusted these people and began running easily at her side. Behind her she heard one of the men shout, "Come on or you'll be killed."

Jeni turned around to see Jorge Vallik standing stock-still where the group had first landed on the ground. He was waving papers in the air and yelling, "But I've got these."

Jeni yelled back, "They won't give you a chance to show them. They'll kill you first and look later."

Jorge obstinately refused to move. He shouted, "I'm in charge of this expedition. I insist you return immediately."

What was wrong with the man? Jeni thought. Med-Comm must have been blind to pick him. But then, Selena had said they were getting old and tired. She yelled back to Jorge, "So stay there and be in charge. I'll tell them you got killed in the line of duty."

But Jorge refused to move. Jeni thought to herself that she must have been blind, too, not to have seen what an incompetent fool he was. She had let herself be taken in by his false bravado, his air of command backed by MedComm authority. But then, until this moment, they had not been involved in a crisis situation. There had been no way of knowing that the man lacked independent judgment and initiative.

Quickly, one of the bearded men ran back, grabbed the papers out of Jorge's hand, and ran forward again. Jorge began running, chasing after his papers rather than running away from danger.

The rebels raced across a courtyard to an alleyway. There, two more men waited who ushered them all down a sewer hole, through an opening into a dark corridor lit by handlamps. Jeni gasped in surprise. She recognized the place as one of the many underground corridors Komsol used to send its comsol units speeding to its destinations. But no comsol would come hurtling through this corridor. Its parent was dead, and, without the Komsol-clone system behind it, every comsol and robo-tech in Palas was useless.

As the last man shut the entrance door, there was a communal sigh of relief. In the shadowy light Jeni noticed that one person was bleeding from his shoulder, and forced to lean heavily on a comrade.

While they bound up the wounded man's shoulder in dirty rags, the leader turned to Jeni and said, "We're safe now. They're too stupid to think of using these places. They can't think how to do things without Komsol running their world."

While Jeni was catching her breath, she noted the term "their world." It was not only two separate political factions fighting, but obviously two separate societies.

Jorge began shouting, "Who do you think you are? You can't kidnap us, just like that. We're . . ."

"Oh, shut up." Jeni had caught her breath. "If it wasn't for you, we wouldn't be in this mess."

The rebel leader turned to Jorge and said in a cold voice, "They were about to execute you."

"Why would they want to execute us?" Jorge sputtered.

"Because they think you knocked out their Komsol."

"No, we didn't," Jorge insisted.

"I know that," the bearded man said. "What I don't know is, who are you and why are you here on Palaster?"

"We're here to capture the ones who did. If some-one would just read those papers." Jorge was practically wailing.

The man turned to Jeni. "Is that true?"

"Yes," Jeni answered. "This isn't an isolated case, you know. It's a galaxy-wide problem."

The man smiled, as if with recognition, and muttered almost to himself, "So you're the one she told me about." He reached into his shirt pocket and pulled out a pair of wide-rimmed eyeglasses, propping them on his nose. "Bad light here, you know," he explained. Then he extended his hand toward Jeni. "You're wel-come to stay with us. If you try to return to your ship they'll not give you any chance to explain."

"I can see that," Jeni said, returning Daven's hand-touch.

"Then you don't mind taking refuge with the Dassils?"

"No, I don't mind." Jeni smiled. And thought to herself, *if you don't mind accepting a clone.* Out loud, she said, "I accept your hospitality."

"What about Soronson?" Jorge yelled.

"Let's find out what can be done, first," Jeni said. "It's obvious we can't just go wandering around out there."

"You make good sense, lady," the man said. "By the way, my name is Daven Migdal, second in com-mand to Barak Rolson, leader of the Bassils."

"I'm Jeni. And this is Nikki." She brushed a wisp of red hair back off the boy's forehead. "That's Jorge Vallik."

"Is he a MedComm agent?" Daven asked carefully.

"He is," Jeni answered. "But we're not. Unfortunate-ly, circumstances have forced us to work together on this mission."

"I understand," Daven said slowly. Then loudly, "Okay, men, let's not sit around on our asses all day. Get going." He started walking rapidly, holding a lamp in one hand and with the other pulling Jeni, who was holding on to Nikki, up ahead of the line of marching men. Jeni looked back and saw that Jorge was following reluctantly, looking over his shoulder as if wanting to bolt, but not knowing where to go. Daven, walking even more quickly, put himself, Jeni, and Nikki a few yards further ahead of the nearest men.

Speaking softly, he said, "I'm also a member of the ConFed Workers' Union and used to be in touch with HOFROC. If I am guessing correctly, this matter is connected to recent events at the Joint Council?"

"Yes," Jeni told him. "We made a deal with Med-Comm. They gave us some things we want, and we're supposed to give them Sven Soronson." She grimaced.

"I take it you're not too happy with your half of the deal?"

"You guessed right," Jeni said.

"Then why do it?"

"MedComm threatened to kill ten clone-children a day if we didn't comply," Jeni answered grimly.

"Yes, I heard about that." Daven shook his head. "That's a heavy one." He was quiet for a few minutes as they walked. Then he looked back at Jeni and said, "I used to know Sven Soronson. I also know Selena Menard."

Jeni's feet stopped moving. But Daven pulled her gently forward. "Got to keep going. No time to stop now." He patted her hand. "I'm sorry if I surprised you just now, but I worked with HOFROC on Trattori for a little while, and knew Sven Soronson when he was first liberated from Mivrakki's Komsol. And recently, when I was on Rivolin, I saw Selena again. What a person she is!"

Jeni nodded her head. But how much had Selena told this Daven Migdal?

"I know it's not really my place to ask, but it seems to me you might be supporting Soronson, rather than trying to capture him," Daven said.

Brusquely, Jeni said, "He's killing clones, too, when he kills Komsols."

Daven looked at her, staring directly into her eyes.

Then he turned forward and they spent the rest of the march in silence.

Had Selena told him too much? Jeni wondered. Did he know Jeni was a clone? She looked sideways, over her left shoulder, at the man walking next to her. In the half-light she could see that Daven was short and skinny, with light skin and dark hair. He seemed to have the build and the nearsighted look of a scholar. But his tone of voice was that of one used to commanding; his stride was purposeful, his muscles wiry underneath the skimpy flesh. But he had been gentle enough, and courteous.

When they reached the end of the long corridor, Daven began barking orders at his men. He acted the same toward Jeni as he had done before, helping her to climb out of the sewer hole into the middle-of-the-night street. "We're probably safe here," he told her, whispering. "But keep as quiet as possible. We're only just inside the perimeters of Lower City. You can never tell when an SPF patrol might be around."

Jeni followed his instructions, walking behind him in single file, as the line of men crept close to the shadowy edges of the brick buildings in an attempt to keep their presences concealed.

A moon cast its rays down into the center of the street. The left-hand side was an eerie mass of light and dark rubble jutting up into the glowing sky in bizarre shapes. This must be part of the city that had gotten burned out, Jeni thought, as she noiselessly followed behind Daven.

As the moon rose higher and higher, they continued walking. The rubble disappeared; taking its place were rundown tenements, small grocery shops, vacant lots. Garbage glinted in the moonlight. A rat ran across the street, almost under their feet, disappearing into an alley.

Nobody else walked the streets. The city was deadly quiet.

It seemed like they had been walking half the night. At first it had been a little chilly, but then the cold had grown stronger until it had numbed Jeni's feet below the ankles. Long ago, Nikki had begun to drag tiredly on her arm. Noticing this, Daven had picked up·the boy, swinging him over his shoulder where Nikki had immediately fallen asleep. Jeni forced her feet to plod along. It was a matter of directing the muscles to keep working, of ordering more adrenalin to be pumped through her bloodstream, of simply putting one foot in front of the other, and not daring to stop to rest.

Finally, Daven called a halt to the forced march, telling Jeni they had arrived. Relieved, Jeni felt herself begin to sink into the aching fatigue that had been threatening to overwhelm her body.

In her haze she felt a man's hand guide her out of the street, into a doorway, a hall, a large room. And then a woman was tucking her into a bed. It felt so soft, so warm, so sweet to lie down and not have to move one muscle. So good to be able to sleep.

A hand was roughly pushing her shoulder. Jeni opened one eye. Purple sunlight streamed into the room. A voice was saying, "Get up. We can't stay here. We should never have come this far." It was Jorge.

"Go away," she mumbled.

"Get up or I'll leave you here."

Jeni sat up, yawning. "What time is it?"

"It's noon. Half the day's gone and we have to decide what to do." Jorge's voice was taking on an irritating whine.

Jeni pushed his hand off her shoulder. "Let me wake up. I can't think yet."

"Hey, you leave her alone." A woman's voice. "Here, honey, drink this."

Jeni gratefully accepted the warm brew. It was stimulating, hot, and satisfying. She opened her eyes now, fully awake. The room was drab, with water cracks and peeling paint, a worn-out rug and furniture held together by wound ropes and tape and cardboard. Her blanket was thin and moth-eaten, and the bed that had felt so comfortable the night before was little more than a pile of old, lumpy springs. The woman standing next to her bed, her hand outstretched for the now empty cup, looked like a drudge. Her skin was wrinkled, her mouth was missing some teeth; strands of unruly gray hair escaped from the tight knot pulled behind her head; her dress was washed-out, colorless, shapeless. Across the room, eight or nine men sat in front of a fireplace. They didn't look much better in their straggly beards and ragged pants and shirts.

Jeni handed her cup back to the woman, asking, "Could I have a little more of that, please?"

The woman shook her head sadly, and said, "Sorry. Rationing, you know."

One of the men rose from the far group and came over to Jeni. She recognized Daven, who had managed somehow to scrape off his scraggly beard, but was still wearing his old-fashioned pair of thick eyeglasses. "She can have my share," he told the woman.

"Oh, no," Jeni said, shaking her head. "I can manage. Where's Nikki?"

"Oh, the boy has been up for hours. He went outside to explore."

"You didn't let him go by himself?" Jeni started to get out of the bed.

Daven laughed. "Relax. There's no danger this far from Upper City."

"But he's not used to being out by himself."

"A boy's a boy," the woman said.

Jeni looked sharply at Daven. The man said, "We have guards posted, even this far away. They'll keep an eye on him."

Just then Jorge's whine broke into the conversation. "What does the boy matter? The point is we've come too far away. And now these idiots think we're going to help them."

Listening to Jorge made Jeni clench her teeth. She decided it would be better to ignore him. She turned to Daven, questioning.

Daven only said, "Go wash up. Then we can talk."

As Jeni stood up, Jorge grabbed her by the elbow, hoarsely whispering, "You're not going to do it, are you?"

Jeni told him she had no idea what he was talking about. "Just go sit down and keep out of my way." She thought to herself that it was ironic how very quickly their roles had become reversed. It was another case to point out how the more frightened and weaker one was at a disadvantage, while the stronger entity took hold of the power. There was some satisfaction in the thought that, at least in this one-to-one encounter, she, a clone, was coming out on top.

Jeni followed the gray-haired woman to the washroom. Her stomach was feeling empty, but she was reluctant to ask for food.

A half hour later Daven introduced Jeni to Barak, leader of the Bassils. He was older than Daven, tired, worn-out, but with a determined set to his shoulders, an insistent look in his eyes.

While Jorge was strategically detained in another room, the situation was explained to Jeni. The Lower City was surrounded, under siege. That, she already knew, she told them. Barak, speaking with effort, slowly told her that there was almost no food or medicine left. A few more days and the people would be dropping like flies.

"What do you want from me?" Jeni asked.

"Your help."

"How?"

"The Lower City of Ista, south of Palas, has sent in a runner offering supplies. They've already started the wagons rolling, but it'll take many days. We need something right now," Barak said. "We need you and your comship."

"But it's too small," Jeni protested, "to do any real good. And besides, it's under guard. We just escaped from there."

"It's not too small to carry concentrated nutrients, vitamins, and a few medical supplies," Barak told her.

"We need whatever we can get to sustain us." His shoulders were proud, but his voice and eyes pleaded for her help.

"What about getting back to the ship?" Jeni asked.

"We can get you there. It's worth the risk to us."

"Where would I bring the supplies?"

"There's a grass field not too far from here. Can you land on grass?"

"If the field is large enough," she told Barak. "I need a little room to maneuver."

"Oh, it is. It is," he reassured her, hope beginning to light up his eyes.

"I don't know," Jeni said. "How long will it take?"

"We can get you into the city tonight. You'd have to hide out for a day. Then the next night we'd get you back to your ship. From then on, it would be a breeze." Barak waved his hand in the air to emphasize this point. "Without Komsol their radar won't be working. Two or three trips, that's all we need. Then you could be off in your ship." Barak stopped for a moment, then continued, "You certainly don't intend to try to contact the Harmins again, do you?"

"Not if I can help it," Jeni said. "I'm not trying to get myself killed."

"That's the girl," Daven said.

Jeni looked up at him, wondering at his phrasing. Should she help them? It would take too much time from her own mission. But just look at them, she thought, look at this miserable room. Look at the way they're living. They're barely surviving. Clones were not the only scapegoats in the universe, not if things like this could happen. These people were humans, but they were almost as badly treated as clones. In a way it wasn't the manner of birth that made people brothers and sisters, she thought, but the common oppressors —the strong, cruel people who took advantage of weaker people.

Yes, she decided, she would help them. If she turned her back on them now, it would be tantamount to signing their death sentence. And a dead person, clone or human, was a dead person. Besides, they would help her to get the comship back. It was really a mutual-aid pact.

"I'll do it," Jeni said. "On two conditions."

Barak looked worried, but Daven was smiling as he unconsciously pushed the rim of his glasses further back on his nose.

"Nothing big," Jeni reassured Barak. "Just keep that Jorge out of my way. And Nikki." She leaned over the table toward Daven. "Keep him safe for me and promise me that if anything happens, you'll take care of him."

"Of course," Daven said, reaching over and grasping her hand. "We'll watch out for him. Now here's our plan."

The same night, 6:00 P.M.: Jeni, Daven, and two other men set off on the trip to Upper City.

The next morning, 4:00 A.M.: They arrived at the closest usable Komsol corridor, ate a light meal, and bedded down for the day.

The second night, 8:00 P.M.: They stormed the landing field, easily overcoming the few unprepared Harmin guards. Jeni and Daven took off while the other two men returned to Lower City.

9:00 P.M.: Jeni and Daven arrived at a field outside the Lower City of Ista. Concentrated nutrients, vitamins, and medicinals were loaded, filling every bit of available space in the comship.

10:00 P.M.: They arrived back at Palas' Lower City with supplies and a message: "Bassil troops in Pietra, Calab, Mifra, Ista, Kitra, and Latos are occupying the Upper Cities. They are sending extra Bassil troops to Palas. Will arrive in a fortnight. Hold out. Help is coming."

A quiet cheer rose up among the people unloading the comship. The rebellion had begun in earnest. This time they would win.

11:00 P.M.: Jeni and Daven picked up the second load from Ista.

12:00 P.M.: The second shipful of supplies was delivered to the Bassils of Palas.

1:00 A.M.: The third load was piled into the ship.

2:00 A.M.: The last run was completed.

4:00 A.M.: Once again, almost morning, Jeni fell asleep.

At dusk the next day four people stood at the edge of the grassy field: Jeni, Nikki, Jorge, and Daven. Jorge was still fuming at being held prisoner, but couldn't protest too much. After all, Jeni had gotten back their ship. He stomped across the field and entered the waiting comship.

Jeni, Nikki, and Daven stood together.

"I hope we brought in enough," Jeni said.

"It'll get us through the worst of it," Daven said, holding her right hand in his two hands. "I want to thank you."

"And I want to thank you, too," Jeni said. "Not just for getting the ship back, but . . ." She couldn't finish.

"I know," Daven said. He raised her gloved hand to his lips.

"You know?" Jeni asked, not sure if he really did know.

"That you're a clone," he smiled at her, still holding her hand.

Jeni, becoming conscious once again of her twisted fingers, jerked her hand away, putting it behind her back.

"Don't pull away," he said softly. He leaned over and kissed her on the cheek.

Jeni murmured, "I didn't mean to. I'm sorry."

"And don't be sorry." He stood close to her body, his eyes looking directly into her eyes. "Be proud of yourself, and don't hide." He reached behind her back and pulled her hand forward. "Don't hide any part of yourself. Stand up for your rights. We'll be with you when you make your stand. Just like you were here with us. We've got more power than you think.

This is only the beginning. Workers all over the galaxy are standing up for themselves. The Workers' Union is organizing worldwide strikes everywhere. You'll see."

"I believe you," Jeni said. "I believe you." She stretched upward, kissing the man on his cheek. "Goodbye," she whispered. She took Nikki's hand and began walking to the comship. Her heart raced. Daven had known all the time. He had known, and he had treated her as if she were a normal human. Yes, she did believe. If there were other people like Selena, like Daven, then she had a chance.

The Bassils were going to win on Palaster.

And the clones would win over MedComm.

Nikki tugged on her hand. "I like him," the boy said.

"So do I."

CHAPTER 16

Jeni

"Well, what are we going to do," Jorge asked in his now-usual whine, "since you've messed up that chance?"

"Let's hang around for a few days," Jeni said, trying to keep her own voice calm. "Soronson might still be down there. And if he is, I don't think he'll be staying too long." She didn't really buy that explanation, but she didn't know any better course of action.

"He probably left days ago," Jorge grumbled.

"Then we've got nothing to lose by waiting. We don't know any better place to look, do we?"

Jorge didn't answer, but turned his back and stalked off to his own cabin.

Good. He was finally leaving her alone for a few minutes. Ever since they had left Palaster, he had been watching her with an eagle eye. Even so, Jeni knew that the balance of power now lay with her. She could intimidate Jorge when the occasion required a forceful decision. In the meanwhile, she would let Jorge play commander, but was happiest when his physical self was removed from her presence.

She leaned back in the pilot's seat, reviewing the little adventure that had taken place on the planet below. Other than the hospital, where life had been routine and she had been branded as a subspecies clone, this had been her first large-scale experience with the human world. Some of it was very depressing —that people could be forced to live in such squalor and filth, that humans were so cruel even to their own kind. But people everywhere were fighting for their rights, and clones were not alone in their struggle against the system. Most of all, she, Jeni, had been treated as a responsible person, able to hold her own among humans, and even more, able to extend much-needed aid to these humans.

One day that's how it'll be all over the galaxy, Jeni thought. Clones will be contributing citizens, respected and accepted by society.

What a nice dream.

But it was still only a dream. Now, today, she was acting the puppet for MedComm, doing their bidding while she waited for events to ripen. She had not even gotten close enough to know the name of the Palaster clone, Jeni realized. But she was sure that the clone had been killed, if not by Sven, then by the Harmins, who would have punished the clone for allowing Komsol to be destroyed. That would be the Harmins' way, retaliation, not compassion.

But Daven and the Bassils on Palaster were taking care of that.

Jeni's job was out here in space, to track down Sven and stop his murdering crusade.

Although expecting that her attempts would once again prove fruitless, Jeni began feeding statistics into the comship's computer. So far, no attempts to chart a pattern had proved successful. Only Sven's deranged mind knew what sector of space would be his next target. As far as Jeni could tell, there was no way to second-guess him. The main chance they had was to arrive as quickly as possible at the scene of the crime, hoping to catch Sven and his crew before they had deserted the vicinity.

Finally, Jeni had to agree with Jorge that they might as well resume searching other star systems. Sven was long gone from Palaster. Jeni admitted she had made a mistake and fumed inside at having been so close and ending up with nothing to show for it.

She returned to her cabin, pacing up and down the few steps that the limited quarters allowed. Nikki tried to divert her with questions and games, but Jeni was too caught up in her own anger and frustration. Nikki ended his efforts to reach his friend, and sat curled up on his bunk bed, trying to block off the waves of anger that assaulted his mind.

Something else was wrong. Jeni realized that the boy was withdrawing back into his shell. The mind contact they shared worked both ways; Nikki was too sensitive to her state of mind. He would have to learn how to rely on his own resources. But that would take time and patience. For now, she forced herself to pay attention to him. They resumed their hours at the library console, and the boy began to unwind. Still, part of Jeni was distracted, going over and over in her mind the events that had led to this point in time, beginning with the surprise attack on Callistra. As the weeks passed, she left the choice of direction to Jorge, who decided which planets to contact, when they should land, and what to say to the officials.

One day her reverie was broken by Jorge's loud voice. "Hey, get out here. Quick."

Responding to the urgency, Jeni rushed into the control room.

"Look at this," Jorge pressed a button. "I just got this transmission from the Komsol on Dante."

A written message appeared on the viscom: AS PER YOUR REQUEST, I AM INFORMING YOU THAT A TRAVELING MEDICAL SALESMAN, DR. LENNY MARKOVAN, HAS JUST TOUCHED DOWN ON DANTE. I WILL PROCEED WITH CAUTION.

At last their efforts were paying out! Where was Dante? Jeni leaned over Jorge's shoulder, studying the starmaps that he had punched into the vis-screen. "There, it's only a few jumps away." Jeni pointed at a small planet in the Aldebaran system.

"I can see it well enough without you shouting in my ear," Jorge grumbled. But he was excited, too. "Get yourselves strapped down. We'll be ready to jump in a few minutes."

Jeni obeyed, thinking that maybe all those months hadn't been wasted after all.

By the time they arrived at Dante, Jeni was edgy. Was Sven really here? Would they be in time?

When they set down on the planet, Jeni headed straight for Komsol. After assuring herself that everything was in order and that the clone was on guard, she decided that she wanted to hear for herself what the bureaucrats had to say. She and Nikki joined Jorge, who was already trying to interrogate a customs official. She entered a gray functional office devoid of any personal feeling. Jorge was asking the usual questions of a man who was tall and spindly, dressed in a formless gray robe.

In crisp, clearly enunciated words, the man answered, "Why no, I don't believe we can help you. As far as I am aware, no persons of that description, except yourselves, have chosen to enjoy the benefits of our humble world. Of course, we have no official watch system."

Jeni interrupted. "But the Komsol told us that they were here."

"If Komsol said so, then it is so," the man answered.

"But we need your help," Jeni insisted, trying to make the official understand. "They are trying to destroy your world."

"Komsol will provide." The tall man bowed his head.

What was wrong with him? Jeni hadn't been taking

notice of the people on the planets they had contacted, leaving that aspect to Jorge. Now, she thought, what irony, here's a planet that reveres its Komsol, but goes overboard to the point of being oblivious to reality.

At that moment Nikki tugged on Jeni's hand. "I think Sven is here," the boy said. "But someone else, too. I'm not sure who."

"Which way?" Jeni asked.

Nikki said, "They're not together."

Jeni turned back to the tall man. "Did you hear that? They're here right now. Hurry up and get a squad out to patrol the grounds."

"We have no such squads," the tall man said. Clasping his hands, he sank to his knees. "They are not needed."

"Then what do you plan to do?" Were all humans crazy?

"Komsol knows All. We do not question."

"Oh, shit," Jeni exclaimed. "Nikki, you stay here. I don't want you to get hurt. Jorge, you go that way, and I'll take this direction. It looks like they're using new tactics. They might be trying to dismantle sensor sections from the outside. I don't think they could get through to Komsol, since I warned the clone."

Leaving the bureaucrat to his devotions, Jeni ran down the hall. Dante natives were standing or kneeling, chanting, "The KOM provides. The SOL is One." Running, Jeni turned a corner.

Suddenly, she saw a woman, tall and thin like the other natives. But, although she was dressed in the same gray shapeless robe as the others, she moved with a diligence and speed that gave away her alien status. Jeni knew, without a doubt, that it was Sindra, who had been her resentful nurse those early days after the Callistra tragedy.

Darting around a corner, Jeni followed. And into a dark closet where Sindra was tugging at a piece of machinery.

Jeni touched the other woman's shoulder. The taller

woman ducked, swiveled, jumped up at Jeni. All too quickly.

Grappling, with Sindra's hands at her throat, Jeni saw a mad gleam in her eyes. And far away she felt the twisted thread of a mind.

"You!" The woman spat. She pushed Jeni hard against the far wall of the closet, leaped back and away, out into the hall. Before Jeni could move, the suction door had been swung back into place.

Entirely in darkness, Jeni groped her way forward. But there was no handle to grasp or key to press or scanner to trigger. The door could not be opened from the inside. Touching the walls and floor, Jeni looked for any item that might be of aid to her. But all the machinery was attached to the wall or too heavy to lift and use as a battering ram.

Gasping, she sat down for a minute to think and touch the sore spot on the back of her head which had been bumped when she fell.

How to get out? First, calm yourself. All these exertions are using up the available air. What about Dante's clone? No. He couldn't help. There was no sign of life in this dark hole. That woman had already managed to dismantle the feedback circuit here. A vital lens was missing. Jeni had noticed that during her search of the closet.

Okay now. You'll have to wait. Nikki will know where you are. He always knows. He'll find you. So just wait. Slow your breathing. Lower your metabolism. Quiet your heart. There now. Rest. Drift. Soon. Soon.

A scratching sound outside the door. Can't move. Arms too heavy. How long have I been here?

The high whine of unoiled machinery. A crack of light. The door pulled open. A small figure, hard to see, crouching over her face. Unintelligible words.

But in the distance, *Don't leave me. Oh, please don't go away.*

Reach for these thoughts. Come closer. Raise the heartbeat, the metabolism. Take a deep breath. Blink the eyes.

I'm here, Nikki. I'm all right. Sitting up now, Jeni felt a little dizzy. Nikki and Jorge, on either side, gripped her arms and pulled her to a standing position. Leaning more heavily on the taller Jorge, Jeni stumbled out of the black closet.

"I couldn't find anyone," Jorge reported.

Still not steady on her feet, Jeni gasped out the words, "Leave me with Nikki. We'll follow. Just get back to the ship. Try to spot them as they take off."

Jorge ran ahead of them. After a few more steps Jeni took a deep breath and stopped leaning down on Nikki's shoulder. "I can walk by myself now. Let's hurry."

They rushed past the gray-clad figures who were kneeling and swaying in front of Komsol's scanners. The damage didn't look too bad. Maybe a few blown circuits.

But once back on the ship, Jeni notified rescue operations. These people needed more than one kind of help.

Simultaneously, Jorge continued scanning. "There they go," he called. Then down to business. The takeoff was smooth. They were in pursuit.

As Jeni relaxed into the web seat, she admitted to herself that Jorge knew what he was doing. In spite of his obtrusive, pedantic personality, he was more than competent as a comtech.

Fifteen minutes later they were free-floating. All the ship's energy was concentrated on the race, leaving nothing extra to waste on simulated gravity. They were not far behind now, with the ship's nose entering the ill-charged particle trail left behind by the rebels.

Then the dot on the screen winked out.

Two minutes later the cold in-between engulfed Jeni's flesh.

They burst out into real space. But there was no sign of the other ship on the scanner.

Unstrapping herself, Jeni pushed over to the pilot console. "Where are we?"

"In the Alpha Crucis region," Jorge answered.

"Do you think they came here?"

"All the calculations point this way. It was the most likely choice. If you don't believe me, sister, I can go over them and show you."

Jeni couldn't help herself. She shot him a look that could have killed. Sister. How dare he call her that! But Jorge was busy with his charts and didn't seem to notice.

Jeni calmed herself and said, "No. We don't have the time. What do you think happened to them?"

"Well, there was a two-minute time differential. That would place us in the same sector, but possibly at some distance from where they emerged."

"Then it's back to the charts," Jeni sighed. "We'll have to search out the likely planets in this area."

"If they stay around here." Jorge sounded doubtful.

"Why? You think they could be planning to vector out?"

"They couldn't do it right away. They would need about three hours to build up to capacity again. But don't think they'll stick around. They know we're on their trail."

"Then the charts are a waste of time. We'll have to find them in less than three hours. Here, let me try something."

Jeni pushed in front of the tech, taking over the pilot's seat. Punching keys, calculating probabilities, feeding and digesting data, she immersed herself in the oh-so-beautifully-familiar world of logic. Not inside now, not actually part of the circuits and relays but oh-so-close. Compare the planetary distribution with the space/time configurations. Possible points of departure in three hours time leading to which more Komsol-oriented sectors. Here, this one, that one, another. Once plotted, the probabilities became limited to three distinct space/time junctures. Okay, send off two scan pods in those directions while we follow the course.

After punching in the last of the code symbols, Jeni leaned back in the pilot's seat. There was now a good

chance that the other ship could be spotted before it
jumped out of this area. She closed her eyes for a moment, resting and savoring the past few minutes.

"What did you do?" Jorge asked.

Jeni explained.

"Wow, you could do that?" Nikki exclaimed.

As Jeni pushed herself away from the console, she
said, "I used to do that all the time when I was with
Komsol."

"And you liked it," Nikki said, following close behind Jeni. "I can feel inside you, you liked it."

"Sure. It's what I know how to do best."

"But I always thought it would be so terrible to be
locked up in those old machines."

"Not always." Jeni laughed. "There were compensa-
tions. And look what I can do now."

"Can I learn, too?" Nikki asked.

"Maybe, I don't know." Jeni's voice was serious
again. "Some of it's good, but some of it isn't."

"Maybe I can learn it all from you," Nikki said,
without having any wires stuck in my head?"

Jeni turned, touching Nikki's chin with her fingers.
She leaned over and kissed him on the cheek. "Maybe
here is a way. When this is all over, we'll find out,
okay?"

"Okay." Nikki smiled back at her. "So long as you're
my teacher."

Jeni hugged him and they tumbled over each other,
a free-fall, laughing, tickling, playing.

Jorge, who had been ignoring all this, interrupted
them. "They're straight ahead of us. On the edge of
the screen."

"Slow down. Let them get further ahead. They might
not have spotted us if they weren't watching too carefully. They may not believe we could be following
them."

"Done," Jorge said. The spot moved off the northeast
corner of the screen.

Calling in the two scan pods, they continued their
dodging maneuvers, periodically catching the ship on

the screen, then slowing up again. When the other ship jumped, they were ready to follow it. The chase carried them through four more jumps. By this time Jeni was certain that their quarry was overconfident, sure that they had lost their pursuers. She could tell by the lazy way the ship moved, as if it were just marking time while the people inside prepared for their next sortie.

And then came the real moment of triumph. They picked up a call from the other ship requesting landing permission for Dr. Lenny Markovan and crew. The rebel ship started moving in for a landing on Lylle.

While Jeni's ship cautiously followed, its occupants viewed the library tape describing the planet Lylle.

It was a well-distributed integration of the pastoral and the industrial. Cities were built low with room for trees and grass inlets spaced among the concrete roways. Farmlands and mining areas were not too isolated. The standard of living was moderated by the government. Nobody was too rich or too poor.

Jeni spotted the Komsol-hospital complex. Why were they always located right next to each other? Time to look into that later. Right now, that's where Sven would be headed.

The question was how to catch him. If Jeni sent in a call to the authorities, the other ship would lift off and the chase would be on again. The only way was to land on Lylle after Sven's operations were well under way. To catch him in the act. But that was risky. If Jeni wasn't quick enough, Sven would be able to complete his mission.

CHAPTER 17

Jeni

Jorge landed the ship and they disembarked.
One of Lylle's officials was waiting at the customhouse
across the landing field. Jeni accepted his welcome,
cutting short a speech the short bald-headed man was
about to make. Instead, she showed her MedComm
papers, explaining the situation and requesting guards,
if any were available. Luckily, these people were better
organized than on Dante. It was arranged that the
patrol units were to be deployed to strategic places,
with orders to stay out of sight until called for. A large
group was to surreptitiously keep an eye on the enemy
ship. Others were to follow after Jeni, and also after
Jorge and Nikki, who would be searching in the opposite direction. Now, there was no time to lose. They
had to stop Sven's group before he accomplished his
mission.

"Tell me how to get to Komsol."

The official handed her a map. "It's not far. The
quickest route is marked in red."

"Thanks." Jeni was off, through the plasticized

191

customhouse, out onto the moving walkways, standing among the ordinary citizens living their everyday lives. The people were dressed casually, both men and women in long flowing colorful garments, each wearing a single gold or silver bracelet. Some faces were serene. Others were animated in lively discussions with friends. One wrinkled old woman held the hand of her grandchild. A young couple was having a heated argument until the woman turned away, refusing to speak. Another woman, in her mid-twenties, was speaking calmly, businesslike, into a small portable viscom. Jeni could have been that woman, living a normal citizen's life, living among other normal human beings.

But she wasn't. And never would be. Not only wouldn't they accept her, but she was so very different from them. Inside. The difference came not only from the label of clone, but because of her connection with Komsol, her entire isolated life, and now her emerging special abilities. All these people had done it to her, through complicity in the use of Komsol, if not in direct participation in the breeding of clones and their surgical adaptation to Komsol. Now she understood why the hospitals and Komsol complexes were always located right next to each other. And why the doctors were so concerned with the technical and bureaucratic side of Komsol operations. The doctors were the ones who produced the clones. They were the ones who surgically adapted them for use in Komsol. Not just MedComm, but the entire medical community's livelihood depended on the continuation of the Komsol system, the use of clones for organ transplants and for other experiments.

It was time to get off the ro-way. Jeni grabbed the deceleration pole, slowed to a stop, and began walking slowly on the grass. Was she doing the proper thing? Should she be helping MedComm? Or was Sven right, that all these people had to be destroyed? No. She quickened her pace. He went too far. Nikki's brother had died; and Jenine, her own clone-sister; as well as masses of humans on Callistra and elsewhere. Whole sale slaughter couldn't be the answer. He had to be stopped.

Now she was inside the Komsol buildings. Always the same design. No need of the map here among familiar corridors. She found herself once again running to the control room. What was he planning this time?

She rushed into the main room. A light-haired man she didn't recognize was leaning over the manual console. But standing over the clone receptacle was Sindra, tall, thin, and lethal. The clone-woman was about to inject something into one of the life-support tubes.

"No, stop!" Jeni shouted.

Startled, both looked up.

"It's her," Sindra said. "You better get out."

The man stared for a moment at Jeni, then began punching the keyboard. Jeni ran toward him, but Sindra, quicker than she, was already blocking her path. Again, they were fighting. But Jeni was better prepared this time. Sliding sideways, she grabbed hold of the other clone-woman's right arm, then jerked it hard, bringing it behind Sindra's back. With her own free arm, Jeni encircled the clone-woman's neck, pressing in, choking her. Sindra clawed at Jeni's arm, ripping skin, but was unable to dislodge the arm from around her throat.

From far down the hall faint footsteps could be heard. Sindra, hoarse from the pressure against her windpipe, said, "Get away while you can."

The man coded in one last sequence, turned to the two women and said, "I'll be back for you."

"Get going."

The man ran past Jeni, out the door.

Jeni pushed Sindra down to the floor, on her stomach. Pressing her own knee into the small of the woman's back, now twisting both arms almost to the breaking point, Jeni asked, "Where's Sven?"

The woman croaked out a laugh. "Honey, he just left."

"But that wasn't him."

"Ever hear of cosmetic surgery?"

Unable to leave, Jeni held the woman down while she waited for the patrol to arrive. Only a few minutes, it seemed forever until she was relieved. But then they were there. Two of the four guardsmen took over the prisoner. Jeni let go, rubbing her own tensed neck muscles.

She asked, "Did you see a man coming from this direction?"

One guard answered yes, but that he had worn the Komsol insignia so they had thought the man was approved.

"That was him." Jeni was off, running back the way she had come. Somehow, the corridors seemed longer now, her feet running and running, but not going far enough fast enough. And then there were the explosions. First distant rumblings. Then closer and closer, until a piece of machinery burst out of its glass-enclosed frame, scattering sharp splinters all over the place. A few stung her arms, which she had thrown up to cover her face. Smoke started fuming, then billowing out of the broken fissure in great gusts. Overloads. Sven had set up a series of overloads. She had to catch him.

On and on she ran, inhaling burning smoke, dodging exploding fire balls. Quickly. Damp down those neurons. Inhibit the pain feedback. Slow the respiration rate. Now, free of the smoke, breathe again, deeply. Slow it again for this next bit of poisoned air.

She saw him. Through eyes that were tearing, warding off the fumes.

He was kneeling over the inert form of a small boy. Over Nikki. The clone-boy must have followed her, even though she hadn't called him. He had to learn to obey.

But what was Sven doing? Jeni ran the last few steps. With a low, almost animal sound, she swooped and pushed Sven away from the boy. He lay sprawled out on the floor while Jeni bent to cradle Nikki in her arms. Over the clone-boy's head she looked at this strange man. He rose up on one elbow, staring back. The face was all different. But there was the faint echo of the familiar mind-aura that she recognized as belonging to Sven.

"I was only trying to help him," Sven said. "He was hit by a flying piece of metal."

"Caused by you," Jeni answered.

"I never meant to hurt him." Sven rose onto his knees.

"Don't come any closer," Jeni warned.

"I can help."

"Why should I trust you?"

"Because I know what to do." Sven ripped off a piece of his sleeve. "Let me."

Jeni realized blood was gushing from an open wound on the boy's head. Looking at Nikki's closed eyes for a long moment, she made her decision. "All right. But I'll be watching."

Sven eased the boy's head onto his own lap, crumpled the torn sleeve into a wad of cloth and held it against the wound. "It needs pressure, you see, from the outside. Until we can get the boy into proper medical facilities."

"And are there any proper medical facilities left on Lylle, Sven?" she asked caustically.

Sven lowered his eyes. "I don't know. It was a rush job. I haven't been as thorough lately as I would like."

"I hope not," Jeni said. "For Nikki's sake."

Just then, the patrol appeared, with the tall clonewoman in tow. One of the guards picked up Nikki, while Sven kept his hand pressed over the wound. Three others walked on either side, escorting the prisoners.

Once out of the building, each person inhaled deeply, drawing fresh air into burning lungs. Now, across the street and to the hospital.

It was chaos. The wounded were stumbling out of the various doorways. No way to tell the difference between patients and staff. A deep thunder rolled, grew louder, exploded into a deafening sound. Flames streamed out of several upper-story windows.

"We can't go in there," one of the guards said.

"But what about Nikki?" Jeni looked uncertain.

"To my ship." Sven coughed as a wave of smoke engulfed the group. "I have medical equipment."

"Okay," Jeni decided. "Let's go."

Back they went, through the city, following almost the same route Jeni had taken to get to Komsol. But this time the ro-ways weren't moving. Although no apparent damage was manifest in this section, everything had stopped working. The overloads and subsequent explosions had done the job. Komsol was immobile. People stood, looking bewildered and staring at the black smoke and red-black flames that were blanking out a portion of their blue-green sky.

Jeni's group marched through the city along the abandoned ro-ways. Nikki didn't move or utter a single sound. Jeni was scared. This was taking too long.

After more than an hour, they finally reached the landing field. It appeared intact. The local government seemed to have everything under control. A call had already been put out to Central Rescue. It would take about three weeks for help to arrive. In the meanwhile, guardsmen were deployed to the Komsol-hospital complex to help with the evacuation. Others were setting up a makeshift medical center at one of the city's parks. Still others were being sent out to calm the general populace and advise them to move temporarily to open country, just until the city began functioning again. Runners, with similar messages, were being sent to other cities. The planet of Lylle would survive the disaster with a minimum amount of anguish.

But there was Nikki. Quickly, Jeni explained the problem. While Sindra was placed under guard with Marcus and Toby, the other two members of Sven's crew who had been captured on the landing field, Jorge began his interrogation.

Meanwhile, Sven was escorted, with Jeni and Nikki, to his own ship. Here, the clone-doctor got down to work, expertly probing, removing a splinter of embedded copper alloy.

"It didn't penetrate too deeply," he reassured Jeni.

He cleaned out the wound, sutured it closed, and bandaged it. Nikki was deep under the anesthetic.

"We'll have to keep him warm and comfortable. Move him as little as possible."

"All right. But I want him back on my own ship."

"It's up to you," Sven said.

"Then we'll move Nikki and whatever medical equipment we need back to my ship. We'll take off tonight and establish an orbit. That way there'll be no chance for you to escape." Jeni turned away from Sven, giving one of the guardsmen her orders.

Back on their own ship, Jeni tucked Nikki into his bed. At least he seemed to be breathing normally.

The four prisoners were entrenched behind opaque force screens. Marcus and Toby inhabited one cabin, while Sven and Sindra shared a second. Jorge still had his own room.

Jeni folded a blanket gently around Nikki's shoulders as he lay dozing in the lower berth. They had succeeded. They were finally on the way back to Trattori. Sven had sabotaged his last Komsol. Nikki was going to recover.

So why did she feel so miserable?

Barely touching the boy, Jeni brushed her fingertips over his thick red hair, then fastened two straps down over his body. She rose and slowly walked out to the control room. Strapping herself into the web seat, she closed her eyes as she felt the initial thrust, then the weight pushing down on her body as they left Lylle's atmosphere.

Opening her eyes, she saw that Jorge was busy with his coordinates, preparing to make a jump.

Fumbling with the straps, she cried out, "What are you doing?"

"The timing's perfect for a jump," Jorge said, turning to glare at Jeni.

"But I thought we discussed that." Why couldn't her

fingers move any faster. "We weren't going to jump for a few days. Not until Nikki feels better."

"What do I care about you lousy chem-slaves? I went along with you all this time. But those were my orders. Give you just enough rope to hang yourselves. But now I'm going to put you all back where you belong." He grinned and turned back to his work.

Harsh, numbing cold. Beyond cold, to nothing. Complete emptiness. Despair. They'd never get back to real space this time. Miscalculations. Sometimes it happened. Why even bother?

But a shiver ran down her spine. And her toes and fingers tingled as they returned to life. Warmth spread painfully once again throughout her body.

A sharp cry. It was Nikki.

Jeni finally pulled loose the straps that held her down. Scrambling out of her web, she pushed herself too high, and rose in a wide arc before descending to the floor. More carefully, but as quickly as possible, she hurried back to her cabin.

Nikki was tossing under his restraints, moaning softly. His bandage was soaked with red.

Leaning over the bed, Jeni tried to reassure him. He didn't seem to hear her words. Reaching out with her mind, she touched his pain. Soothed it. Told him he would be better soon. *Just lie quietly. I'll be right back.*

Out in the hallway, she hesitated, then extracted a small stunner from her pocket. Pressing her hand to the opening scanner, she told herself it had to be done.

The force field lifted from the entrance. Sindra was sitting on the top berth, dangling her legs, and now watching warily as Jeni took one short step into the room.

"Ha," Sindra said. "So the bitch dares to show herself."

Sven, undoing his own straps, stretched and looked around.

"That's not called for," he said sharply. He sat up, hunched over under the second berth, pushed himself out of the bed.

Sindra glared down at him. "How can you still take her side? After what she did. Turning against her own kind."

"She didn't know any better," Sven answered. "It was really my fault for leaving her in their hands."

Jeni didn't know which was worse, Sindra's outright hostility or Sven's patronizing paternalism. Cutting the discussion short, she said, "Nikki's bleeding again. Will you come?"

Sven picked up his medical pouch and took the few steps that brought him out into the hallway. Jeni palmed the scanner, closing Sindra back in behind the force field.

"No tricks," Jeni said. "I've got this." She showed him the stunner.

"My only concern is for Nikki's health." Sven turned sharply away from her and proceeded to Nikki's cabin. Jeni followed.

Two sutures had dissolved prematurely, from the cold-in-between, and had to be replaced. Sven advised a few more days' delay before exposing the boy again to the danger of a jump.

Sven rose to leave, then turned back to Jeni. "Can we talk?"

"What about?"

"About you and me. About this whole thing."

"I don't think there's anything to be said."

Sven shrugged. "Not if you don't think so." He rubbed the side of his head, as if trying to push away some kind of pain. Turning, he walked back to his own cabin. Jeni let him through the shield, closing it after him, and went back to her own room.

She sat, watching Nikki, trying not to think. Who did Sven think he was, anyway? Whatever he had to say, it didn't matter. He was convinced he was right. And was also convinced he could show Jeni the light, if she would only let him. That much was evident in his manner. The arrogant bastard. Why did she still let him get to her? After all he had done. After he had abandoned her on Trattori.

Slowly, the tears seeped out. She blinked her eyes against the burning. Shivering, she felt a freezing knot form deep inside her, as if her body hadn't relinquished all the cold from in-between. It was so cold. So empty. There was no Komsol. No Sven. And Nikki lay so still. She was all alone. Jeni clutched her middle, trying to reach in to the cold knot, to pound it out of her. And then crumpled over, holding herself, crying. What was she supposed to do?

When her body stopped shaking, Jeni found that her limbs felt heavy; her mind seemed to be engulfed by a lethargic fuzzy mass. Somehow, she managed to drag herself up onto her own top bunk, where she fell into a deep sleep.

Dreaming. Of her three clone-sisters standing in a line facing three dark-haired men. They had Sven's earlier features, before the cosmetic surgery. Each pair, a Jeni and a Sven, held one end of a long piece of rope. Each side tugged, trying to pull her/his opponent over to her/his side of the room. Each was equally strong. Each refused to let go.

The first Jeni decided to push instead of pull. The rope turned into a long piece of metal tubing. The Sven changed tactics, pushing, too. The edge of the metal tubing was sharp against her stomach. But she pushed against it, unwilling to give up. The Sven pushed back. Suddenly, she felt her skin break, the metal entering coldly, deep into her guts. She gave one final push before collapsing over the metal rod.

The other two pairs of Jeni/Svens watched in horror as the first pair impaled themselves. Then, with renewed determination, each Jeni fought her Sven, until all six figures lay dead upon their unbendable metal tubes.

The tubes glistened, brightened, and then abruptly dissolved. The figures fell over, clutching their stomachs. They looked down at themselves. There were no longer any deep gashes. No longer any ropes or tubes. Nothing was there. Nothing was between them but a very small bit of empty space. Jeni looked longingly at that space. If only she could take a step forward. But no, he didn't want her. He had left her behind.

I'm sorry, she heard Sven think. *I love you, I need you.* Sven reached out a hand. Jeni stretched out her own hand, felt his fingers around her wrist, grasping.

And then nothing. Jeni was awake, holding her head that was pounding with impossible pain. Staring at the blank ceiling, it took her a few minutes to realize it had only been a dream. There was only one Jeni and one Sven. Right here and now, in this ship. She got up, relieved herself, and splashed cold water over her forehead. She concentrated on the bright candle flame and told her muscles to relax. But nothing she did helped to relieve the all-encompassing pain in her head. Okay, she told herself, okay already.

She opened the door of her cabin, crossed the hall, and palmed the scanner. As the opaque force field lifted, she saw Sven standing in front of her, waiting, rubbing his forehead as he tried to push away the pain.

"Did you dream?" she asked.

"Yes," he replied.

"Can we talk now?"

He nodded and followed Jeni back to her cabin.

They seated themselves in the small space that the floor allowed, close but not touching. Jeni's headache receded a little into the background.

Sven described his dream.

Jeni nodded, *yes,* hers was the same.

"But how?" Sven asked.

"Telepathy," Jeni answered. "Do you remember when we heard each other's thoughts, back on Trattori?"

"I thought I'd imagined that."

"No. We entered each other's minds. But Nikki can do it best. He was still so close to his siblings that being isolated and then immersed in Komsol he didn't have a chance to bury his ability to mind-speak."

Sven shook his head, still not exactly believing.

"Don't you remember, back with your own brothers,

how you always did everything together, always knew what the other was feeling?"

"Yes. But that was so long ago."

"My guess is," Jeni continued, "that a clone group with identical genes also has identical thought patterns. They're all on the same wavelength. And as long as they are all together, subjected to the same environmental conditions, they continue that way. I'm not even sure if we had truly separate identities." Jeni stopped, reminiscing. "I seem to have mainly collective memories. Nothing particularly personal until I became part of Komsol."

"And not having very strong egos," Sven began to get excited, "made us vulnerable to the drugs."

"And to immersing ourselves into the Komsol unit," Jeni finished.

They both stared at each other for a moment. "But how about you and me?" Sven then asked.

"I'm not sure," Jeni said. "If you remember, Nikki was able to follow you everywhere. Then, when you left, he started to do even more with me. I suppose, being so close to it, needing so much, he could pass through whatever thought barriers usually exist. But it's erratic. A lot depends on the degree of need. And maybe then our wave patterns search out a mutual level, begin coinciding. So we can communicate. When I found my sister I did it almost automatically. She . . ." Jeni stopped.

"Your sister?"

"Jenine. She was on Whitsun. You killed her." Jeni turned away from him.

"I didn't know. I'm sorry."

Jeni turned back to face Sven. "How many of your own brothers have you murdered?"

Jeni flashed her anger like a stab of lightning deep behind Sven's eyes. She saw him roll over on his side on the floor of the small cabin, clutch his temples with both hands. She could feel him try to squeeze out the pain that throbbed so deeply within his skull.

She could hear him scream. *Siven!* Scream at the fire shooting through his brother's brain.

A blank space expanded within Jeni's brain as Soren and Sven moved their bodies close to one another, merging their minds against the empty hole where Siven used to live.

But the pain in Sven's head would not go away. It seared Jeni's brain, too, as she now saw Soren's body arch in agony with the current as it ran up and down his spine; as Jeni heard Soren's last piercing scream; as she saw Soren's lifeless body, eyes glazed, convulsing in death spasms against the hard examiners' tabletop. Sven was screaming, "I'm sorry. It's not my fault!"

No, Jeni pulled her mind's-eye away from Sven's images, but stayed within. *It's not your fault they're dead. You didn't kill your brothers.* Unrelenting, she continued. *But you did kill my sister, Jenine.*

I'm sorry, I'm sorry. Sven was screaming inside. His throat made tiny moaning sounds.

"Sorry doesn't do anyone any good," Jeni spoke the words out loud, but so softly, she was barely whispering.

Sven heard the words in his mind and answered, "Yes, dammit, I was trying to kill them all, to kill those MedComm bastards for what they did to us. Don't you understand?" Sven was screaming.

"And what good did that do you?" Jeni asked. "They're still there." She sent back to Sven the feel of Siven's brain on fire, the sound of Soren's last scream, and then that final emptiness, that deep black hole of nothingness.

Sven's arms were groping in the air. Jeni could feel inside his mind. The endless eternity, the loneliness, the pain of remembered closeness, the pain of being wrenched apart.

It hurt so much.

For both of them.

Jeni sent a quivering thought, tentative, not sure of

her reception. *Let me help you,* she reached out her hand through the black emptiness.

Despairing, Sven answered. *But I killed your sister, too. Why should you want to help me?*

Because it wasn't your fault. They drove you to it, to do those kinds of things.

But I'm still the one who did it, Sven moaned. *How can you ever forgive me?*

Trust me, and Jeni felt herself swallowing the last vestiges of her own anger as she reached out, more strongly this time, to comfort Sven's pain. *Believe me,* she thought to him, *I do forgive you.*

She reached out to touch Sven, physically brushing his hair back with her fingertips, purposefully, sending emanations of love and compassion, all that now filled her heart to overflowing.

"Oh!" Sven moaned and thought at the same time. *I never felt like this before.*

Jeni, in Sven's mind, felt the ever-so-gentle touch against his forehead; felt the sensuality of another person's skin brushing his skin; heard the screams gradually growing softer as a woman/mother cradled the lost boy in her arms; saw the black hole receding to a tiny dot in infinity; saw coming toward him this fluffy ball of warmth, of love opening, enveloping, spreading out its wings in a gentle embrace, protecting. And knew that she/he were no longer isolated individuals. The giant chunk of her that had died with Komsol was slowly being filled, was slowly opening to receive Sven's returning love.

He lifted his head from the cabin floor and looked at Jeni with wondering eyes. "I never thought I could feel like this again," he said.

"Nor I," Jeni said, cuddling him on her lap, feeling his arms encircle her waist as he drew her near. She bent down and they kissed a long passionate kiss, a kiss of returning home, a kiss all-fulfilling in itself.

They settled quietly in each other's arms, neither speaking for a long while, just feeling, absorbing the newness of each other's presence.

Finally, Sven broke the silence.

"Even if they had been still alive," Sven said thoughtfully, "I would have done the same thing. I really believed that as long as clones served MedComm they were traitors to their own people."

"Most of them have no idea what's going on."

"I always said that if I was in their place I would have been willing to sacrifice my life if it helped destroy the Komsol system. I wasn't doing anything to anyone that I wouldn't have been willing to have done to myself."

Jeni was quiet, gathering her thoughts. Then she said, "That's very noble of you. But you weren't giving us any choice in our own lives or deaths. And I don't believe it's possible to build a new, healthy society based on murder and destruction. If we don't like what MedComm does, we have to try to change it, from the beginning, with what we believe are good values."

"I never thought of it exactly that way." Sven stroked Jeni's shoulder.

"All you thought about was revenge." Jeni's words held no rancor. They were a simple statement of fact.

"But what was I supposed to do? I didn't know any other way."

"Sven." Jeni reached out to hold his hand. "It wasn't right."

"I know," Sven said softly. "I know that now." He kissed her gently on the breast. "But I had all those facts. They seemed to make so much sense. Before this, before you."

"What kind of sense?" Jeni asked. "Tell me. I want to know everything."

"What I wanted to tell you before. About how clones are made. Bought and sold."

"Go on."

Sven told her not only about the clones used for Komsol, but what he had learned about the clone farms, where replicas of wealthy patrons were kept on ice for organ transplants. He told her about the atrocities, in the name of science, performed on children.

He told her that their flesh and bones, cloned from MedComm doctors, were owned by MedComm. They were no more than slaves.

"But I know all this. That's why HOFROC was formed," Jeni said, "to legally fight MedComm, without using violence."

"With all the money they've got, and the promise of immortality, what can mere words do? Nobody's going to vote against them," Sven said.

"You're wrong. Mivrakki stood up against them at the Joint Council and won."

"I heard about that," Sven admitted. "But it wasn't a major issue. MedComm was only throwing them a bone to keep them quiet."

"I think it was more important than that," Jeni insisted quietly.

"Look, MedComm has too much at stake." Sven drew in his breath, let it out slowly, then said, "They've got everything invested in Komsol. They're not going to let us go."

Jeni said, "But that doesn't mean that their actions give us the right to behave the same way. If we plant our own seeds of evil, the evil will only grow bigger as our power grows. We'll end up no better than MedComm."

"What's the alternative?" Sven asked, seriously wanting to know.

"We can continue to fight them, but legally and non-violently, when possible. We certainly shouldn't be killing any of our own people, and hopefully, not any of theirs, either."

"You're asking us to be saints."

"No. Just not murderers. I don't want to populate a world with clone-murderers. I don't want to have a family and bring up my children by that kind of eye-for-an-eye ethic."

"Then you do want a world for ourselves?"

"Of course I do," Jeni said softly. *Of course I do,* she thought, and opened up to him all her dreams of a home, a quiet house, green grass, trees, and children playing like normal True Borns.

Sven touched her hand, then resettled her head against his chest. He stroked the back of her neck, her hair, her eyelids with his lips. Jeni thought to him, *I wanted a world where you and I and Nikki could have lived together.*

We can still do that, Sven thought back to her.

No. The single word carried with it all of Jeni's anguish. *No.* She pushed herself out of Sven's arms, into a sitting position, feeling her mind reflexively closing off from Sven's presence.

"Why not?" he said out loud. His face held a hurt expression, perplexed at Jeni's reaction.

"Because MedComm threatened to kill ten children a day if we didn't turn you over to them."

"The bastards! If I only knew where to find them." He turned his anger back to its usual target.

"I know where one of their bases is located," Jeni said, not knowing exactly why she was telling him.

"Where?" Sven asked, roughly grabbing Jeni's hand again.

She let him hold her hand, but didn't return the touch. "On Trattori. But I don't see how it helps you to know that."

"Don't you know I've been trying for years to find them?" He was squeezing her hand, hard.

"If you remember," Jeni said sarcastically, as she pulled her hand away, shaking it loose from his grasp, "you never told me anything about your plans when we were back on Trattori. You just sabotaged the Komsol and disappeared. Anyway, you can't do anything about it now."

"You could let us go."

"I can't. I just told you why."

"Can't we find some kind of compromise?"

"I don't know how." Jeni shook her head. "You yourself just told me they're too powerful."

"Too powerful at ConFed. But not militarily, not anymore," Sven said. "I've been destroying Komsols for more than three years, and they had to ask for help in order to capture me."

"That's true," Jeni agreed. "But I still think they're weakening in both areas. Selena said they're getting old and tired, that their minds aren't as sharp as they should be."

"That woman." Sven grimaced. "But her observations are usually correct. Maybe"—Sven stood close to Jeni, wanting to touch—"maybe we have a chance. We just have to think of a way."

"But how?" Jeni asked, feeling the electricity from his body cross the few inches of empty space between them, feeling her mind beginning to relax its too-tight barrier.

Sven said, excited, "I have clones from the Clone Organization for Freedom scattered all over ConFed, just waiting till the time is ripe. If we could just get in touch with them, we'd have a good nucleus for a fighting force. And then, maybe the Workers' Union and HOFROC people would join us?"

"But I want to avoid violence, if possible," Jeni insisted.

"Sometimes there's no other way," Sven said reluctantly.

"Can't we try not to kill?"

"We can try," Sven said, "but I can't promise that it wouldn't become necessary."

"Just promise that you'll try." Jeni touched his cheek gently. *Promise,* she thought to him.

I promise, Sven thought, kissing her on her mouth, once, quickly. Then he returned to the spoken word. "But this whole discussion is only theoretical. We have no way of contacting COFF and our human sympathizers without alerting MedComm."

Jeni sat still, thinking. Finally, slowly, she said, "I have an idea, I don't know if it'll work. But we could try."

"I'm willing to try anything," Sven urged her. *Out with it,* he thought to her, encouraging.

Jeni told him her plan. "First we'd have to get as

close as possible to Trattori's space, not more than one jump away as a minimum distance. Then, with Nikki as the focal point, you and I, Toby and Sindra, could link up together. Hopefully, with the amplification produced by our four adult clone-minds, we'd be able to mind-speak to Melanie on Trattori. Our collective mind would then have the power to reach out through space to all our clone-sisters and -brothers. The mobile ones could buy or steal ships, joining our comship on the outskirts of Trattori's space. And even more important," Jeni was waving her hands with excitement, "maybe, at our signal, they can close down their energy outlets, put their planets in a state of siege. We'd really have bargaining power." Jeni's eyes were gleaming.

"Yes, we certainly would." But Sven was much calmer than Jeni. "If we can manage that first thing and coalesce into a single telepathic unit."

We're doing it right now, Jeni reminded him.

Yes, he agreed. "But it's erratic even with the two of us as close as we are. Then we'd still have to be able to project immense distances."

"If we can manage to reach Melanie," Jeni said, "the power behind Trattori's Komsol could give us quite a bit of amplification. She and I already began experimenting with that, and I believe it can be done."

"Well," Sven said as he stood up, "we've got nothing to lose. Let's try it."

Jeni rose, grabbing his arm. "There's just one thing, Sven. What about the clone-children?"

"If we win, they're safe. If we lose, I'll turn myself in." *Okay?* he projected.

Okay. Jeni could feel it was the truth, that he had committed himself to the children's safety. "Let's get going." Jeni squeezed Sven's hand and kissed him lightly on the forehead.

He patted her curly hair, gently tracing a line behind her ear, down her neck, her shoulder, over to her breast.

"Not here." She looked at Nikki.

"Later?"

"Yes."

Walking with their bodies brushing up against each other, sharing the same mind-space, they crossed the hall to Sven's cabin. Jeni palmed open the force field. Sindra was sitting inside, scanning a library tape.

"So you're finally back. All cozy, too, I see."

"Cut it. She's on our side," Sven said.

"Ha. I don't believe it." Sindra stood up, catlike, ready to pounce.

"It's true," Jeni said, modulating her voice to a calm level. She still didn't like this one, clone or not.

"How'd you do it?" Sindra shot a look at Sven.

"We just needed to talk, that's all," he said.

"Well, she still has to prove it to me," Sindra replied.

"I am. Now. You're free." Jeni turned, leaving the force field up. Walking down the hall, she palmed open the second force field. Marcus and Toby were seated on the open lower berth, heads bent together, earnestly talking. They looked up as Jeni, followed by Sven and Sindra, entered the room. While Jeni sketched her plan to the three other people, Sven interjected bits of background information. Completely immersed in their discussion, they had forgotten about Jorge.

"What in the galaxy is going on in here?" A deep voice boomed from the doorway.

Jeni swung around, her stunner out of her pocket and into her hand, aimed. "Just associating myself with my fellow chem-slaves," she answered. "My brothers and sister." She motioned the others out of the cabin. "Just get in here," she told Jorge.

"It's a good thing MedComm warned me to watch you," Jorge said.

"I don't see how that helps you now," Jeni said.

"You'll see," Jorge sounded smug.

"What do you mean by that?" Jeni asked.

"Just that there's no way you can win." Jorge glared at her. Defiantly, he said, "Are you going to kill me?"

"No. Just lock you up. Keep you out of the way,"

Jeni said, as she backed up and palmed the force field down into place. She turned to the group waiting behind. "Okay, the ship is ours."

"I don't trust him." Sven gestured toward Jorge's cabin. "He might have sent a message to MedComm."

"Does it really matter?" Jeni asked. "If our plan works, we can control every Komsol on every planet. What can they do to stop us?"

For the next few days they practiced. Even Marcus, who wasn't a clone, insisted on being part of the group. As he pointed out, telepathy was not unknown among normal humans, and there was no reason to assume his latent ability might not be stimulated by the closeness of viable forces.

They sat in a circle, holding hands, trying to bring themselves close to one another. But nothing exceptional happened. Sven and Jeni had sporadic deep contacts, but each of the others remained closed off within her or his own thoughts. After a week of this, everyone was getting on each other's nerves, and popping painkillers for all the headaches. But finally, Nikki was better, walking around, talking to everyone. The rebel group moved their comship as near to Trattori's space as they dared, hoping no patrol ship would accidentally spot them.

"Do you think he's strong enough?" Jeni asked.

"He's almost completely healed," Sven said. "It was just the cold that caused the setback. He's okay now." Sven held Nikki on his lap. They had been drawing pictures together.

"What makes you think it's going to work this time?" Sindra broke in, with a shrill grating voice. "How is he any different?"

"Just give it a chance," Sven answered.

"I've been doing that. All week long," she retorted.

"Calm yourself," Jeni said. "Nikki's the catalyst, I hope. Let's see what happens."

They sat down in a circle, one more time. Nikki was between Jeni and Sven.

"You remember what I explained?" Jeni asked the boy.

"Sure. You just want me to mind-speak," Nikki answered. "That's easy."

"Well, go ahead," Jeni told him.

And there he was, in her mind, all young and playful and happy to be sitting with his two best friends. *Can you reach Sven?* Jeni asked.

Here already. Sven's personality, still determined, ruthless in its goal of freedom, yet newly-compassionate, colored the thought.

And then a motley of other mixed thoughts jumbled together.

Okay, everyone. Jeni. *One at a time.*

Marcus, the human, was the first. He projected fascination and amusement with this new ability. *Listen to me. I'm not so different from the rest of you after all.*

Toby here. Logical. Computer equations in the background. Curiosity. *What happens next?*

Sindra. Cold and hard, like the in-between. *So what good is this new toy? It won't make them accept us. We're better than them, anyhow. Let's just kill them all.*

No. I promised. Besides, this might really work. Sven, really getting excited.

She's got you so you can't think straight. Sindra.

He knows what he's doing. Jeni.

That's what you would say. Sindra, boiling with jealousy. *Ever since he met you he hasn't looked at me.*

So that's it. I didn't know. Sven.

You're blind to everything. You only see what you want to see. Bitterly, Sindra.

That's true enough. Laughing, Jeni.

Shut up, you bitch. Sindra, exploding. Then cutting her mind off from the circle, Sindra rose and walked out of the control room. Sven began to stand up.

Let her go. It won't work with her anyway. Her hate would probably block out our real message. Jeni.

I don't know. I wish she wouldn't cut herself off like this. Sven.

We can take care of her later, when this is all over. Jeni.

I hope so. Sven.

Okay. We know we can talk to each other. Let's find out what else we can do. Toby, interjecting.

Nikki, help us look for Melanie. Can you reach out past the ship? Jeni.

At first, no discernible change. Just Nikki and the four adult minds, linked together, close.

Nikki. *I don't know what I'm supposed to do.*

Here, let me help you. Jeni. She projected an image of her hand, taking Nikki's hand, guiding him to float out in empty space, between the stars that were distant tiny dots of brilliant light. *This way.* She showed him the path toward Trattori, the direction their comship would have to travel in real space. As Nikki got the idea, their journey picked up speed. An immense sense of freedom permeated Jeni's being—something entirely different from her physical body running free in a grassy meadow, or the ultimate superpower of Komsol bolstering her neural functions. It was a letting go, a dropping of power, moving beyond it to an ethereal state of the spirit. Such an unfathomable word. So was this experience.

Jeni realized she had been floating in a cloud of euphoria, forgetting the original purpose of their mission. Now, in an indistinct transformation, she and the others could see Trattori's planet mass loom under their mind's eye. They had made it. They had actually reached Trattori!

Melanie was there, welcoming them, embracing them all. *I'm so glad you're safe. I was worried.*

Jeni returned the mind-embrace. All the others joined in with their own feelings of warmth, shared companionship. Now, the power behind Komsol pumping through Melanie, through Jeni, Sven, Nikki, Marcus, Toby. Their awareness expanding, coming closer together, becoming one Unified Awareness stretching outside the usual limits of time and space.

Now, a dark emptiness. A feeling of speed, but no

way to measure it. Moving quickly. Searching. Different minds, growing closer with the need to achieve the same goal. To reach across the light years. To find more clone-mates. To tell them of this marvelous new discovery. To give them hope. To promise freedom. To overcome. To succeed.

We.

In the distance, a sparkle, a light not part of us. Get closer. Find it.

Who's there? The other.

Clone-mates. Calling to you from far away. Us.

Brent. Clone for Kiridon's Komsol. The other.

Now one of us. Part of our Unity.

The basic essence and power of Jeni's group reached beyond the years of isolation, beyond artificial barriers, into Brent's deepest being. There was no resistance. He joined the Unity. Jeni felt a renewed surge of computer logic, of a second Komsol bringing its memory tapes to her/their mind-essence.

Sven. Nikki. Marcus. Toby. Melanie. Now Brent. All of us. With two Komsols to back us up. One total Being. One Unity. Surging forward. Onward. To find another. And yet another. Latori. Sirna. Kopol. Fiella. Dolek. Mithra. More and more Komsol clones. And comsol clones, free-moving clones. All sorts of clones. The power of the universe at our feet. We can't lose.

How many hours they spent traveling, they didn't know. But finally, one by one, the connections began dropping out. Jeni, only herself again, lay in an exhausted heap upon the floor. All were in the same condition. They slept.

And woke to find Sindra worriedly shaking Sven awake. Their recent experience had brought them so close together that each immediately responded to feelings projected by any one of them. They'd have to learn to control this new force, Jeni realized. Not just for communication, but to be able to retain privacy. Just now, it was nerve-racking to be awakened by Sindra's shrill voice, and feel, through Sven's shoulder, Sindra's relentless grasp.

"Okay, okay. I'm awake." Sven's voice, grating on their ears. His feelings of annoyance magnified by four other minds.

Damp down. Try to get off this wavelength. Jeni.

Nikki. *Don't think so hard.*

But the voices crowded in, louder and louder in Jeni/Nikki/Sven/Toby/Marcus' skulls. All those voices of all those clones in all those Komsols. All those chemically altered metabolisms, all those physically deformed bodies, all those clone legs, arms, livers, stomachs, hearts, all those organs being ripped out of the living, breathing bodies, all those tissues bleeding, muscles torn, bones broken; all that immortality being stolen from their owners and given to MedComm thieves who didn't deserve it.

"I don't deserve it. I don't deserve this. I don't belong here."

Who was screaming? Jeni realized one mind among the four had begun to dominate. She recognized the flavor as belonging to Marcus. What was wrong with him? She tried to contact Sven, but the noise from the ex-MedComm doctor was too strong, too powerfully compelling. It drew her in, closer, closer to . . .

. . . images of red-hot firebrands burning skin to the bone; the smell of stinking, rotting flesh, the breathing in of poisons to make you vomit; the sinking down into a mud swamp filled with slimy creatures tentacling themselves around your throat until you couldn't breathe, until . . .

No! No! She sent the thought in waves of negation, pushing away the mud swamp with her vehement denials. Forcing her eyes open, she saw that Sven was standing still, staring, sweat beading on his forehead. Sindra was trying to shake him awake.

Jeni pushed Sindra aside, slapping Sven across the face, simultaneously shouting his name out loud, "SVEN!" while silently screaming *Sven! Wake up!* "WAKE UP!" *Come back to me.* She pushed past the oozing mud creatures, found Sven's mind, wandering, grabbed hold of him. *Here I am.*

Jeni. His thoughts leaped with recognition, jumped into her mind-space. *Are you all right?*

Yes. Help me find Nikki. Hurry.

The two pushed away the choking mud, heard a tiny crying sound. *Nikki. Here we are. This way.*

Jeni, don't leave me, the boy pleaded.

I won't. Come with us. Come on. Jeni led the way. The three closed the gaps between them and became as one mind, one stronger being fending for itself in the stinking hellhole they had fallen into.

Stroking their way upward, they found Toby, floundering, striking out in all directions. Their three minds called out to his one. He heard and joined them. A few short, quick strokes, and they broke through the surface slime, into the air.

Gasping, Jeni looked around the ship's main cabin.

Sindra was backing away from Sven, saying, "You look so strange."

Sindra was right, but Sven was coming out of it, his eyes beginning to focus. Nikki was grabbing hold of Jeni's left side, burying his head just under her breast, his arms circling her waist. He was crying softly, but he was all right, too. A few feet away Toby stood, taking one tentative step and asking, in a cracked voice, "What was that?"

Jeni's throat was dry. But she forced the sounds out of her mouth. Right now she wasn't taking any chances. No more mind-speaking until they knew what had happened. "I don't know," she answered, looking at Toby, then, hopefully, at Sven.

But then she saw Marcus, sitting on the floor between Toby and Sven. His eyelids were wide open, but the pupils had disappeared. Only the red bloodshot whites of his eyes remained, staring blindly.

"Marcus," Jeni said softly. Then louder, "Marcus?"

But he didn't answer. When she crossed the room to touch his shoulder, he didn't move. He sat, stock-still, staring endlessly.

Inside his own head, Jeni realized. That's where he's lost. Inside the stinking swamp of his own head. That's where we were, being dragged down by his guilt, his self-hatred. "Our telepathic bond must have broken some internal switch," Jeni croaked in her hoarse voice. "He just couldn't take it."

"We can't leave him like this," Sven said.

"I don't know what to do for him, do you?" Jeni asked.

"No," Sven said reluctantly. "I don't know."

"Then he'll just have to wait. Maybe, as we learn more about this thing, this mind-reaching, maybe we'll learn how to help him. Then there's always the chance that Selena will know what to do."

"I don't think so," Sven said. "Not this time." He looked at Marcus, not wanting to, not able to draw his eyes away.

Sindra spoke now, her voice on the edge of hysteria. "I don't understand what's going on!" She stood apart, looking warily at everyone.

Jeni forced a half smile and said, "Sindra, it's okay. Everything's okay. We've done it. All the clones are, even now, preparing to shut down services. We've won. That's what you've been fighting for." Jeni stood up and began to move toward Sindra.

"No!" Sindra screamed. "Not this way." She turned and fled out of the room.

Sven looked at Jeni, felt the mutual response, *go after her*. Giving Jeni's hand a squeeze, Sven followed Sindra out of the control room. Nikki and Toby and Jeni simply stood together for a while, not knowing what to do next. Jeni could sense the other two nearby, without actually hearing their thoughts.

Finally, Jeni spoke out loud. "I think we should start using words again. We won't be able to function on a practical level if we don't separate out."

Toby agreed. "Yes, and I'll take care of him." Gingerly, Toby helped Marcus to his feet and guided the unresisting True Born to his cabin.

Jeni and Nikki, alone, returned to their own cabin. Stretching out on her bed, planning to think about all the implications, Jeni fell asleep.

The smell of food aroused her. Nikki was eating a poulette sandwich. Umm. Her mouth watered. Rising from the bed, Jeni found herself laughing about how wonderful it was to be alive, to see the light shine off the ship's silver walls, to hear Nikki munching on his bread, to taste the here-and-now physicality of this world. She reached for the second sandwich on the plate. At this moment nothing, either inside Komsol or outside in limitless space, could equal the delicious sensation of hunger being satisfied.

CHAPTER 18

Jeni

During the next few days Jeni's group consolidated their plans, coordinating the Komsol shutdown with the mobile clone rendezvous in Tiattoil's star system. In two weeks' time, they calculated, everything would be ready.

While they waited, they practiced controlling their thought emanations, learning to open up or close down according to each person's desire. Marcus' tragedy had taught them a painful lesson, and each of the four clones on Jeni's ship was very careful to keep his or her personal mind-space separate and distinct. Sindra sulked, listening to the others' spoken plans, but never commenting. Sometimes Jeni would catch Sven's eyes upon the other clone-woman, as if he were expecting one of Sindra's caustic remarks.

One day, after they had learned to sufficiently close down their thoughts, Jeni found herself alone with Sven.

He touched her cheek, caressing, questioning, "Now?"

"Now," Jeni agreed.

Nikki was out playing in the control room. They closed the door.

Once again Jeni felt the thrill of fantastic explosions erupting inside her, the thrill of interlocking bodies and minds. Afterward, she lay close to Sven. This time he didn't run away, but stayed a long time, holding her. Selena had been right. There had been no pain, and now there was no sad epilogue. It was good.

Finally, rising from the bed, they washed and dressed. Soon it would be time to take that last space/time jump that would bring them to their destination. And their ultimate goal of freedom.

Jeni was at the control board, piloting. She touched the appropriate switch.

The freezing cold. The timeless nothingness. Forever and not-ever.

They emerged into real space, not far from Trattori. Coming at them from the planet's surface was a cotillion of comships bearing the Komsol insignia. There was no sign of their own small clone-force.

Within minutes, they were surrounded. Inside the control room Sven and Nikki and Toby formed the telepathic circle. Sindra waited on the sidelines. Jeni opened up a channel. On her viscom was Proctor Girot's face, angry, but smug.

"Did you think, my dear," Proctor Girot said, "that we were as stupid as all that?"

"How did you find out?" Jeni asked.

"Jorge called us, as you were turning traitor."

"I'm not a traitor," Jeni said, "to my own people."

"Let's not bandy words, clone," Proctor Girot said. "Are you ready to give yourselves up?"

"Not so quickly." Jeni steeled herself for what was to come. "Maybe you had better listen to our terms," she said.

"You have no terms."

"And you, Sir," Jeni retorted, "have no Komsol."

"What are you talking about?"

"We are in control now. If we choose, every piece of equipment on your planet will stop functioning."

"Idle threats."

"I'll show you." Jeni turned to look behind her, nodded to the group, turned back to the viscom set. "Everything is now shut down, except for emergency facilities and communication outlets. Try your own door, see if the electro-eye works."

Proctor Girot looked away, giving orders, turned back again. "How did you do that?"

"Every clone on every planet in ConFed, including Trattori, is cooperating with us," Jeni said.

"Impossible," Proctor Girot said, his lips pressed down in a grimace.

"You had better believe it," Jeni answered.

Proctor Girot cut off the communication. Nothing could be heard in the dead silence that lasted for minutes while Jeni and the others waited. Then the proctor's visage reappeared on the screen.

"It's irrelevant whether I believe it or not," Proctor Girot continued. "The only thing that should matter to you is that you are now surrounded by the MedComm fleet, and that their weapons are aimed at you. I've already given orders to destroy your ship in five minutes if they receive no countercommand from me. I expect you to bring your ship planetside. Immediately."

This time it was Jeni who cut off her viscom, turning to Sven and the others. "Any word?" she asked.

Sven answered, "Our force is on its way, but won't be here for at least another hour. Better play for time and do what he says."

Jeni switched the viscom back on. "We're coming down," she informed Proctor Girot.

"I thought you would." Proctor Girot leaned back in his chair. "Don't make any false moves. My fleet still has instructions to blast you if they don't hear from me every five minutes."

Jeni began piloting the ship down toward Trattori's second continent. Sven came to stand beside her. He patted her hand saying, "It will work out."

"Yes, I think it will," Jeni agreed. She smiled up at him, then returned her attention to the control board. Sven rejoined the others who were strapping down for the landing.

When both sides were standing on the landing field of Trattori's second continent, Jeni's group surrounded by the two squads of MedComm troops dressed in the galaxy-wide military colors of black and silver, Jeni said, "We're ready to negotiate."

Proctor Girot was standing a short distance away with a group of people marked by the richness of their attire. Facing the small clone-faction, Girot said, "Oh, you are, are you?" The proctor waved his hand to indicate the black-and-silver guards.

Jeni said, "We're part of your world. Sooner or later you'll have to learn to accept us."

"What makes you think that?"

"You forget. We're at a stalemate. If you kill us, every Komsol on every planet will be shut down."

"But you'll all be dead," Girot said.

"And so would the ConFederation," Jeni answered.

"What is it you want?"

"Freedom for all clones. Our own planet. Equal rights as citizens of ConFed."

"We will not accept clones masquerading as humans."

"We're cloned from human beings, from the cream of humanity, and from yourselves, as you well know," Jeni said. "And in time I hope we will be accepted. But in the meanwhile we are willing to leave you alone, to go off and find our own world, to live by ourselves."

"Under those circumstances we would be no better off than if you carried out your threat to shut down our Komsols."

"We only want our rights. We would still be willing to work with Komsol. But only as paid citizens and under our own terms."

"All this is very complicated."

A voice started laughing, behind Jeni. It was Sindra. "You can't talk to them. I told you this wouldn't work.

We should have killed them all. We . . ." Sven slapped her. Sindra hit back, fighting with him. He grabbed her arms, pinioning her.

Suddenly there were shouts from the other members of Jeni's group. Jeni looked up to see that the True Borns had moved, closing in, stunners aimed at the clones. But her people were ready, with their own weapons out.

"No." Jeni moved toward the nearest guardsman. She spoke to him saying, "Don't listen to her. That's not what we plan. We only want respect. We'll keep working with you." Desperately, "Don't you know we're part of you? We're cloned from you people. We're your own grandfathers and fathers. Your own mothers and sisters. We're no different from you. The same bodies. The same brains. The same feelings." Jeni took another step forward, hands outstretched, pleading.

A low whirring sound. A stream of light. An intense feeling of heat on her left thigh just above the knee. Grabbing at her leg, Jeni collapsed to the ground. Weapons aimed, the MedComm troops began to close in.

Sven ran toward Jeni, yelling, "Stop! Just listen to her!" Before he could reach Jeni, a beam of light shot out, hitting him directly in the chest. Without another word, he crumpled over, falling heavily onto the concrete pavement.

Suddenly there was a droning sound, high above the landing field, which grew into an almost deafening roar. Everyone stopped, in mid-action, looking up. The guardsmen still encircled the small group of clones, but stood, indecisive, not knowing whether to advance or to expect an attack from above. Proctor Girot and the other MedComm officers gave no orders, simply standing still, dumbfounded. Within minutes the other clones had landed their ships and were streaming toward the MedComm troops. The guardsmen were sandwiched between the original group and this new one. Outflanked, and outnumbered, the MedComm troops began firing in both directions. The smell of burning flesh permeated the air.

But Jeni could only see Sven, lying on the concrete, in the empty space between her group and the guards, only a few feet away. She felt the pain in her leg as she reached toward Sven. She didn't notice the sudden silence, didn't see that the guards had dropped their weapons, surrendering. All that mattered was Sven, lying on the ground, so very still.

Gritting her teeth, she traced the nerve endings to her damaged leg. Inhibiting the feedback, she minimized the pain. But the leg wasn't working properly. With both hands and her good right knee, she dragged herself over to Sven's inert body. He lay on his stomach with his face twisted sideways, toward her. Jeni lowered herself to his level, putting her face next to his and an arm around his back. "Sven," she said softly. *Sven,* she thought to him. And then, *Nikki, help me find Sven.*

I can't. Nikki's thoughts, scared, bewildered, searching.

You have to help me. Jeni, demanding, desperate.

I don't hear him anymore, Jeni. He's gone. Nikki, wailing.

Go after him. Help me go after him. Jeni.

I don't know how. Nikki, screaming in her mind. Wanting to run away and hide. But afraid to leave Jeni in case he lost her also.

Help me find him, Nikki. Help me. Jeni.

And the others—Toby, Melanie, Brent, all the Komsol clones, the mobile clones in the landing field —soothing Nikki, telling Jeni. *He's gone. There's nothing more you can do for him. But we're still here. We need you.*

And Nikki crying. *Jeni, don't go away. You promised me you'd stay.*

Melanie. *We're almost there. But we need your help.*

I can't. I want Sven. Jeni.

Don't give up now. Toby. *Sven fought all his life for this moment.*

But he's dead. Jeni.

He died keeping his promise to you. Trying to stop the killing. Make his death count. Melanie again.

They killed him. Jeni pushed herself up on one elbow. Then out loud, screaming, "They killed him." She tried to stand up, but her leg wouldn't support her weight. She fell down on her hands and knees, crying, "They killed him."

A woman's figure separated itself from the MedComm group and walked over to Jeni. Selena reached down, touched Jeni's shoulder, saying, "It'll be all right."

Jeni looked, angry lines twisting in her face. "No," she shouted. Then in a quiet tense voice, "No, it won't be all right."

Toby came over now, and together he and Selena helped Jeni to stand. Jeni didn't look anymore at Sven's body. She didn't seem to be looking at anyone or anything. Her eyes just stared blindly. In a flat monotone, she said, "Sindra was right. We'll show them who's got more power. It can't work any other way." And in a louder voice, commanding, "Shoot them. Kill them all. We'll never be free while they live."

The other clones aimed their weapons, but didn't fire. They waited.

Selena spoke. "Will you kill me, too?"

"Yes. Kill them all." Sindra's shrill voice screeched into the silence. And then Sindra was running, leaping at Selena, hitting her.

No. Nikki.

No. Jeni echoed. Then out loud, "NO!"

Toby released his hold on Jeni, letting her drop gently to the ground. He forced himself between the other women, grabbing Sindra, pulling her away. Holding the struggling clone, he said to Jeni. "In the end Sven came to believe in you, in your way. He died trying to keep his promise not to kill. Would you betray his trust in you now?" He was silent for a moment, then continued. "Let's show them who is human. Who can feel mercy."

Choking on her words, Jeni said, "I can't forgive."

"Neither can I," Toby said. "Not yet. But maybe our children will, one day. In the meanwhile"—Toby looked up at the sky, then back down at Jeni—"there are all those other True Borns on all those other planets. Will you keep trying to kill them all? Will you keep making the same mistakes Sven made, that I made? There are just too many of them," Toby ended up whispering.

"Or learn to live with us?" Selena said softly, looking down at Jeni.

"Not you." Jeni shook her head. "I never meant to hurt you."

"But what about all the others like me?" Selena continued.

"No. I guess not."

"Then come now." Selena reached down to help Jeni stand up. "We've only just won the first battle. There's a lot more that needs to be done."

Jeni looked once more at Sven, lying so still, so quiet. But then there was Nikki, tears streaming down his face, grabbing at Jeni's hand with his own small fingers. Jeni felt the tears beginning to well up in her own eyes. But, no, she had to be strong. It was not all right to cry in front of these bastards. It was not all right to show weakness. Clones could no longer allow themselves to be put into the roles of scapegoats. To let themselves be used and killed.

Leaning heavily on Selena, Jeni rose to face the MedComm contingent. Proctor Girot was led out from the safety of the center of the human group where he had been hiding. Jeni remembered that these people had invested their whole lives in the avoidance of death. Now, threatened with the immediate loss of their supposedly immortal bodies, they were frightened beyond reason. Their fear was their Achilles heel. Forcing the words out of her tight throat, Jeni said, "Now, as to our terms."

"I have no choice," Proctor Girot said. "You'll get what you want. But we'll see if you can keep it."

Slowly, carefully enunciating each word, Jeni said, "I want this all recorded in a legal document."

"If you'll just come inside." Proctor Girot turned his back and began walking. His pace was a slow waddle. He was not going to be rushed.

Leaning on Selena, with Nikki at her other side, Jeni followed.

Sven's gone. Nikki's mind still cried.

Jeni felt the boy's despair merging with her own—a total sense of loss and emptiness.

But we're still here. The thoughts came from Toby and Melanie. From her other clone-mates. *We know it hurts. But we're here, with you. Together. You're not alone.*

I'm not alone. The thought echoed in Jeni's mind. But it would be a long while before that feeling would begin to fill the void so deep inside her. Silently now, only to herself, she cried out: Sven.

And kept walking. To fulfill Sven's dream—her own dream. To live freely as a human citizen. To be respected. To live on a world with her own people.

But not with Sven.

He had said it wasn't too late. But it was too late. For him.

CHAPTER 19

Excerpt from Selena Menard's *Out of My Father's Seed: A Personal History of the Clone Wars, Vol. I.*

As I entered the hotel suite my ears were buffeted by the noise of arguing voices, and my eyes by a view of multicolored, bizarre outfits that came in all styles from the far reaches of the galaxy. Here, HOFROC, COFF, the Workers' Union, and other concerned citizens were meeting to finalize their plans for the Joint Council meeting tomorrow afternoon. I was sure that there were as many different opinions as there were people loudly discussing the situation.

Although Girot had signed the papers relinquishing ownership of the clones, the actual state of affairs was much more complicated. Entire planets depended on the Komsol clones for their technological existence, while the wealthy aristocracy was terrified of losing their source of immortality. Still, HOFROC intended to place before the Council their demands for equal citizenship, a home world, and medical assistance.

If the clones didn't get medical supplies, their theoretical freedom would do them no good. Most of those that had been freed on Trattori had no place to go and were in poor physical condition. They would not survive long without outside help.

I remembered only too vividly what had been found on Trattori's second continent. It had been appalling, even worse than we had expected. One after another of the storage rooms had been unlocked—there were layers of frozen adult clone-bodies waiting to be cut up to fit the needs of their recipients. The children's rooms were even more grotesque: small bodies lay in cubicles, drugged into insensibility, while pipelines permanently attached to their arms fed them the necessary nutrients that would bring their bodies to maturity. Further on, there were the nurseries where first consciousness was allowed, but not encouraged, until the age of three, when the little bodies were deemed sufficiently developed to be able to handle the drugs and liquid nutrients that provided sustenance in the induced-coma state.

Beyond the regeneration center, as it was called, was the research department. Here we found clones who were being literally starved to death in various attempts to record the stage of disintegration as the human body reached the limits of its endurance; here also were clones who had been surgically experimented upon, without anesthetics, in order to better watch the unhampered neural reactions; clones who had been impregnated with recombinant-DNA fetuses in order to see if new mutations could survive; along the same lines, other pregnant clones had been subjected to various types and amounts of radiation; still others had been injected with animal hormones in order to determine possible compatibilities; others were used as guinea pigs for new drugs, new hallucinogens, new sterilization techniques.

Many were beyond redemption, and I was faced with the difficult decision of whether to put the clones out of their misery. But Jeni, rubbing her leg where the recent wound had healed rapidly according to her inner commands to the tissue cells, insisted that as many as possible be saved. Even the frozen clones, who were no more than vegetables in human form, were to be salvaged. In a way, I was relieved. Since Marcus had returned to Trattori in his psychotic state, the work of organizing the entire medical rescue operation had fallen to me. Although I was not a doctor, I was the most qualified person available. But it was a heavy responsibility, one which I did not relish. I was happy to have Jeni make this decision, and I was glad not to be required to stop the lives, no matter how minimal, within these helpless bodies and blank minds.

But it was the new crop of clone-babies that my heart turned to with hope. These had not yet been drugged or tortured into mindlessness. The young ones were the future hope for a clone-nation. They were to be nurtured and coddled and loved.

I remembered standing over the cribs of three five-month-old brown-haired clone-brothers. My hands were clenched at my sides as I looked down at one of the children. I unclenched my hands and reached over the bars to rearrange a blanket around one baby's shoulders, and thought to myself that the clone-child seemed to be perfectly normal. Through no help of my own, I remembered thinking.

I removed my hands from the crib, shocked by my thought. I had done nothing to harm this child. Was I so lost in my father's guilt I couldn't see the difference between us?

It was my father, I reminded myself, who had closed his eyes to all the torture. Not me. It was doctors like Marcus who killed clones for their organs. Not me.

There's good reason for my father to hide in his study, I thought. There's good reason for Marcus to run away deep into the guilty sea of his disturbed mind.

But I am innocent. The declaration was like a clear bell on a foggy night. Why hadn't I ever seen this before?

It was so obvious. I had not chosen to be born Paul Menard's daughter.

But I had chosen to search out these people, to find them and help them to the best of my ability. I was here to do what I could do best—to help them find a way to live. This was my job and I felt lucky to have been given this chance.

A sense of security settled within me as I looked around. I knew what I'd be doing in the years to come. I had found my clones, thousands of them.

True, there were more than I could possibly handle alone. I would have to train a corps of therapists from the mobile clones, and some of them would have to be ready too soon—before I went to Rivolin in three months to finalize the political arrangements. I was going to be very, very busy.

But I was needed—for my medical guidance back on Trattori, and now, here on Rivolin, to negotiate for the clones.

I had not felt easy leaving Trattori, wanting to initiate treatment for each clone victim as soon as possible. But then I realized that those who had survived this far could last another few months without a fully-organized rehabilitation program. It was more important that I make sure that they all get their chance in the larger arena, or my little ministrations would end up useless. But I missed them. I missed doing my real work, missed the intimacy of constant contact with human bodies and emotions. Indeed, I was surprised to find out how lost and alone I felt, and how tired. I had been so busy on Trattori that I had thought the trip to Rivolin would give me a chance to rest. Instead, it all seemed to be catching up.

I couldn't stop thinking about all the problems I had left behind. But I was glad, at least, that I had made the decision to send for Daven Migdal to come to Trattori to help organize the evacuation operation. The clones would be in good hands with him. I only regretted that I had to leave before he arrived and had missed the chance to say hello to him once again.

Now I stood in the hotel suite full of noisy people, but felt completely separate and alone. A speedy, nervous feeling was twirling in the pit of my stomach, and an aching fatigue was spreading through my arms and legs. Last time I had been on Rivolin the results had been disastrous. The deal had been made with MedComm that had forced Jeni out on her terrible mission. Sven had ended up dead and Jeni had been hurt, perhaps irrevocably.

I remembered how, almost two weeks after Sven's death and after the papers had been signed by Girot, I had found Jeni sitting in an empty room staring at the blank walls. We had all been pampering the clone-woman, petting her, caring for her. But there had been no response. My patience was coming to an end.

"How long are you going to sit there like a lump?" I asked, knowing how harsh the words sounded. "You're no better than those mindless bodies Med-Comm has in storage."

Jeni just looked up at me, glaring.

"You can't just give up," I pressed on. "You're a Komsol clone come back to life. You've already done the impossible. You've won the biggest battle." I paused, looking at the hate-filled eyes. Then I leaned over and grabbed Jeni by the shoulders, letting out all my pent-up frustration by shaking her. "Look at me, you silly fool. He isn't worth it. He was mad. They did it to him. But he was mad." The words were out of my mouth before I realized fully what I was saying.

Jeni jumped from her chair, eyes blazing. "How dare you? What do you know?"

I stood up to face Jeni. "At least I got a rise out of you. But I do know. You forget, I knew him from the moment we helped him escape his Komsol. And I loved him, too, for a little while."

"You could never know him the way I did." Jeni's tone was filled with scorn.

"No. He never really loved me." Even now, this was difficult for me to admit.

"Not just love."

"You mean the mind-link?" I said reluctantly, not wanting to talk about this special ability belonging to the clones. My lack of it made me feel so very apart from Jeni.

"Yes," Jeni answered.

"You still have others who can do that." I heard the jealousy in the tone of my voice. "And Nikki. I know it's not the same, but . . ."

"Yes," Jeni interrupted. "That's why I'm going on. For them."

"But what about yourself?"

"I don't care what happens to me."

"I do," I said. I could still let Jeni know how much I cared about her with spoken words. It was the best I could do. "And that's why I said he's not worth it. You're still young, and you have your whole life to lead. Mourn him, yes. But don't stop living." *Jeni, please hear me,* I pleaded silently.

Answering as if she had heard my silent prayer, Jeni said, "I don't want to hear anymore about this." The clone-woman turned her back on me and stomped out of the room.

I remembered thinking to myself that at least I had gotten Jeni to feel something again besides self pity. But after that last conversation Jeni would no longer speak to me, or to any of the other few human beings helping out, except when absolutely necessary.

I noticed something else. Although no words had been spoken out loud, I could see, through their behavior, that the other clones were following Jeni's lead, that she was becoming their unnamed leader as the clones separated themselves more and more from us humans.

Now it seemed to me that I had failed Jeni, and myself, as a therapist. What had happened to the golden dream of nurturing Jeni into a healthy woman? It had been shunted aside for political expediency and destroyed, along with Sven, on Girot's landing field. I think I resented Sven's death more for what it had done to Jeni than for the actual fact of the loss of his life.

I was. angry at Sven for letting himself get killed. I was angry at myself, and at Jeni, too, as the second party to my failure. The anger was echoed in the loud voices that finally began to penetrate my conscious mind.

"MedComm is dangling lower rental rates and more Komsols before ConFed." It was Vera's voice, one of the delegates who had been with me on Rivolin the last time.

Willis answered, "We can counter that with promises that the clones won't leave their Komsols as long as they're paid like other workers, until a non-human technology can be developed. My worry is Med-Comm's latest bribery attempt. They've been approaching certain statesmen, in secret, with offers to prepare a new set of clones for transplant parts."

"We can counter that one, too," the scientist, Bertil Renson, said. "We'll soon be able to provide cloned organs at affordable prices that will be available to everyone, without restriction to rank or position."

"And I plan to withdraw my support from Med-Comm's procedures, totally and publicly."

I recognized my father's voice, but it shook with the wavering sound of old age as he spoke these words. I turned to look at him, for although I had known he was supposed to be on Rivolin, I had not yet had a chance to seek him out.

What I saw horrified me. An old and feeble man, dressed in gray, was rising from his armchair to greet his daughter. Was it less than a year since I had last seen my father? I rushed to embrace him, and was further shocked at the trembling weakness I could feel in the touch of his arms around my back. I held him close, thinking, this may be the last time. I don't want him to die.

My father whispered in my ear, "It's all right, daughter. I am content."

I tried to blink away my tears before releasing him from my arms and letting him see my face. I felt very tired but I forced myself to smile. "It's good to see you again."

"I'm glad I can be here for this," Paul Menard said.

"Don't talk like that," I said. "You could still have years."

"Ssh," he said. "I have very little time left. I just hope I'm here long enough to see this thing through to the end. Then I'll be happy to go. I'm very, very tired."

I looked at my father, not knowing what else to say.

"But come over here," he told me, disregarding my look of concern. "Sit down with me and talk." Leaning heavily on my arm, my father walked with me to a corner of the room where we could sit in relative privacy.

"What I want to know is, how are you?" Paul Menard asked, patting my hand. "You don't look too well."

Fighting back the tears, I sat quietly. Here was my father, about to die any day, and he was concerned with my health! I felt like a fool, worrying about ridiculous things.

When I didn't answer, my father continued. "I just wanted to tell you," he said, "that I'm proud of you. Because of what you've done, I can die easy."

This was too much. "What I've done!" I exclaimed. "All I've done is hurt the people I love best. I walked out on you. I got Sven killed. I turned Jeni into a human-hater. I left thousands of inexperienced clones behind, on Trattori, who don't know anything about living in the True Born world. I can't manage anything right." I turned my face sideways, crying against the back of my armchair.

"There's nothing to blame yourself for," my father said. "You've helped guide this whole issue to its proper resolution. You've done a good job of it. After all, it was you who triggered me into action. If you hadn't walked out on me I wouldn't be here today fighting with you for the clones." He touched my cheek, stroking it. "Come on, say it out loud. You know I'm right."

I remembered my father sitting, years ago in his study, tired and dead to the world. I looked at him today, in an old man's body, but with his spirit vitally alive.

"Yes, you're right," I finally admitted both to myself and to my father.

Paul Menard continued. "Sometimes drastic situations require drastic actions. You're good at stimulating people that way."

Yes, I thought. At least Jeni was up and around with her clone-mates on Trattori, not sitting quietly drowning in self-pity.

"Can't you see how much you've done, girl? You've got the whole of ConFed paying attention. No one in three hundred years has been able to do that!"

Now I looked at my father. I felt silly, like a tired little girl who had been drowning in an imaginary pool of quicksand, my own well of self-pity. I was supposed to be the perfect therapist, the perfect negotiator. Well, I wasn't God. My father was right—I had done my best. That was as much as anyone could do. And it was okay, sometimes, to let myself feel like a little girl. I realized that, right now, the little girl hiding inside my grown-up body was immensely proud. My father was praising me. He liked what I had done. I was a good little girl.

Maybe, after all, everything was going to be all right. Since coming to Rivolin I had been very tired and lonely, and those feelings had made everything seem worse that it was. I felt as if a veil had been lifted from my eyes.

The truth was that MedComm was being brought to its knees. The clones had been freed and had a good chance of becoming ConFed citizens. I had made sure Jeni's people on Trattori were in good hands, with Daven Migdal to watch over them. Jeni herself was still alive, and I had every reason to hope that our relationship was strong enough to survive recent events. And I had been reunited, in more ways than one, with my father.

I squeezed the old man's hand that was holding my own, leaned forward and whispered to my father, Paul Menard, "I'm proud of you, too."

CHAPTER 20

Jeni

Jumbled thoughts from several minds pushed into Jeni's brain. One thought became more distinct, louder, separate from the others. *Jeni. Jeni. Help.* It was Nikki. Somebody was hurting him. Jeni rushed toward the source of the confusion, hearing Nikki's thought-cries grow louder as she came closer to the boy's physical body. As she ran down the hallway, there were other footsteps, and Jeni could feel the comforting mind-auras of other clones also hurrying to help Nikki.

Suddenly, in front of her was a crowd of bodies. Jeni pushed through the warm arms and torsos, past the door and into the storeroom. Here boxes and crates were being inventoried for usable medical supplies that could be taken with them when the clones left Trattori. But right now all work had stopped. Two clones stood on one side of the room, glaring at the three human workers who were backed against the wall of the opposite side of the room. In the center of the storeroom, on an overturned crate, sat a short, thin man wearing archaic thick glasses. It was Daven Migdal, and he had Nikki turned over his knee. The boy was being spanked!

What's going on here? Jeni, projecting her question to all the clones. Almost instantly, she began receiving mind-messages back from Nikki and the others.

I was only playing. Nikki wailing.

How dare he touch the boy! One clone inside the storeroom answered, indignant.

Just because he's True Born, does he think he can still get away with things like that? Another.

We won't stand for this. From a clone standing in the doorway, behind Jeni.

Somehow, the fact that it was Daven, not just any human, who was hurting Nikki, annoyed Jeni even more. It had been Selena who had sent for Daven to help organize the clone evacuation, not Jeni. The clones were no longer in real trouble. If they had had a little more time, they would have been able to figure out what to do for themselves. But it didn't seem as if Jeni and the other clones had been given much choice. Now that negotiations were in full swing on Rivolin, it was HOFROC that had the upper hand— Selena and HOFROC and all those humans who were willing to reap the benefits of what Sven had done, but not give him any of the credit. When the clones found their own planet, Jeni thought to herself, they would make themselves totally independent of the human universe. Meanwhile, she reluctantly admitted, she had to accept their help if the clones were going to be safely evacuated from Trattori. But she didn't have to like it. And she didn't have to let things like this go on. If she had expected better from any of the humans, it would have been from Daven. If there was anyone who owed anybody anything, it was he who owed the clones a favor, after what she had done for him on Palaster.

"Put him down," Jeni said harshly to the man who was in charge of the human evacuation force.

"Don't you want to know what was going on?" Daven asked, in that voice that was always so surprisingly strong for such a thin and wiry body. But he released Nikki, who stood up gingerly and walked with mincing steps across the room to stand next to Jeni.

"I don't need to hear it from you," Jeni retorted.

"A child's story is likely to be a little one-sided, don't you think?" Daven stood up, crossed his arms in front of his chest, and calmly faced Jeni and the group of clones who had gathered in the hallway outside the storeroom door.

"Nikki couldn't lie to me," Jeni said, beginning to turn away.

"Because he mind-speaks to you?" Daven sounded skeptical. "It is just possible he could see things differently, from a child's perspective, you know. And the boy is beginning to get really wild."

"I don't think it's any of your business."

"It becomes my business when my men start getting bruised fingers from snaptraps hidden in with the crates."

"Why would Nikki do a thing like that?"

"I'm sure I don't know," Daven said with a sarcastic ring to his voice. "I guess for the same reason that you and your group think you've got everything coming to you, just for the taking; for the same reason that you think you own the air we all breathe; for the same reason that we humans have become the targets of your verbal cat-and-mouse games."

"I don't know what you're talking about," Jeni said, and turned away. She stalked down the hallway, hoping the man would learn to stick to his own business and leave her alone. The clone-woman and boy turned a corner, and, after Jeni absentmindedly ruffled Nikki's red hair, she sent him outside to play.

Her body ached with tiredness, physical and emotional exhaustion. Although one part of her mind noted this, another part of her brain kept pushing her on and on. She could instruct her muscles to move, increase the adrenal flow, cause her body to respond to her neural commands, until it performed far beyond normal human limits. This was one of the things she had learned to do from Komsol. This was another one of those things that separated clones from simple humans.

She had to do it this way now; she had to call on every ounce of strength she could summon. There were more than 1,800 clones in semivegetable states. The lucky ones were like childen with undeveloped three-year-old minds. All those had to be cared for, their survival ensured against such do-gooders who might think they would be happier put out of their misery. Then there were all the escaped comsol clones arriving in small comships, converging on Trattori from all over the galaxy. Quarters had to be arranged, and instructions given to these beings who had never lived truly free lives. But mostly Jeni was occupied with maintaining the inner communications network between clones on Trattori and the Komsol clones on various planets of ConFed. It was still their greatest source of power— the threat of shutting down Komsols, of depriving the humans of the energy and technology they were so completely dependent upon.

All this Jeni had to worry about. She had no time to sit and be still, no time to be alone, no time to think about Sven, to remember him. No time to stop and feel the pain, feel the loss. She had to keep going. On and on. To push the humans out of her way. To fight for all people who needed her.

Suddenly, the air seemed to grow thick, hard to breathe, almost fluid in its consistency. The walls were spinning. What was happening?

And then Jeni didn't care. It all felt so soft, warm, safe, as her body slid down the wall and sank into a crumpled heap on the floor.

She woke to find herself lying in a soft bed. The first distinct sensation was the crisp touch of clean sheets under her hands. A blurred form stood at the side of the bed, injecting something into her arm.

"Are you awake?" Daven's voice asked. Jeni could see him better now, his thin bony face looking worried behind his thick glasses as he peered into her eyes. "How long since you've eaten anything?" Daven asked Jeni.

Jeni's voice croaked, then formed the words, "I don't remember."

"Well, you better remember." Daven's voice was harsh, but not really angry. "You're not a machine. You're a human being, as well as a clone."

Jeni turned her head away.

Daven reached out, putting his hand on Jeni's shoulder, in what was obviously meant to be a comforting gesture.

A flash memory came and passed—the first time Sindra's nonmetallic hand had touched Jeni, back on Callistra, after the explosion. The revulsion that Jeni felt was the same. She shrugged her shoulder, slipping out from under the man's fingers.

But Daven was not going to be turned away. He reached down and gripped her arm above the wrist. Speaking softly, he said, "Old friends should take a few minutes every once in awhile, just to say hello. I've been here for weeks and you've managed to completely avoid me."

Jeni tried to pull her arm away, but was too weak. She said nothing.

"I told you I'd be around when you needed me."

This time Jeni answered. "Why bother?" She practically spat up at his face. "You're not really involved in this. It's just a game for you. You can leave whenever you want."

Daven looked shocked. But he spoke. "I think you know that's not true. I'm proud to be able to help where I can. Especially you. And—" he paused, then continued, "I wanted to tell you I cared. That I was sorry to hear about Sven's death."

"What can you know about that? You're human!" Jeni turned her head away. Why wouldn't this man leave her alone?

But she could feel Daven's weight as he sat down on the bed and slid his arm behind her back. He began to cradle her against his chest. She could feel the warmth of his skin, even through her clothes. Was she imagining the beat of his heart against her own? What was he doing?

"No, let me go." Jeni pushed at Daven's chest, feebly screeching out the words.

Daven held her firmly in his arms as he asked, "What's wrong?"

"Don't try anything like that with me again," she said, fury making her voice shriek in her own ears.

"If you think I'm after your beautiful body, you're completely off course," Daven said. Jeni felt his fingers digging into the soft flesh of her upper arm. "I am only trying to help you." He loosened his grip a little and, with his other hand, touched Jeni's cheek, turning her face so she would have to look at him. His voice was more gentle this time. "We're all very worried about you, you know."

"Why don't you just leave me alone," Jeni said. "I don't need any of you True Borns."

"I don't give a damn what you think you need," Daven said. "You're going to listen to me."

Jeni began to struggle in Daven's grasp, anger giving her more strength than her weakened body should have been capable of summoning. She screamed again. "Let me go." But she couldn't get free of his hold on her. Changing direction, she lunged toward him, began biting and kicking, losing herself in an animal fury.

Daven pushed her shoulders down on the bed, swung one leg over her body, and sat down on her stomach. Then he let go and gave her a hard slap across the face; and another slap and another one. Suddenly, the strength seemed to ebb from Jeni's body; she stopped fighting but lay still under Daven's arms and legs, crying. Long loud sobs shook her body. Daven changed his position to sit once again on the side of the bed. Lifting Jeni, he cradled her in his arms.

"I don't want to live without him," Jeni managed to say between the sobs that racked her body. "I don't want to live."

"I know," Daven said, gently holding her, rocking her. "I know."

"How can you know?" Jeni cried out. "How can you know?"

"I lost my parents the same way," Daven told her. "There was a famine. My people rose up. But the rich planetowners brought out their guns and massacred my people. I was a child of twelve, standing in a doorway, when I saw my mother and father gunned down. I saw their blood streaming out over the cobbled stones of the road. I saw their heads smashed open by the butts of guns. I saw . . ." Daven stopped, still looking down at Jeni, but also caught in the vision of his own past.

Jeni felt his arms go rigid over her body. She heard his words and their meaning began to penetrate. She wasn't the only one. He was human and he had lost, too. But how could he go on living, how could he bear the pain? She could hear, in his voice, that he still carried it with him. Jeni turned to look up at Daven, saw him staring at her, the pain twisting his features. With a cry, she flung herself closer to him, holding him, feeling his arms tightly around her back. She clung to him, and she cried. Finally, she cried. She cried for Sven, for Daven's parents, for all those who had been killed, and all those who had to live with their memories. Letting herself go, she heard the wailing sounds, felt the depth of her loss, and cried.

It seemed like she would never stop, but, at last, her body ceased its jerking in time to her sobs. Her sounds grew lower, less intense. It was almost comforting to cry, quietly, to feel Daven's strong arms around her body, to know that she had, at last, accepted the fact that Sven was dead.

Finally, Jeni felt her body relax into quietness. In the momentary peace she became aware of Daven as a separate entity, holding her, touching her, hearing and feeling her pain. She began to grow ashamed of her outburst, afraid to look up at the human who held her.

Once she had sworn never to be weak; but this time she hadn't been able to stop herself.

Quietly, Daven asked, "Are you all right now?"

Still not wanting to look, Jeni nodded her head, yes.

"Can you sit up?" he asked.

Jeni nodded again and began to rise. Daven helped her, and when she sat on the edge of the bed, he said, "Why won't you look at me?"

Jeni realized she was staring pointedly at her feet. She shook her head, not knowing how to answer.

Daven's finger touched under her chin, pushing her face up toward his. He said, "I once told you never to be ashamed. And I meant that. It's perfectly okay to cry. It's a normal reaction."

Jeni looked at him and saw that his cheeks were wet, that his eyes were red. "You've been crying, too," she said.

"Yes. For you. For me. There was a lot to cry about," he said. He began to smile. "But there's a lot to live for, too. And a lot for us to do so that there'll be less reason for others to cry. Don't you agree?"

"Yes," Jeni said, and was amazed at how strong the word sounded, amazed at the weight that had lifted itself from her heart. The unrelenting pain, the all-absorbing hate, had been washed away with the tears. Selena was right, Jeni thought to herself. Mourn for Sven, but live.

Jeni moved her hand to wipe away her tears, and found that her eyes burned, inside and out. But she was smiling. "I'll go wash up," she said, "if you help me to stand up."

"Good." Daven kissed her on her wet cheek. "Then we're going to feed you a healthy human meal."

_____

Excerpt from Selena Menard's *Out of My Father's Seed: A Personal History of the Clone Wars*, Vol. I.

My father and I, with several other people, entered the great round hall of the Forum. Delegates all over the floor, dressed in the colors and styles of their various worlds, were standing and shouting while the Speaker raised and banged his electronic gavel. As the sonic hum penetrated, I held my hands over my ears, even though I had learned by previous experience that nothing could effectively muffle the sound.

"This way," my father mouthed silently, pointing. He leaned heavily on my shoulder as we walked through several aisles until we reached HOFROC's seating area.

We had only a few minutes to wait before the Speaker announced that Paul Menard was next on the agenda.

As I stood up to help my father walk to the podium, he waved me back down into my chair. I was reluctant to let him go alone, but sat still, watching with respect and anguish as my father painfully and slowly made his way to the center of the Forum. At that point a member of the audience did stand up and help the old man climb the few steps to the podium.

Paul Menard began to speak, in an old crackling voice amplified by the Forum's sound devices. I knew that other devices were already beaming these proceedings through the relay system, to all the planets of the ConFederation. Trattori would be hearing these words with only a seven-hour delay.

"My fellow citizens, we are not only asking for a vote for citizenship for clones, but at the same time it must be acknowledged that such a vote will, by implication, be one asking for the condemnation of those crimes perpetrated against a human segment of the galaxy. We are faced with a grave responsibility. The wrongs which we seek to set aright have been so calculated, so malignant, and so devastating, that Civilization cannot tolerate their being ignored any longer, because it cannot survive their being repeated.

"We, the people, and our governments, cannot allow ourselves to be further implicated in these crimes. The men of MedComm, who possess themselves of such great power, and have made deliberate and concerted use of it to set in motion evils which have left no home world untouched, must be stopped. It is a cause of this magnitude that is being presented before this Joint Council.

"The real complaining party is Civilization. On all our planets it is still a struggling and imperfect thing. What has been done to the clones is symbolic of forces all good citizens abhor—racial hatreds, slavery, and violence. MedComm's acts have bathed the galaxy in blood and set Civilization back centuries. They have subjected the clones to every outrage and torture, every spoilation and deprivation that insolence, cruelty, and greed could inflict.

"Civilization is asking whether it must be helpless to deal with crimes of this magnitude by criminals of this order. It does not expect that you make such actions impossible. It does expect that your decision will put its sanctions on the side of peace, so that men and women of all kinds in all the worlds may be able to enjoy this peace to which they are entitled. But this peace must be worked for, sacrificed for, and gained by interplanetary cooperation on the widest scale.

"The ConFederation is a precarious institution, based on the goodwill of its member planets. It has too long suffered this group of power-seeking individuals to dictate its course of action. In good conscience, we must now take a stand against MedComm, a forceful one, and be willing to back up our decision. It will be a momentous event, for, with this decision against these forces of evil and for humanity, the ConFederation will gain a unity that it so far has been unable to achieve.

"And with this unity all people shall one day enjoy peace.

"Thank you."

As Paul Menard finished speaking these last words, the delegates rose to their feet, filling the round hall of the Forum with a tumultuous roaring. I could not tell whether it was all one roar of approval, or whether the shouts and stomping included noises of anger. The Speaker's gavel descended, its sonic vibrations finally managing to bring silence. I waved to my father for attention and pointed to the tape I was holding in my hand.

Paul Menard nodded that he understood, and said, "Mr. Speaker, our delegation has another voice to be heard. It belongs to Jeni. She is one of the clones we have been talking about, an ex-Komsol clone who now walks in her own body. Although she could not be here in person, she has sent this tape."

I rose and walked to the podium, climbed the steps, and handed the tape to my father, who inserted it in a prepared slot. The room darkened as Jeni's face appeared.

"I wish to speak to you today, clone to human, human to human," Jeni's voice said. "For although I am a clone, I am a human being, too." I smiled to myself as I watched Jeni's relaxed face on the screen. I had already prescreened the tape and knew, from Jeni's behavior, that all was well back on Trattori.

Jeni's voice continued. "I believe there can be peace and harmony between clones and natural-born humans. Are we so different from those humans who are children born out of artificial insemination or the ectogenetic chamber, or from children whose characteristics have been predetermined by genetic engineering?"

Or from the child of a cloned organ, I thought to myself.

"I want the same things you do," Jeni continued. "Meaning in my life, a home, a mate, a child. I have two hands, two feet, two eyes, a heart, lungs, all the same organs, the same feelings, the same hopes and desires. I was conceived differently from most of you. At birth I was an exact genetic copy of my mother. But now I am me, no one else, a human being just like all of you, and unique unto myself just as each one of you is truly yourself.

"I am a human being. And I don't deserve to be cut up for spare parts, to be experimented upon, to be used as slave labor. I deserve the same rights and privileges as all other human beings as a citizen of the ConFederation. I deserve a home of my own, a land of my own, the right to hold my head up among equals.

"I have no wish to harm humans. I only wish to live in harmony with all my sisters and brothers of all races and worlds.

"Anselm Gabrol once said, 'Let there be peace among all peoples.' Now I say unto you, 'Let my people join you in peace.'

"That is all I have to say. Now I leave it to you to vote on my future. Am I to be a free citizen or a slave?"

As the tape faded and the lights grew bright, the Forum broke into pandemonium. Shouts filled the air as fists were raised in the age-long salute to victory. I was sure now the people were with us, with the clones. The Speaker's gavel sounded, the sonic hum vibrated, and soon the hall became almost quiet. As I walked down the aisle and helped my father down from the podium, another woman's voice rang out.

"May I be recognized, Mr. Speaker?"

"Who calls?" the Speaker asked.

"Lista Colman of Mivrakki."

"You are recognized."

"My speech is short and to the point. There are only several hundred thousand colonists on Mivrakki. It is a green and lush world. We wish to extend a welcome to all those clones who might want to make our world their home."

Now the shouting was deafening. Delegates waved their arms in the air, screaming across the aisles to their neighbors. The sonic gavel had no effect at first. People put their hands over their ears but kept yelling, as if the other person could still hear. The Speaker gave up and stood helplessly on his dais in an attitude of 'What do you expect me to do?' He waited another five minutes before banging down on his gavel again. This time the delegates listened, closed their mouths and sat back down in their chairs. But there existed an almost tangible air of expectancy.

"Okay, folks, are you all settled down?" the Speaker asked amiably. Then his voice changed and boomed out, "There will be no more uncontrolled outbreaks or this session will be recessed for the rest of the day. Is that understood?" He paused for effect and listened appreciatively to the silence. "Good. Now, first things first. We have not yet taken a vote on the question of clone citizenship. If everyone is agreed, we will proceed to call the roll."

I sat, leaning forward and tightly gripping the top of the chair in the next row. I focused my eyes on the Speaker in the center of the Forum, and strained my ears to make sure I heard every sound.

"Abenard votes yes."

"Aculla says no."

"Andor votes for clones' rights."

And on and on, through Mivrakki, yes, and Trattori, still legally owned by MedComm, no, until all three hundred and thirty-six worlds had voted.

The victory was obvious. I wished I could be back on Trattori when Jeni viewed the transmission. We had done it! Myself, Jeni, all of us, clones and humans alike,

Everyone in the Forum felt it, too. It was not just a victory for the clones, but a coup against MedComm's tyranny over all of ConFed. Delegates were roaring and leaping to their feet, congratulating one another, pushing across aisles to talk to friends.

The Speaker didn't even bother to pound his gavel, but laid it down, smiled, and walked down one of the aisles.

I hugged my father, Willis, Vera, others who were strangers. Everyone embraced one another, pounded one another's backs, yelled words that were lost in the noise of all the voices echoing Civilization's victory throughout the great hall.

Excerpt from Selena Menard's *Out of
My Father's Seed: A Personal History
of the Clone Wars, Vol. I.*

A caravan of ships traveled the spaceways;
two thousand clone bodies were divided up among the
four large trawlers and the numerous small comships
that followed like minnows in the wakes of the great
whales of Terra. Through financial and material contributions, the many planets of ConFed had helped to
support the evacuation from Trattori and provide the
trawlers, food, and medical supplies. I had also con-
tributed a large portion of my father's estate.

Now, five months after our departure from the Med-
Comm planet, our new home, Mivrakki, was finally in
sight.

Jeni, ex-Komsol clone, myself, Paul Menard's daughter, Nikki, who had lost his clone-brothers, and Toby,
ex-comsol clone, stood lightly in the half-grav of the
lead comship's pilot room. There were only the four
of us, now. Sven was dead. Marcus was holed up inside his own crazy nightmares. And Sindra had left
us, running half across the galaxy to continue her

private war against what was left of MedComm. Jeni's voice broke through my thoughts.

"There it is," Jeni whispered, awe keeping her voice low.

A porthole had been opened, and through it shone the reflected light of Mivrakki, a small sphere gradually growing larger.

"We're only just beginning," I reminded her, trying to hold back my own growing enthusiasm.

"Oh, but what a beginning!" Jeni said.

Toby added, "I still can't believe it, MedComm legally stripped of all its power! The vote was almost unanimous."

"But we still have to see if ConFed has the strength to implement its decision against MedComm," I said. "And what will happen when we find out how to free the Komsol clones from their machinery." I couldn't help feeling a little doubtful. I had lived with the spectre of MedComm's power all my life. It was hard to realize that the balance of power was actually shifting.

"Things are changing already," Toby insisted. "It won't take long for us to get all that we want."

"Yes," Jeni said. "And we're starting with our own world—a green world where we can stretch our legs and bask in the sun. I wish Daven could have come with us," she added.

I touched my friend's shoulder, purposefully ignoring the implications of Toby's statement. "Daven's gone where he's needed," I said. "He's a professional organizer and gets itchy if he stays in one place too long. But he knows—" I paused for a second, then added, "and I think my father knew, too, before he died." With these words I breathed a sigh of relief, feeling a wave of relaxation pass through all the muscles of my body. It was now three hundred and fourteen years since my father had first created the Komsol clones. Finally, it could be said that his work was truly bearing fruit. Paul Menard was now being hailed as the man who had talked the Joint Council into defying MedComm and freeing the clones. And he had freed me, too. Freed me of the guilt. Freed me to feel his pride in me. Freed me to enjoy hope in the future. Freed me to let him rest in peace.

I was grateful to feel Jeni slipping her arm around my waist as she answered, "Your father was happy when he died."

"I know," I said. I squeezed Jeni's hand.

Jeni returned the hand squeeze and for a moment, hands interlocked, we gazed into each other's eyes. "I never said I was sorry," Jeni said to me, "for the way I was acting."

"Ssh," I whispered, surprised at myself for feeling embarrassed.

"And I think Sven knows, too," Jeni said, very quietly. Nikki, who had been standing nearby, grasped Jeni's hand. Toby drew closer, too. The four of us stood together, sharing our losses.

But I felt the need to say something else, to finish the apology. "I never should have said he was mad," I told Jeni. "He was disturbed, because of what they did to him. But he could have been healed."

"I know that," Jeni reassured me. I was thankful to hear her tone of voice, calm and sane. She continued. "But what happened to Sven, to Nikki, to all these thousands of clones, can never again happen to one of us." She pointed out to the shining orb in the porthole. "We've got our own world now."

"Yes," I said, rejoicing in these precious shared moments.

"And you're here with me," Jeni added.

I reached out to hold Jeni's other hand, and began circling in a quiet dance. Nikki broke into our circle, joining us, and then Toby joined, too. Three clones and one True Born danced together, swaying to a common, unheard, but sensed rhythm. It was a dance of oneness, of solemn rejoicing, of togetherness. Four people traversed the circle, gathering momentum, going faster and faster. Our bodies joined in the movement, our feet flew across the floor, our hands grasped the flesh of other human hands.

As we spun around in our tightly-knit circle, I lost myself completely to the physical sensation of the moment. I could feel, emanating from flesh to flesh, a certain elemental sort of electricity. I could sense Nikki's childish abandon to the force of the movement propelling his feet across the floor; and Toby's exultation in his absolute freedom; the lifting of guilt from my shoulders as I leaped into the air; and Jeni, flying free, loving Sven, picturing him standing straight and tall before he was killed, and then, finally, letting him go.

Welcome. I heard the word, but no one had spoken. I looked around me, wondering. Jeni smiled. Again I heard the word. *Welcome. Welcome, my sister.* The thought was in my mind. From Jeni?

She shook her head, *yes, verifying.*

Then from Nikki. *Love you, Selena.*

Toby. *Good to have you with us.*

And Jeni again. No words. Just the physical impression of her arms, holding me tightly, closely.

I spun around in the circle, wonder and gratitude overflowing. I reached out and I could truly feel them —Jeni, Nikki, Toby—beyond the finite physical world of touch and sound.

We were four people, our bodies dancing to the same rhythm. Together, we moved as a single unity. One thought, in four joined minds, surged forward, growing stronger with the physical speed of the dance.

We're coming home.

To a new beginning. For all of us who are my father's children, the fruit of his seeding.

And I was going to be with them, with Jeni and all

the other clones, to watch their rooting in Mivrakki's verdant soil. To watch them grow, to stumble, to find their own way to the sun.

If only the True Borns would give them enough time.

But I pushed that thought to the back of my mind. That day, that moment, I only hoped that Toby and Jeni were right, that nobody could stop them now.